What People Are Saying
about the Left Behind Series

"This is the most successful Christian-fiction series ever."
—**Publishers Weekly**

"Tim LaHaye and Jerry B. Jenkins . . . are doing for Christian fiction what John Grisham did for courtroom thrillers."
—**TIME**

"The authors' style continues to be thoroughly captivating and keeps the reader glued to the book, wondering what will happen next. And it leaves the reader hungry for more."
—**Christian Retailing**

"Combines Tom Clancy–like suspense with touches of romance, high-tech flash and Biblical references."
—**The New York Times**

"The most successful literary partnership of all time."
—**Newsweek**

"Wildly popular—and highly controversial."
—**USA Today**

"Christian thriller. Prophecy-based fiction. Juiced-up morality tale. Call it what you like, the Left Behind series . . . now has a label its creators could never have predicted: blockbuster success."
—**Entertainment Weekly**

"They can be fun and engaging, with fast-paced plotting, global drama, regular cliffhanger endings, and what has to be the quintessential villain: Satan himself."
—**abcnews.com**

"Not just any fiction. Jenkins . . . employed the techniques of suspense and thriller novels to turn the end of the world into an exciting, stay-up-late-into-the-night, page-turning story."
—**Chicago Tribune**

Tyndale House products by
Tim LaHaye and Jerry B. Jenkins

The Left Behind® book series
Left Behind®
Tribulation Force
Nicolae
Soul Harvest
Apollyon
Assassins
The Indwelling
The Mark
Desecration
The Remnant
Armageddon
Glorious Appearing
The Rising
The Regime
The Rapture
Kingdom Come

Other Left Behind® products
Left Behind®: The Kids
Abridged audio products
Dramatic audio products
and more . . .

Other Tyndale House books by
Tim LaHaye and Jerry B. Jenkins
Perhaps Today
Are We Living in the End Times?
The Authorized Left Behind® Handbook
Embracing Eternity

**For the latest information on individual products, release dates,
and future projects, visit www.leftbehind.com**

Tyndale House books by Tim LaHaye	Tyndale House books by Jerry B. Jenkins
How to Be Happy Though Married	*Soon*
Spirit-Controlled Temperament	*Silenced*
Transformed Temperaments	*Shadowed*
Why You Act the Way You Do	

KINGDOM COME

KINGDOM

THE FINAL VICTORY

COME

TIM LaHAYE
JERRY B. JENKINS

Tyndale House Publishers, Inc.
CAROL STREAM, ILLINOIS

To Jesus, the Christ,
who saved us from our sins
and promised to return
as King of kings and Lord of lords

Our Father in heaven,
Hallowed be Your name.
Your kingdom come.
Your will be done
On earth as it is in heaven.
Give us this day our daily bread.
And forgive us our debts,
As we forgive our debtors.
And do not lead us into temptation,
But deliver us from the evil one.
For Yours is the kingdom and the power
and the glory forever. Amen.
MATTHEW 6:9-13

REVELATION 20

THEN I SAW an angel coming down from heaven, having the key to the bottomless pit and a great chain in his hand. He laid hold of the dragon, that serpent of old, who is the Devil and Satan, and bound him for a thousand years; and he cast him into the bottomless pit, and shut him up, and set a seal on him, so that he should deceive the nations no more till the thousand years were finished. But after these things he must be released for a little while.

And I saw thrones, and they sat on them, and judgment was committed to them. Then I saw the souls of those who had been beheaded for their witness to Jesus and for the word of God, who had not worshiped the beast or his image, and had not received his mark on their foreheads or on their hands. And they lived and reigned with Christ for a thousand years. But the rest of the dead did not live again until the thousand years were finished. This is the first resurrection. Blessed and holy is he who has part in the first resurrection. Over such the

second death has no power, but they shall be priests of
God and of Christ, and shall reign with Him a thousand
years.

Now when the thousand years have expired, Satan will
be released from his prison and will go out to deceive the
nations which are in the four corners of the earth, Gog
and Magog, to gather them together to battle, whose
number is as the sand of the sea. They went up on the
breadth of the earth and surrounded the camp of the
saints and the beloved city. And fire came down from
God out of heaven and devoured them. The devil, who
deceived them, was cast into the lake of fire and brimstone where the beast and the false prophet are. And
they will be tormented day and night forever and ever.

Then I saw a great white throne and Him who sat on
it, from whose face the earth and the heaven fled away.
And there was found no place for them. And I saw the
dead, small and great, standing before God, and books
were opened. And another book was opened, which is
the Book of Life. And the dead were judged according to
their works, by the things which were written in the
books. The sea gave up the dead who were in it, and
Death and Hades delivered up the dead who were in
them. And they were judged, each one according to his
works. Then Death and Hades were cast into the lake of
fire. This is the second death. And anyone not found
written in the Book of Life was cast into the lake of fire.

A NOTE FROM
DR. TIM LAHAYE

THE MILLENNIAL kingdom gets its name from the twentieth chapter of the book of Revelation. *Millennium* is derived from the Latin words *mille* (one thousand) and *annum* (year).

The Millennium defines the duration of Christ's kingdom following the Rapture and Tribulation and prior to His creation of a new heaven and new earth. During the Millennium, Christ will physically reign on earth.

Not many details are provided about Christ's millennial kingdom in Revelation 20, except the final order of last-days events, the windup of history as we know it, and the length of the reign. There are, however, enough details to provide an idea of the way things might unfold. Many passages in the Old Testament and the New tell of the future kingdom of Israel within Christ's kingdom.

I feel the need to clarify that the millennial kingdom is not heaven. While in some ways it can be seen as a fore-taste of heaven, sin will still exist. Those who enter this period after already having been in heaven are the redeemed saints, of course. And those who survived the Tribulation are also all saints. So the first few days of the Millennium will be idyllic, with Christ on the throne and all citizens of the earth believers.

But as newborns come along, obviously, they will be sinners in need of forgiveness and salvation. I believe the scriptural prophecies indicate that anyone who does not trust Christ by the age of one hundred will be accursed. And while some may disagree, popular consensus among those of us who take the Bible literally wherever possible is that such people will die on their hundredth birthdays, thus exposing themselves as unbelievers.

You may also find it instructive to see the Millennium as yet another of God's efforts to reach the lost. He started by providing the perfect environment, the Garden of Eden.

But sin invaded.

Then came the faith age, in which Old Testament heroes acted on their trust in God. The New Testament book of Hebrews contains a faith Hall of Fame, each description of each saint's acts preceded by the phrase "By faith."

But sin invaded.

Then came the age of the law, during which God's people tried to please Him by following meticulous rules.

But sin invaded.

Then came the age of grace, when Jesus died for our sins and all we had to do was trust Him and His work on the cross for our salvation.

Still men and women rejected God.

Then will come the Rapture and the Great Tribulation, and despite these obvious signs that God is sovereign, humans will turn from Him and go their own ways.

Finally, the Millennium will put Jesus Christ on the throne of the earth. His light will illumine the globe. His justice will prevail. It seems inconceivable that anyone could still reject Him, and yet scriptural prophecy is clear. When Satan is again loosed for a season at the end of the Millennium, despite that the earth is massively populated with more believers than have ever lived, there will still be those who live for themselves and constitute the army of the rebellion against God.

Only heaven itself will finally be populated with only believers.

It should be plain from our treatment of this great future period that we are the opposites of anti-Semites. Indeed, we hold that the entire Bible contains God's love letter to and plan for His chosen people. If Israel had no place within the future Kingdom of God, we could no longer trust the Bible.

I have been studying the prophecies of the Word of God for my entire adult life—more than six decades—and still I thrill anew at what is in store. Now come along as Jerry tells the story of how this could all play out. Even so, come, Lord Jesus!

AT THE DAWN OF THE MILLENNIAL KINGDOM

The Principals

Abdullah ("Smith" / "Smitty") Ababneh, former fighter pilot, Royal Jordanian Air Force, Amman; lost divorced wife and two children in Rapture; former first officer, Phoenix 216; a principal Trib Force pilot assigned to Petra; witnessed the Glorious Appearing; now residing near the Valley of Jehoshaphat, Israel

Yasmine Ababneh, wife of Abdullah, mother of daughter **Bahira** and son **Zaki;** all raptured; returned to earth with the heavenly hosts at the Glorious Appearing; glorified bodies

Bruce Barnes, former assistant pastor and original member of the Tribulation Force; martyred; returned to earth with the heavenly hosts at the Glorious Appearing; glorified body

Tsion Ben-Judah, former rabbinical scholar and Israeli statesman; revealed belief in Jesus as Messiah on international TV—wife and two teenagers subsequently murdered; former spiritual leader and teacher of the Tribulation Force; had cyberaudience of more than a billion daily; teacher of the Jewish remnant at Petra; slain defending the Old City in Jerusalem; returned to earth with the heavenly hosts at the glorious appearing of Jesus, the Christ; glorified body

Cendrillon Jospin, worker at Children of the Tribulation ministry (COT), Valley of Jehoshaphat

Ignace and **Lothair Jospin,** cousins of Cendrillon; devotees of the Other Light, Paris

Qasim Marid, friend of Zaki Ababneh; worker at COT

Montgomery Cleburn ("Mac") McCullum, former pilot for Global Community supreme potentate and Antichrist, Nicolae Carpathia; chief Tribulation Force pilot assigned to Petra; witness to the Glorious Appearing; residing near the Valley of Jehoshaphat

Ekaterina Risto, Greek believer; worker at COT

Dr. Chaim Rosenzweig, Nobel Prize–winning Israeli botanist and statesman; former *Global Weekly* "Newsmaker of the Year"; murderer of Carpathia; leader of the million-plus Jewish remnant at Petra; witness to the Glorious Appearing; now residing near the Valley of Jehoshaphat

Irene Steele, wife of Rayford; mother of Chloe and Raymie; raptured; returned to earth with the heavenly hosts at the Glorious Appearing; glorified body

Rayford Steele, former 747 captain; lost wife Irene and son Raymie in the Rapture; lost second wife, Amanda, in plane crash; former pilot for Carpathia; original member of the Trib Force; witness to the Glorious Appearing; now residing near the Valley of Jehoshaphat

Raymie Steele, son of Rayford and Irene; brother to Chloe; raptured; returned to earth with the heavenly hosts at the Glorious Appearing; glorified body

Cameron ("Buck") Williams, former senior writer for *Global Weekly*; former publisher of *Global Community Weekly* for Carpathia; original member of the Trib Force; lost wife, Chloe, to Global Community guillotine; slain defending the Old City in Jerusalem; returned to earth with the heavenly hosts at the Glorious Appearing; glorified body

Chloe Steele Williams, daughter of Rayford and Irene; wife of Cameron; mother of Kenny Bruce; original Trib Force member; guillotined by the Global Community in Joliet, Illinois; returned to earth with the heavenly hosts at the Glorious Appearing; glorified body

Kenny Bruce Williams, son of Cameron and Chloe; witnessed the Glorious Appearing from Petra

Gustaf ("Zeke"/"Z") Zuckermandel Jr., former member of the Trib Force; farmer and youth worker, Tiranë, Albania

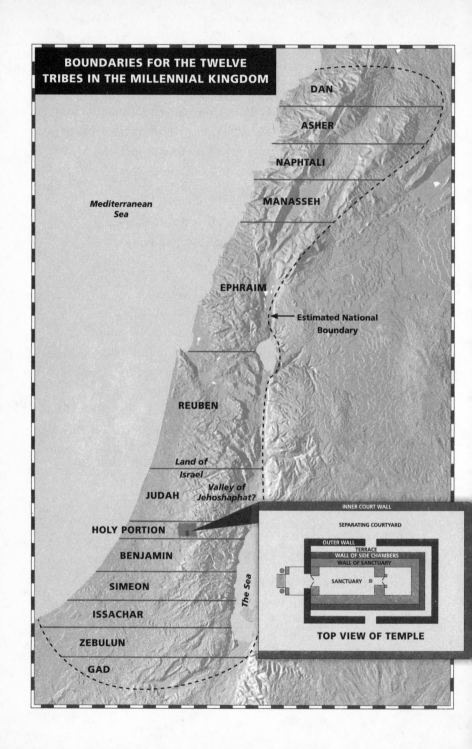

BOUNDARIES FOR THE TWELVE TRIBES IN THE MILLENNIAL KINGDOM

DAN

ASHER

NAPHTALI

MANASSEH

Mediterranean Sea

EPHRAIM

← Estimated National Boundary

REUBEN

Land of Israel

JUDAH

Valley of Jehoshaphat?

HOLY PORTION

BENJAMIN

SIMEON

The Sea

ISSACHAR

ZEBULUN

GAD

INNER COURT WALL

SEPARATING COURTYARD

OUTER WALL
TERRACE
WALL OF SIDE CHAMBERS
WALL OF SANCTUARY

SANCTUARY

TOP VIEW OF TEMPLE

PROLOGUE

From Glorious Appearing

RAYFORD TRIED to stay with Chaim. The men had left the Rosenzweig home without breakfast and without a word, as if they all somehow knew where they must go. Rayford decided that whatever was to come, he wanted to be close enough to Chaim to ask questions. The others must have had the same idea, as they all stuck together despite the crowds.

"When you see My throne, join those on My right, your left."

The words of Jesus were more than impressed on Rayford's heart. He had actually heard them. He moved to his left without question, and as waves of people moved both directions, suddenly the view before Rayford became clear. Directly below and centered under the vast heavenly hosts, saints, and angels, a great platform bore a throne on which Jesus sat. Behind Him stood the three angels of mercy. On either side of Him stood the archangels Michael and Gabriel.

Rayford knew instinctively that every living person on earth was gathered in that valley.

Chaim explained: "Half a billion or more were raptured seven years ago. Half the remaining population was killed during the Seal and Trumpet Judgments during the next three and a half years. Many more were lost during the Vial Judgments, and millions of believers were martyred. What you are looking at is probably only one-fourth of those who were left after the Rapture. And most of these will die today."

Indeed, Rayford realized, those assembling on Jesus' right were scant compared to those on His left.

It took most of the morning for the masses to find their places and settle. To Rayford it appeared that those to Jesus' left were puzzled at best, frightened at worst.

Gabriel stepped to the front of the platform and stretched out his arms for silence. "Worship the King of kings and Lord of lords!" he shouted, and as one the millions on both sides of the throne fell to their knees. In a cacophony of languages and dialects they cried out, "Jesus Christ is Lord!"

Those on the left of Jesus began rising to their feet, while all around Rayford, everyone remained kneeling. "Clearly two different groups here, eh, Chaim?"

"Actually three," the old man said. "Those are the 'goats' over there, the followers of Antichrist who somehow survived to this point. You are among the 'sheep' on this side, but I represent the third group. I am part of Jesus' 'brethren,' the chosen people of God whom the sheep befriended. We are the Jews who will go into the Millennium as believers, because of people like you."

Gabriel was gesturing that all should stand. When everyone was in place and quiet, he spoke in a loud voice:

"John the revelator wrote: 'I saw an altar, and underneath it all the souls of those who had been martyred for preaching the Word of God and for being faithful in their witnessing.

"'They called loudly to the Lord and said, "O Sovereign Lord, holy and true, how long will it be before You judge the people of the earth for what they've done to us? When will You avenge our blood against those living on the earth?"

"'White robes were given to each of them, and they were told to rest a little longer until their other brothers, fellow servants of Jesus, had been martyred on the earth and joined them.'

"People of the earth, hearken your ears to me! The time has been accomplished to avenge the blood of the martyrs against those living on the earth! For the Son of Man has come in the glory of His Father with His angels, and He will now reward each according to his works! As it is written, 'At that time, when I restore the prosperity of Judah and Jerusalem,' says the Lord, 'I will gather the world into the 'Valley Where Jehovah Judges' and punish them there for harming My people, for scattering My inheritance among the nations and dividing up My land.

"'They divided up My people as their slaves; they traded a young lad for a prostitute, and a little girl for wine enough to get drunk.'"

The group to Jesus' left immediately fell to their knees again and began shouting and wailing, "Jesus Christ is Lord! Jesus Christ is Lord!"

Jesus stood and walked to the edge of the platform.

With anger and yet sadness, He said, "Depart from Me, you cursed, into the everlasting fire prepared for the devil and his angels: for I was hungry and you gave Me no food; I was thirsty and you gave Me no drink; I was a stranger and you did not take Me in, naked and you did not clothe Me, sick and in prison and you did not visit Me."

The millions began shouting and pleading, "Lord, when did we see You hungry or thirsty or a stranger or naked or sick or in prison, and did not minister to You?"

Jesus said, "Assuredly, I say to you, inasmuch as you did not do it to one of the least of these, you did not do it to Me. You will go away into everlasting punishment, but the righteous into eternal life."

"No! No! No!"

But despite their numbers and the dissonance of their bawling, Jesus could be heard above them. "As the Father raises the dead and gives life to them, even so the Son gives life to whom He will. For the Father judges no one, but has committed all judgment to the Son, that all should honor the Son just as they honor the Father. He who does not honor the Son does not honor the Father who sent Him."

"We honor You! We do! You are Lord!"

"Most assuredly, I say to you, he who hears My word and believes in Him who sent Me has everlasting life, and shall not come into judgment, but has passed from death into life.

"But My Father has given Me authority to execute judgment also, because I am the Son of Man. I can of Myself do nothing. As I hear, I judge; and My judgment is righteous, because I do not seek My own will but the will of the Father who sent Me."

"Jesus is Lord!" the condemned shouted. "Jesus is Lord!"

Gabriel stepped forward as Jesus returned to the throne. "Silence!" Gabriel commanded. "Your time has come!"

Rayford watched, horrified despite knowing this was coming, as the "goats" to Jesus' left beat their breasts and fell wailing to the desert floor, gnashing their teeth and pulling their hair. Jesus merely raised one hand a few inches and a yawning chasm opened in the earth, stretching far and wide enough to swallow all of them. They tumbled in, howling and screeching, but their wailing was soon quashed and all was silent when the earth closed itself again.

Everyone on the platform moved back into place, and from the throne Jesus said, "Surely, as I have thought, so it shall come to pass, and as I have purposed, so it shall stand."

Gabriel came forward again. He said, "God's Son, Jesus Christ our Lord, was born of the seed of David according to the flesh, and declared to be the Son of God with power according to the Spirit of holiness, by the resurrection from the dead.

"Through Him you have received grace. You also are the called of Jesus Christ; grace to you and peace from God our Father and the Lord Jesus Christ. In His gospel the righteousness of God is revealed from faith to faith; as it is written, 'The just shall live by faith.'

"The wrath of God has been revealed from heaven against all ungodliness and unrighteousness of men, who suppressed the truth in unrighteousness, because what may be known of God was manifest in them, for God had shown it to them.

"For since the creation of the world His invisible attributes were clearly seen, being understood by the things that were made, even His eternal power and Godhead, so that they are without excuse, because, although they knew God, they did not glorify Him as God, nor were thankful, but became futile in their thoughts, and their foolish hearts were darkened. Professing to be wise, they became fools, and changed the glory of the incorruptible God into an image made like corruptible man— and birds and four-footed animals and creeping things.

"Therefore God also gave them up to uncleanness, in the lusts of their hearts, to dishonor their bodies among themselves, who exchanged the truth of God for the lie, and worshiped and served the creature rather than the Creator, who is blessed forever. Amen."

"Amen!" the assembled shouted.

"These who have been cast into outer darkness and

await the Great White Throne Judgment a thousand years hence were indeed without excuse. God sent His Holy Spirit as on the Day of Pentecost, plus the two preachers from heaven who proclaimed His gospel for three and a half years, plus 144,000 witnesses from the twelve tribes. Endless warnings and acts of mercy were extended to these who continued to be lovers of themselves rather than of God."

It hit Rayford that all who were left were believers, worshipers of Christ, and that he himself was among those who would populate the millennial kingdom.

Gabriel gestured that everyone should sit. When all were situated, he smiled broadly and pronounced loudly, "Blessed and holy is he who has part in the first resurrection. Over such the second death has no power, but they shall be priests of God and of Christ, and shall reign with Him a thousand years.

"The Mighty One, God the Lord, has spoken and called the earth from the rising of the sun to its going down. Out of Zion, the perfection of beauty, God will shine forth. Our God has come, and shall not keep silent; He shall call to the heavens from above, and to the earth, that He may judge His people!"

With that Jesus stood, and Gabriel moved to stand behind the throne with the other angels. And Jesus said, "Gather My saints together to Me, those who have made a covenant with Me by sacrifice! Come forth!"

From everywhere, from the earth and beyond the clouds, came the souls of those who had died in faith, whom Chaim and Tsion had often referred to as "the believing dead" and whom Rayford knew now also included Tsion himself—along with many more of Rayford's friends and loved ones.

Jesus began by honoring the saints of the Old Testament, those Rayford had only heard and read about. Rather than handling this the way He had the individual audiences with the tribulation saints—supernaturally dealing with them all in what seemed an instant—Jesus this time gave the spectators His strength and patience. The ceremony must have gone on for days, Rayford eventually decided, but he felt neither hunger nor thirst, no fatigue, not even an ache or a cramp from sitting in the sand that long. He loved every minute, knowing that when Jesus finished with the Old Testament saints, he would get to the tribulation martyrs. Waiting for his friends and loved ones to be recognized would be akin to waiting for Chloe's name to be called when she graduated from high school, but the reunion afterward would make it all worthwhile.

He glanced at his watch every few hours and realized how long it had taken to cover most of the Old Testament saints. Many he had never heard of—either he had not studied enough or these were some whose exploits had not been recorded. And yet God knew. He knew their hearts, knew of their sacrifice, knew of their faith. And one by one Jesus honored them as He embraced them and they knelt at His feet, and He said, "Well done, good and faithful servant."

As they came to Him one by one, Jesus said, "Without faith it is impossible to please God, for he who comes to

My Father must believe that He is, and that He is a rewarder of those who diligently seek Him."

There was Noah, humbly kneeling, receiving his reward. Jesus said, "By faith, being divinely warned of things not yet seen, you moved with godly fear, prepared an ark for the saving of your household, by which you condemned the world and became heir of the righteousness which is according to faith."

Hours later it seemed everyone roused when it was Abraham's turn. Jesus said, "By faith you obeyed when you were called to go out to the place you would receive as an inheritance. And you went out, not knowing where you were going. By faith you dwelt in the land of promise as in a foreign country, dwelling in tents with Isaac and Jacob, the heirs with you of the same promise; for you waited for the city which had foundations, whose builder and maker was God."

Sarah was right behind him, and Jesus said to her, "By faith you yourself also received strength to conceive seed, and you bore a child when you were past the age, because you judged Him faithful who had promised. Therefore from one man, your husband, and him as good as dead, were born as many as the stars of the sky in multitude—innumerable as the sand which is by the seashore."

Jesus addressed the spectators. "These all died in faith, not having received the promises, but having seen them afar off were assured of them, embraced them and confessed that they were strangers and pilgrims on the earth. For those who say such things declare plainly that they seek a homeland. And truly if they had called to mind that country from which they had come out, they would have had opportunity to return. But now they desire a better, that is, a heavenly country. Therefore I am not ashamed to be called their God, for I am preparing a city for them.

"By faith Abraham, when he was tested, offered up Isaac, and he who had received the promises offered up his only begotten son, of whom it was said, 'In Isaac your seed shall be called,' concluding that God was able to raise him up, even from the dead."

Later Jacob approached the throne, and Jesus said, "By faith, when you were dying, you blessed each of the sons of Joseph, and worshiped, leaning on the top of your staff."

And behind him, Joseph. Jesus told him, "By faith you, when you were dying, made mention of the departure of the children of Israel, and gave instructions concerning your bones."

All around, Jews began to stand. Soon everyone was on their feet. Moses himself was kneeling at the feet of Jesus with a man and a woman, and the Lord embraced them and said, "Well done, good and faithful servants. By faith, when your son was born, you hid him three months, because you saw he was a beautiful child; and you were not afraid of the king's command.

"And you, Moses, when you became of age, by faith refused to be called the son of Pharaoh's daughter, choosing rather to suffer affliction with the people of God than to enjoy the passing pleasure of sin, esteeming My reproach greater riches than the treasures in Egypt; for you looked to the reward. By faith you forsook Egypt, not fearing the wrath of the king; for you endured as seeing Him who is invisible.

"By faith you kept the Passover and the sprinkling of blood, lest he who destroyed the firstborn should touch them.

"By faith you led My children through the Red Sea as by dry land, whereas the Egyptians, attempting to do so, were drowned."

A woman knelt before Jesus. He said, "By faith, Rahab, you did not perish with those who did not believe, because you received My spies with peace."

When all the heroes of the Old Testament, including Gideon and Barak and Samson and Jephthah, also David and Samuel and the prophets had been honored, Jesus stood and said, "These through faith subdued kingdoms, worked righteousness, obtained promises, stopped the mouths of lions, quenched the violence of fire, escaped the edge of the sword, out of weakness were made strong, became valiant in battle, turned to flight the armies of the aliens.

"Women received their dead raised to life again. And others were tortured, not accepting deliverance, that they might obtain a better resurrection.

"Still others had trial of mocking and scourgings, yes, and of chains and imprisonment. They were stoned, they were sawn in two, were tempted, were slain with the sword. They wandered about in sheepskins and goatskins, being destitute, afflicted, tormented—of whom the world was not worthy. They wandered in deserts and mountains, in dens and caves of the earth.

"And all these obtained a good testimony through faith."

"It might be a little late to be asking this, Chaim," Rayford said, "but what kind of a relationship will I have with Irene now? And Amanda. I know that's the kind of question Jesus was asked when the Pharisees were trying to trip Him up, but I sincerely need to know."

"All I can tell you is what Jesus said. 'In the resurrection they neither marry nor are given in marriage, but are like angels of God in heaven. For when they rise from the dead, they neither marry nor are given in marriage. But those who are counted worthy to attain that age'—meaning this time period right now—'and the resurrection from the dead, neither marry nor are given in marriage.' I cannot make it any plainer than that."

"So only the people who reach the Millennium alive will marry and have children."

"Apparently."

Rayford also looked forward to meeting his heroes from the Old Testament. "We *do* get to interact with those guys, don't we?"

"Absolutely," Chaim said. "In Matthew 8:11 Jesus says, 'Many will come from east and west, and sit down with Abraham, Isaac, and Jacob in the kingdom of heaven.' "

But for now the Old Testament saints were not mingling. They too had become spectators, because the multitude that no man could number was lined up at the throne, awaiting their rewards.

"Those who were killed for the testimony of Jesus," Chaim said, "which pretty much covers any believer who died during the Tribulation, will be honored. But those who were actually martyred will be given a special crown."

Gabriel stepped forward one more time and announced, "John the revelator wrote, 'And I saw the souls of those who had been beheaded for their testimony about Jesus, for proclaiming the Word of God, and who had not worshiped the Creature or his statue, nor accepted his mark on their foreheads or their hands. They had come to life again and now they reigned with Christ for a thousand years.' "

Chaim's assessment proved accurate. Somehow the Lord arranged it so that only those who knew each tribulation saint witnessed them getting their reward. So, rather than Rayford's having to wait through the ceremonies for a million or two strangers to see a friend or loved one, as soon as the festivities began, Bruce Barnes approached the throne.

"Bruce!" Rayford called out, unable to restrain himself, and he stood and applauded. All around him others were doing the same, but they were calling out other names. "Aunt Marge!" "Dad!" "Grandma!"

After Rayford witnessed the honoring of many old friends and acquaintances and loved ones, finally there was Chloe, and right behind her Buck and Tsion.

Rayford kept shouting and clapping as his daughter, son-in-law, and spiritual adviser received their *well-done,* their embrace, and their martyr's crown. The entire heavenly host applauded each martyr.

Of Chloe, Jesus said, "You too suffered the guillotine for My name's sake, speaking boldly for Me to the end. Wear this for eternity."

Of Buck he said, "You and your wife gave up a son for My sake, but he shall be returned to you, and you shall be recompensed a hundredfold. You will enjoy the love of the children of others during the millennial kingdom."

Jesus took extra time with Tsion Ben-Judah, praising him for "your bold worldwide proclamation of Me as the Messiah your people had for so long sought, the loss of your family—which shall be restored to you—your faithful preaching of My gospel to millions around the world, and your defense of Jerusalem until the moment of your death. Untold millions joined Me in the kingdom because of your witness to the end."

Rayford enjoyed Jesus' welcome to dozens of others whose names he had forgotten, underground believers in various countries who had worked through the co-op, hosted Trib Force people, and sacrificed their lives in defense of the gospel.

Only by the miraculous work of God through Jesus, the honoring of more than two hundred million tribulation martyrs and saints was suddenly over. Jesus stood at the front edge of the vast platform and spread His arms, as if to encompass the mighty throng of souls, most with glorified bodies, the rest mere mortals who had survived the Tribulation.

"I will declare the decree," He said. "The Lord has said to Me, 'You are My Son, today I have begotten You. Ask of Me, and I will give You the nations for Your inheritance, and the ends of the earth for Your possession. You shall break them with a rod of iron; You shall dash them to pieces like a potter's vessel.'

"Now therefore, I say be wise, O kings; be instructed, you judges of the earth. Serve the Lord with fear, and rejoice with trembling. Kiss the Son, lest He be angry, and you perish in the way, when His wrath is kindled but a little. Blessed are all those who put their trust in Him.

"I welcome you, one and all, to the kingdom I have prepared for you. Rayford, welcome."

"Thank You, Lord."

How anyone found anyone else in the endless mass of souls was a miracle in itself. Rayford saw Chaim making a beeline to Tsion, who was already in the embrace of his wife and two children. Albie and Mac were laughing and shouting and hugging.

There were Buck and Chloe running to Kenny as he ran to them.

And seemingly out of nowhere, at Rayford's elbow stood Irene. One thing he could say for the glorified body: She looked herself, and as if she had not aged. Indeed, she looked younger. No way could he say the same for him.

"Hi, Rafe," she said, smiling.

"Irene," he said, holding her. "You're permitted one cosmic I-told-you-so."

"Oh, Rayford," she said, stepping back as if to get a good look at him. "I've just been so grateful that you found Jesus and so thrilled at how many souls are here because of what you and Chloe and the others did." She looked behind him. "Raymie," she said, "come here."

Rayford turned and there was his son, suddenly full grown. He scooped him in a tight embrace. "Even you knew the truth that I didn't," he said.

"I can't tell you how great it is to see you here, Dad."

Rayford pointed to Buck and Chloe and Kenny. "You know who that is?"

"Of course," Irene said. "That's my grandson—your nephew, Raymie."

They approached shyly, but it was Buck who broke the ice as Chloe gathered in her parents. "So nice to meet you, finally," he said, shaking his mother-in-law's hand. "I've heard so much about you."

As they laughed and hugged and praised God for each other and for their salvation, Amanda White Steele approached. "Rayford," she said. "Irene."

"Amanda!" Irene said, pulling her close. "Would you believe I prayed for you even after I was raptured?"

"It worked."

"I know it did. And you and Rafe were happy for a time."

"I was so afraid this would be awkward," Rayford said.

"Not at all," Irene said. "I didn't begrudge you a good

wife and companionship. I was so thrilled that you both had come to Jesus. You're going to find that He is all that matters now."

"And I," Amanda said, "am just so happy you made it through the Tribulation, Rayford." She turned back to Irene and took her arm. "You know, your witness and character were the reasons I came to the Lord."

"I knew that was your testimony," Irene said. "But I hadn't recalled making any impression on you."

"I don't think you tried. You just did."

Rayford had the feeling that his family would be close, affectionate friends throughout the Millennium. He didn't understand it all yet, in fact hardly any of it. But he had to agree with Irene: Jesus was all that mattered anymore. There would be no jealousy, envy, or sin. Their greatest joy would be in serving and worshiping their Lord, who had brought them to Himself.

THE SEVENTY-FIVE-DAY INTERVAL

DANIEL 12:11-12 indicates a seventy-five-day interval between the glorious appearing of Christ on earth and the start of the thousand-year kingdom: "And from the time that the daily sacrifice is taken away, and the abomination of desolation is set up, there shall be one thousand two hundred and ninety days. Blessed is he who waits, and comes to the one thousand three hundred and thirty-five days."

Jesus returns at the end of the "seventieth week" (Daniel 9:24-27), which is divided into halves of 1,260 days each. A careful reading of the entire chapter of Daniel 12 tells us that Christ's return occurs at the end of the second set of 1,260 days.

Daniel 12:11 speaks of something accomplished at the end of 1,290 days—thirty days beyond the Glorious Appearing. As the verse deals with temple sacrifices and the "abomination of desolation," it is safe to conclude that the first thirty-day interval relates to the temple.

Ezekiel 40–48 tells us that the Lord will establish a temple during the Millennium, thus the thirty days will likely be when He accomplishes that.

Daniel 12:12 tells of those "blessed" who reach 1,335 days, which adds another forty-five days to the interval. The "blessed" are qualified to enter the thousand-year messianic kingdom.

From this we conclude that the seventy-five-day interval is a time of preparation of the temple and for the kingdom. Because so much of the earth will have been destroyed during the judgments of the Tribulation, and because the earth will have been leveled except for the area surrounding Jerusalem, it seems logical that the Lord would renovate His creation in preparation for the kingdom.

THE MILLENNIAL
KINGDOM

WHILE MOST everything our fictional heroes experienced during the Tribulation would be different after the Glorious Appearing, a few things will remain the same. As in the days before the Rapture and the Tribulation, the sun will rise in the east and set in the west. But what a sun! It will be so bright that people will have to wear sunglasses any time they are outside, twenty-four hours a day. The Scriptures foretell this in Isaiah 30:26: "Moreover the light of the moon will be as the light of the sun, and the light of the sun will be sevenfold." It should not be beyond speculation that these orbs will be supercharged by the Shekinah glory of Christ.

With the moon as bright as the sun is now, people will have to get used to sleeping while it is light outside.

And everyone will speak Hebrew fluently, even if they are unaware of knowing a word of it. In Zephaniah 3:9, the Lord said, "For then I will restore to the peoples a pure language, that they all may call on the name of the Lord, to serve Him with one accord."

Hardly anything else, however, will remind anyone of the past. Those who had died and been in heaven with Jesus will recount for the others stories of the spectacular marriage of the Lamb.

Everyone will be assigned temporary housing until Jesus reconstructs the earth. Eventually they will build their own dwellings, but first they will occupy countless structures left empty by the "goat" judgment.

During the seventy-five-day interval that precedes the thousand-year reign of Christ, Jesus will set about re-creating Eden on earth. As the second person of the triune Godhead, long before Jesus first came to earth in human form, He had created the entire earth in six days, merely speaking into being everything that existed.

Between the Tribulation and the Millennium, it appears He will be content to take His time. Jesus will have as His canvas an entire globe that has been shaken flat—except Israel. Around the world, debris from the planetary earthquake will lie hundreds, sometimes thousands, of feet deep. Rock, foliage, buildings, and water will create a residue that coats the earth, leaving everything at sea level. That means, naturally, that in some places the altitude of the sea will have increased with the leveling of mountains. In others, the sea will disappear under new landmasses.

The only place elevated will be the Holy City itself, where the Mount of Olives will have been rent in two and Jerusalem raised hundreds of feet. How appropriate that the new, holy capital of the world should stand high above all other cities and nations, more than a thousand feet high and gleaming, pristine, and ready to be redesigned and decorated for and by the Lord Jesus Himself. Every day the landscape will change as full-grown greenery appears.

Do you ever wonder whether this thousand years that precedes the new heaven and the new earth might be boring? Yes, Jesus will be there, He whom we all have longed to see and worship in person ever since we became believers. But with only the like-minded there—at least initially—what will everyone do? Sit around and worship?

Perhaps. But imagine euphoria that shows no sign of abating. We'll feel full of the glory and presence of God through Jesus. In our current lives, we are aware of our sin and lowliness. But in the presence of Jesus, the contrast between us and our Savior will be even starker.

Perhaps Jesus will not allow us to dwell on that. Every moment should be filled with joy and wonder and worship, as Jesus continually impresses upon our hearts that He died for us, arose for us, and is preparing a place for us. The Millennium will be all about Jesus, worshiping the Lamb who was slain and now lives forevermore.

The newly developing city of Jerusalem will see its boundaries expanded to accommodate the new temple eighteen miles north of the city, near Shiloh. It will be massive. A paved causeway will lead all the way from Jerusalem to the new temple, where the courtyard alone will be larger than the Old City had been, more than a mile square. The holy neighborhood for the priests and Levites will encompass an area forty by fifty miles, more than six times the size of greater London and ten times the circumference of the original ancient, walled city.

The reason for this immensity is that the millennial temple will be the only temple, and the entire population of the earth will make use of it at one time or another. Daily during the seventy-five-day interval will come reports of vast creations throughout the rest of the world. Entire continents will become lush and green with rich, black soil extending down hundreds of feet to seas of pure water that spring up to irrigate the land.

As the vast new temple grows each day in the distance, so will the pristine farmlands and orchards throughout the world.

Jesus will be ever present, physically in the city of Jerusalem, soon occupying the temple and retaking the throne of David. The nations will have been granted to Him as an inheritance, and He is to rule the world with an iron rod. People will occupy themselves planting and harvesting and building their own homes.

During the seventy-five-day interval between the Glorious Appearing and the actual start of the millennial kingdom, every day, everywhere we look will bear the divine handiwork of Christ. Everything will be perfect, from the plants and shrubs and trees to the grasses and fields and orchards. The earth will teem with produce and animals of all kinds.

Strangely, all of us will lose any desire to eat meat. Animals will no longer be our meat. Our sustenance will come from the bounty of the trees and bushes and vines and from what we ourselves harvest from the earth. God says, "Be glad and rejoice forever in what I create; for behold, I create Jerusalem as a rejoicing, and her people a joy. I will rejoice in Jerusalem, and joy in My people; the voice of weeping shall no longer be heard in her, nor the voice of crying. No more shall an infant from there live but a few days, nor an old man who has not fulfilled his days; for the child shall die one hundred years old, but the sinner being one hundred years old shall be accursed.

"They shall build houses and inhabit them; they shall plant vineyards and eat their fruit; they shall not build and another inhabit; they shall not plant and another eat. For as the days of a tree, so shall be the days of My people, and My elect shall long enjoy the work of their hands. They shall not labor in vain, nor bring forth children for trouble; for they shall be the descendants of the blessed of the Lord, and their offspring with them" (Isaiah 65:18-24).

As for what prayer will be like in that day, the Lord says, "Before they call I will answer; and while they are still speaking I will hear" (Isaiah 65:25).

You may be a stellar student or an athlete or even a bit of a techie, but you will not have to be good with your hands. You may not be a gardener let alone a farmer, and perhaps you always pay to have carpentry, wiring, or plumbing done around the house. But in that day God will plant within you the desire—and the acumen—to do all those things yourself. On the first day of the Millennium, you will exercise new muscles, new ideas. You will plant vast acres, tend massive orchards, and build houses. All the knowledge, and the desire, will be poured into you.

You will meet for worship and praise with friends and loved ones, joined by new acquaintances of all colors and nationalities. Some will be compelled to tend animals, and not just tame ones. You will need fear no creature anymore, as "the wolf also shall dwell with the lamb, the leopard shall lie down with the young goat, the calf and the young lion and the fatling together" (Isaiah 11:6).

O N E

RAYFORD STEELE had to admit that the first time he saw
a bear and then a leopard moving about in public,
something niggled at him to keep his distance, to not
show fear, to make no sudden movements. But when he
saw the bear and the cat cooperate to climb a tree and
make a meal of leaves and branches, he was emboldened
to trust God for the whole promise. It wasn't just he
who had become a vegetarian. It was true of all former
carnivores.

Rayford moved quietly to the trunk of the tree and
watched the animals cavort and eat. And when a branch
fell, he himself tasted the leaves. He enjoyed fruit and
vegetables more, but he could see what the creatures
found in the plants. He trusted Christ to calm him when
the great leopard leaped down and nuzzled his leg the
way a house cat would, purring, then sitting to rest.

As for the bear, it ignored him and stretched out beside the big cat. Talk about a whole new world. . . .

Rayford deduced that the sun was brighter without being hotter, because Tsion Ben-Judah taught that its light was somehow enhanced by the ever-present glory of Jesus. A simple contraption out in the open allowed Rayford to concentrate the light through a magnifier and heat vegetables he and Irene and Raymie had gathered for a special feast. Irene had made butter from milk she had collected from a cow, so when everyone had assembled, they were met with steaming piles of fresh produce, drenched in butter.

And when they had eaten their fill, they retired outside to hear Irene's account of the marriage supper of the Lamb.

Like everyone else, Cameron Williams was fascinated with all that had gone on and what was yet to come. Of course, as a late martyr, he had spent very little time in heaven—just long enough to reunite with his wife, Chloe, and look forward to seeing their son back on earth at the Glorious Appearing. Now he anticipated the special dinner where his mother-in-law was to tell yet another story of Jesus.

No one called Cameron *Buck* now, because, he said, "there's nothing to buck here." And strange about Cameron and Chloe's relationship was that they still loved each other, but not romantically. Their entire hearts' desires were on the person of Jesus and worshiping Him for eternity. In the Millennium, they would live and labor together with Kenny and raise him, but as there would be no marrying or giving in marriage, their relationship would be wholly platonic.

"It's bizarre," Chloe told Cameron. "I still love and admire and respect you and want to be near you, but it's as if I've been prescribed some medicine that has cured me of any other distracting feelings."

"And somehow that doesn't insult me," Cameron said. "Does my feeling the same offend you?"

She shook her head. Her mind, like his, must have been on Jesus and whatever He had for them for the rest of time and eternity.

"Do you realize, Chlo', that we still have to raise Kenny in the nurture and admonition of the Lord and see to it that he decides for Christ?"

Only true believers and innocents had survived the Tribulation and the sheep-and-goats judgment to make it into the kingdom. "How many children of the Tribulation must there be," Chloe said, "who still have to choose Christ over living for themselves?"

"Children of the Tribulation," Cameron said. "I like that."

"God has been impressing on me that Kenny will be only one of many children in our charge."

"Me too, Chloe. I find that amazing."

As they talked, it became clear that the Lord had shown them both that their recompense for giving their lives and—in essence—losing their son for a time because of that would be the blessing of a hundredfold more children to love. Cameron could only imagine where these children would come from, but his old mentor Tsion Ben-Judah reminded him that "a hundredfold" in the Scriptures very likely meant many more than a hundred.

"I cannot imagine the havoc unbelievers could wreak in this new world. I hope God grants us the strength to do with them what He wants."

"Oh, you know He will."

One morning Cameron was praising Jesus with psalms and hymns and spiritual songs when he noticed Kenny was not playing alone. Half a dozen other kids—all seven or under, of course, because youngsters alive at the time of the Rapture had been taken and returned as grown-ups at the Glorious Appearing—had joined him and were getting acquainted.

In a flash it came to Cameron to call this group COT (Children of the Tribulation), and as negative as the name sounded, it didn't grate on him. It was merely fact. Here were representative children born after the Rapture who had survived to enter the kingdom. As the thousand years progressed, of course, kids would be born who could still be called children of the Tribulation, because someone in their ancestry had to have lived through it.

When Cameron rushed out to greet them, it was as if they knew he was coming. They immediately quit running and jumping and playing and sat in a semicircle, looking up at him expectantly.

They're ready. Am I?

"I'm Cameron," he said.

A boy raised his hand. "So, start telling us all about Jesus. She can tell us too."

Cameron glanced behind him to find Chloe, who had also apparently been drawn to the kids.

"Lord, where do I start?" Cameron prayed silently.

"In the beginning," Jesus told him. "Where we always start."

"But surely these kids know the basics."

"Start at *your* beginning. They don't know you. They know only that they're to listen. And be prepared. Tomorrow there will be more."

Cameron sat in the grass, and two youngsters immediately climbed into his lap. Others leaned against Chloe.

"I had heard about God and Jesus all my life," Cameron began, and he was struck by the lack of fidgeting and distraction. These kids hung on his every word. "But I never really gave faith a serious thought until seven years ago, when I found myself on an airplane bound for England in the middle of the night. . . ."

TWO

IRENE WAS overcome with joy that her family and friends and many other loved ones and acquaintances were with her. And when she began to tell the unsearchable story of the greatest wedding ceremony in the annals of the cosmos, in the theater of her mind she was transported back to heaven and the wedding itself.

She was able to describe the very portals of the house of God, a great, cathedral-like expanse where the redeemed of the ages were arrayed in purest white, comprising all those born again between Pentecost and the Rapture, marshaling expectantly in a staging area.

"You'd have to have been there yourself to see the limits of this seemingly endless throng. The thrill, the anticipation, were palpable as this bride of Christ readied herself to be presented to the Bridegroom.

"God Himself officiated the ceremony and welcomed all

present to the marriage of the Lamb. As Jesus appeared, bright and shining as the sun, the Father intoned, 'Christ loved the church and gave Himself for her, that He might sanctify and cleanse her with the washing of water by the word, that He might present her to Himself a glorious church, not having spot or wrinkle or any such thing, but that she should be holy and without blemish.

"'I, the King, have arranged this marriage for My Son, in whom I am well pleased. I sent out My servants to call those who were invited to the wedding, but they were not willing to come. I sent out more servants, saying, "Tell those who are invited, 'See, I have prepared my dinner; my oxen and fatted cattle are killed, and all things are ready. Come to the wedding.'" But they made light of it and went their ways, one to his own farm, another to his business. And the rest seized My servants, treated them spitefully, and killed them. I was furious. And I sent out My armies, destroyed those murderers, and burned up their city. Then I said to My servants, "The wedding is ready, but those who were invited were not worthy. Therefore go into the highways, and as many as you find, invite to the wedding." So those servants went out into the highways and gathered together all whom they found, both bad and good. And the wedding hall was filled with guests. He who has ears, let him hear.'"

Rayford understood that God had repeated Jesus' parable of the Wedding Feast and that it had been a prophecy of this very event. The wedding hall was filled with guests good and bad because "there is none righteous, no, not one." Those in attendance were not perfect, but forgiven, as was the bride herself.

Irene continued: "As Jesus stretched His arms to encompass the mighty throng that constituted His bride, God said, 'The Bridegroom loved you with an everlasting love, though you were unworthy and rebellious and disobedient. He redeemed you by leaving His home, only to be rejected by His own, and laying down His life for you. He returned here to prepare a place for you, that where He is, you may be also. And He left His Spirit to teach and protect you and to prepare you for this day.

"'The genuineness of your faith, being much more precious than gold that perishes, has been tested by fire and found to praise, honor, and glory at the revelation of Jesus Christ, whom you loved before ever you saw Him. Yet believing, you rejoiced with joy inexpressible and full of glory, receiving the end of your faith—the salvation of your souls.

"'Henceforth now and forevermore, you and the Bridegroom are one.'"

Rayford wished he could have been there to hear the crescendo of the heavenly hosts as the saints and angels praised God. How he longed for that day, a thousand years hence, when he would ultimately experience the complete wonders of heaven.

"And what about the feast, Irene?" he said. "What was that like?"

"Oh, Ray," Irene said, "that is yet to come. It will

usher in the Millennium at the end of these seventy-five days. For people have been invited to that celebration who were not in heaven for the wedding itself."

———————

Thirty days into the interval between the Glorious Appearing and the millennial kingdom, Tsion told Rayford and the others to expect something dramatic.

"More dramatic than what we have witnessed so far?" Irene said.

"That's a matter of perspective," Tsion said. "But I had expected to awaken today to something wholly different on the landscape of the horizon, and yet the abomination of desolation remains."

"Where the Antichrist defiled the temple?" Cameron said.

Tsion nodded. "The prophecies are clear. Daniel 12:11 says, 'And from the time that the daily sacrifice is taken away, and the abomination of desolation is set up, there shall be one thousand two hundred and ninety days.' That, my friends, is today."

———————

Late that afternoon, Rayford was startled by the sky turning black and lightning and thunder rolling in. He felt compelled to venture out and was surprised to see that everyone else seemed to have the same idea. Natural phenomena were simply not as terrifying as they had once been, and based on Tsion's teaching, Rayford was convinced this was hardly natural. This was an act of almighty God.

When it appeared that the fiery show had riveted the attention of all, a great bolt of lightning streaked from the sky and vaporized the temple. There seemed to be not even a speck of dust remaining, no chunks of stone flying, no fire. Where the temple had once stood, the black sky rolled back to reveal blue and nothing on the horizon.

And the reshaping of the geography continued.

By the time Rayford first visited what Cameron and Chloe had come to call COT, their temporary home was crawling with children—more than two hundred. And how they loved Cameron and Chloe!

"Some reward, eh, Dad?" Chloe said. "We were without Kenny for a little while, and now we have more loving children than we can handle. We need a structure for them."

"Way ahead of you," Rayford said. "The Lord has already put that construction on my agenda."

As the renovated earth took spectacular shape over the next forty-five days, Rayford found himself curious about the upcoming opening of the new temple. At another banquet of fresh fruit and steaming, buttery vegetables, he discussed this with Chaim and Tsion and Irene and several others. "Will Jesus explain it all?" Rayford said.

Chaim and Tsion nodded. "Think of Jesus Himself as

the government, Rayford," Tsion said. "He will put in place princes and governors under His authority, but obviously, everything and everybody will report to Him. Any munitions left over from anywhere on the earth will be dismantled and eliminated. The temple will be full of priests, and the nations will be called to worship and sacrifice there."

"But you taught me that Jesus was the sacrificial Lamb who rendered the sacrifices obsolete. With Him here and in charge, what is the need for a temple, and especially for sacrifices?"

Suddenly there came a long, loud blast from a sheep's horn, and all at the table stood as one and hurried out.

"You are about to get your answer from the ultimate authority," Chaim said, hurrying along.

As on the day of the sheep-and-goats judgment, Rayford could tell that the others knew instinctively that they were being called to assemble. They knew by whom and they knew where. It was merely their obligation to go.

From all over the region, people streamed from their dwellings, many piling into vehicles, others walking toward the new temple site. Rayford headed for the eighteen-mile causeway to take in all of Jesus' creativity along the way. As far as he could see, happy people were eager to see Jesus—not to mention His latest project.

The seventy-five days since the sheep-and-goats judgment had flown so quickly that Rayford wondered at God's economy of time. It wasn't as if now, here on earth, a thousand years was as a day and a day a thousand years. But clearly that was true for God.

Now, as Rayford and his friends and loved ones were passed by rolling caravans of people on their way to the new temple, the last thing on his mind was hitching a ride. A brisk walk of several miles was just what he needed.

Paths and walkways that just days before had been sandy and dusty and desolate now teemed with lush green growth. Animals of every size and kind frolicked. Children ran and laughed.

"What is that glorious smell?" Rayford said.

Chaim pointed to the mountains and hills in the distance. "It smells like what it looks like," he said.

"Do we have time for a detour?" Rayford said.

They left the route to the causeway, and many followed them to the foothills, where the streams had become pure white milk. Having only half finished his meal, Rayford knelt and cupped both hands in the white cascade, the icy flow hitting his taste buds like nectar.

He rinsed his hands in the pure springwater of a nearby brook. "But milk is not what I smell," he told Chaim. "I smell wine."

Again Chaim pointed, this time past the new foothills and to the rocky elevations that surrounded the city. There, gushing down the mountainsides were deep purple channels, collecting in great, beautiful pools below. "Do you believe this, Chaim?" Rayford said.

The older man stood staring, then quietly quoted: "'And it will come to pass in that day that the mountains shall drip with new wine, the hills shall flow with milk, and all the brooks of Judah shall be flooded with water.'"

Rayford closed his eyes and lifted his hands toward

the temple, gleaming in the sun on the vast, elevated plain. "Hallelujah!" he cried. "We're *living* the Bible!"

He and Chaim turned back to the route that would take them to the causeway and eventually to Jesus, and all around them people shouted, "'Blessed is He who comes in the name of the Lord! The Lord will be a shelter for His people, and the strength of the children of Israel!'"

When finally Rayford reached the northern end of the causeway, the millions pouring from the pavement to surround the seemingly endless temple stopped hundreds of feet below it in order to take it all in. Jesus the Christ needed no public address system, no microphone, no amplifier, no bullhorn. His voice was like the sound of many waters, and all Rayford could do was stand with arms outstretched, reaching toward Jesus. Though the Lord had to be miles away, Rayford saw Him clearly, and the earth shone with His glory.

"So you shall know that I am the Lord your God, I dwell in Zion on My holy mountain. Jerusalem shall be holy, and no aliens shall ever pass through her again. Judah shall abide forever, and Jerusalem from generation to generation. For I, your Lord, dwell in Zion.

"The mountain of My house is hereby established and shall be exalted above the hills. All nations shall flow to it. Many shall say, 'Come, and let us go up to the mountain of the Lord, to the house of the God of Jacob; He will teach us His ways, and we shall walk in His paths.' For out of Zion shall go forth the law, and My word from Jerusalem."

Rayford could barely take his eyes from the Lord, but the beauty of what He had created there overwhelmed him. Cypress trees decorated the expanse, next to pines and box trees.

Jesus said, "All this to beautify the place of My sanctuary. I have made the place of My feet glorious. Now come and see what I have wrought."

Pristine white marble walls extended as far as the eye could see, and yet Rayford felt no compulsion to move—and neither, it was clear, did anyone else. He suddenly knew what the prophets meant when they used such language as "the hand of the Lord was upon me and He took me there in the visions of God."

Rayford felt transported to the top of a nearby mountain, from which he looked to the south and could take in the entire structure, akin to a city in itself.

Jesus said, "Look and hear and fix your mind on everything I show you."

Only from this perch could Rayford take in the wall that extended all the way around the temple, its width and height equal. The gateway that faced east lay at the top of a set of stairs that was also the width of the wall. Each gate chamber was the same length and width, as was the vestibule of the inside gate.

The eastern gateway bore three gate chambers on one side and three on the other; again, all the same size. From the front of the entrance gate to the front of the vestibule of the inner gate were beveled window frames in the gate chambers and in their intervening archways on the inside of the gateway all around, likewise in the vestibules and all around on the inside. On each gatepost were palm trees.

In the outer court, thirty chambers faced a pavement that extended all the way around. These same features appeared on all four sides of the temple. Gateposts faced the outer court, and palm trees stood on its gateposts on both sides, and seven steps led up to it. There Rayford saw a chamber that appeared to have been equipped with tables on which to process offerings.

Rayford had thought Jesus was the sacrificial Lamb, so he was surprised to see offering tables. But Jesus said, "Here is where the priests will slay the burnt offering, the sin offering, and the trespass offering. There are eight tables on which they will slaughter the sacrifices. There are also four tables of hewn stone for the burnt offering, and on these they will lay the instruments with which they slaughter the burnt offering and the sacrifice."

Rayford remained puzzled, but he knew the Lord would somehow make it clear why all this was necessary. Inside he saw hooks fastened all around; and the flesh of the sacrifices was already on the tables.

Jesus said, "Outside the inner gate are the chambers for the singers in the inner court. This chamber, which faces south, will be for the priests who have charge of the temple. These will be the sons of Zadok, from the sons of Levi, who come near Me to minister to Me." The altar lay in front of the temple.

Then the Lord showed the sanctuary and said, "This is the Most Holy Place."

The beauty of the architecture washed over Rayford,

and despite his questions, he was speechless. The width
of the structure increased as one went from the lowest
story to the highest. The doors of the side chambers
opened onto a terrace, one door toward the north and
another toward the south. Three stories opposite the
threshold were paneled with wood from the ground to
the windows made with cherubim and palm trees, a
palm tree between cherub and cherub. Each cherub had
two faces, so that the face of a man was toward a palm
tree on one side, and the face of a young lion toward a
palm tree on the other; thus it was throughout the
temple all around.

The doorposts of the temple were square, as was the
front of the sanctuary. The altar was of wood. And Jesus
said, "This is the table that is before the Lord." Cherubim and palm trees were carved on the doors of the
temple, just as they were on the walls.

Before Rayford could ask again the reason for the
continuance of animal sacrifices, Jesus brought him out
into the outer court by the way toward the north, into
the chamber opposite the courtyard. Chambers had been
built into the thickness of the wall of the court toward
the east. There was a walk in front of them also.

Jesus said, "The north and south chambers are the
holy chambers where the priests who approach the Lord
shall eat the most holy offerings. There they shall lay the
most holy offerings—the grain offering, the sin offering,
and the trespass offering—for the place is holy. When
the priests enter them, they shall not go out of the holy
chamber into the outer court; but there they shall leave

their garments in which they minister, for they are holy. They shall put on other garments; then they may approach that which is for the people."

Rayford still had questions, of course, but he was speechless as the glory of the Lord entered the temple by way of the gate that faced east. Jesus said, "This is the place of My throne and the place of the soles of My feet, where I will dwell in the midst of the children of Israel forever. No more shall the house of Israel defile My holy name, they nor their kings, by their harlotry or with the carcasses of their kings on their high places. When they set their threshold by My threshold, and their doorpost by My doorpost, with a wall between them and Me, they defiled My holy name by the abominations which they committed; therefore I have consumed them in My anger. Now let them put their harlotry and the carcasses of their kings far away from Me, and I will dwell in their midst forever. Now that I have judged those who rejected me, those who remain shall keep the temple's ordinances and perform them. This is the law of the temple: The whole area surrounding the mountaintop is most holy."

The altar hearth had four horns extending upward from it. And Jesus said, "Thus says the Lord God: 'These are the ordinances for the altar on the day when it is made, for sacrificing burnt offerings on it, and for sprinkling blood on it. A young bull shall be given for a sin offering to the priests, the Levites, the seed of Zadok, who approach Me to minister to Me. They shall take some of its blood and put it on the four horns of the altar, on the four corners of the ledge, and on the rim around it; thus they shall cleanse it and make atonement for it. Then they shall also take the bull of the sin offering and burn it in the appointed place of the temple, outside the sanctuary. On the second day they shall offer a kid of the goats without blemish for a sin offering; and they shall cleanse the altar, as they cleansed it with the bull. When they have finished cleansing it, they shall offer a young bull without blemish and a ram from the flock without blemish. When they offer them before the Lord, the priests shall throw salt on them, and they will offer them up as a burnt offering to the Lord.

"'Every day for seven days they shall prepare a goat for a sin offering; they shall also prepare a young bull and a ram from the flock, both without blemish. Seven days they shall make atonement for the altar and purify it, and so consecrate it. When these days are over it shall be, on the eighth day and thereafter, that the priests shall offer their burnt offerings and their peace offerings on the altar; and I will accept you.'"

Surely these were the words of God, and while they left Rayford still wondering why burnt offerings were required when Jesus Himself had been the sacrificial Lamb, he was unable to speak.

Then Jesus showed the outer gate of the sanctuary that faced east, but it was shut. He said, "This gate shall not be opened, and no man shall enter by it, because the Lord God of Israel has entered by it. As for the prince, he may sit in it to eat bread before the Lord; he shall enter by way of the vestibule of the gateway and go out the same way.

"Son of man, mark well, see with your eyes and hear with your ears all that I say to you concerning all the ordinances of the house of the Lord and all its laws. Mark well who may enter the house and all who go out from the sanctuary.

"The Levites who went far from Me when Israel went astray, who strayed away from Me after their idols, they shall bear their iniquity. Yet now they shall be ministers in My sanctuary, as gatekeepers of the house and ministers of the house; they shall slay the burnt offering and the sacrifice for the people, and they shall stand before them to minister to them. And they shall not come near Me to minister to Me as priest, nor come near any of My holy things, nor into the Most Holy Place; but they shall bear their shame and their abominations which they have committed. Nevertheless I will make them keep charge of the temple, for all its work, and for all that has to be done in it.

"But the sons of Zadok, who kept charge of My sanctuary when the children of Israel went astray from Me, they shall come near Me to minister to Me; and they shall stand before Me to offer to Me the fat and the blood. They shall enter My sanctuary, and they shall come near My table to minister to Me, and they shall keep My charge. No priest shall drink wine when he enters the inner court. They shall not take as wife a widow or a divorced woman, but take virgins of the descendants of the house of Israel, or widows of priests. And they shall teach My people the difference between the holy and the unholy, and cause them to discern between the unclean and the clean. In controversy they shall stand as judges, and judge it according to My judgments. They shall keep My laws and My statutes in all My appointed meetings.

"My princes shall no more oppress My people, but they shall give the rest of the land to the house of Israel, according to their tribes. O princes of Israel, remove violence and plundering, execute justice and righteousness, and stop dispossessing My people.

"In the first month, on the first day of the month, you shall take a young bull without blemish and cleanse the sanctuary. In the first month, on the fourteenth day of the month, you shall observe the Passover, a feast of seven days; unleavened bread shall be eaten. And on that day the prince shall prepare for himself and for all the people of the land a bull for a sin offering."

Rayford only hoped he wouldn't have to wait a thousand years to know the mind of God. He knew the Lord's ways were beyond finding out for a mere mortal, but still he longed to know why Jesus was so specific about all the sacrifices required of His chosen people.

Rayford saw the door of the temple; there was water flowing from under the threshold of the temple toward the east.

Jesus said, "This water flows toward the eastern region, goes down into the valley, and enters the sea. When it reaches the sea, its waters are healed. And it shall be that every living thing that moves, wherever the rivers go, will live. There will be a very great multitude of fish, because these waters go there; for they will be healed, and everything will live wherever the river goes. Fishermen will stand by it from En Gedi to En Eglaim, spreading their nets. Their fish will be of the same kinds as the fish of the Great Sea, exceedingly many.

"This land is holy to the Lord. The rest shall be for general use by the city, for dwellings and common-land; and the city shall be in the center. Its produce shall be food for the workers of the city, who shall cultivate it.

"I have made a covenant of peace with My people, and it shall be an everlasting covenant with them; I will establish them and multiply them, and I have set My sanctuary in their midst forevermore. My tabernacle also shall be with them; indeed I will be their God, and they shall be My people. The nations also will know that I, the Lord, have sanctified Israel, now that My sanctuary is in their midst forevermore. The name of the city from this day forward shall be: The Lord is There."

Rayford, amazed and confused, found himself gazing upon the great temple from afar. Had Jesus not done away with the sacrifices by His own death?

The Lord said, "The sacrifices My Father required long ago were but a shadow of these good things to come. These same sacrifices, which My chosen ones are to offer continually year by year, cannot make those who approach perfect. But in these sacrifices there is a reminder of sins every year, just as the celebration of My supper is in remembrance of the price paid of My body and of My blood. The blood of bulls and goats could never take away sins. You have been sanctified through the offering of My body once for all. And every priest daily offering repeatedly the same sacrifices can never take away sins. But after I offered one sacrifice for sins forever, I sat down at the right hand of My Father, waiting till My enemies were made My footstool. For by one offering I perfected forever those who are sanctified. My chosen ones must continue to present memorial sacrifices to Me in remembrance of My sacrifice and because they rejected Me for so long."

THREE

CAMERON WILLIAMS was convinced that in a thousand
years he would never get used to the bizarre supernatu-
ralism of everyday living now. He and Chloe had
traversed the paved temple causeway with Abdullah
"Smith" Ababneh from their Tribulation Force days.
Cameron and Chloe and Abdullah's wife, Yasmine,
possessed glorified bodies, as did the Ababnehs' two
beautiful children—daughter Bahira and son Zaki—
who were now, of course, fully grown.

The former Jordanian fighter pilot and eventual
convert—after he lost Yasmine and their children to the
Rapture—quickly told Cameron of the glorious reunion
with his family. "And, as you know, marriage is not the
same as it was before all this. Which, in our case, is
fortunate."

Bahira was a beautiful, tan-faced girl who took after

her mother; Zaki was darker, like Abdullah, and seemed shy, if not aloof. They were fourteen and thirteen in real years, but their new bodies reminded Chloe of how her little brother, Raymie—twelve at the time of the Rapture—looked now, as though he were in his midtwenties.

When Jesus had begun showing everyone the new temple, Cameron was primarily drawn to the vast geographical changes that had wholly recast the landscape.

"I have opened a fountain for the house of David and the inhabitants of Jerusalem," Jesus said. "The time is now, when the moon shines as the sun and it is neither day nor night, but at evening it is light. I have caused living waters to flow from Jerusalem, half toward the eastern sea and half toward the western sea. In both summer and winter this shall occur."

To the Mediterranean and the Dead Sea! Cameron wondered what this divine freshwater supply would mean to the Dead Sea, having long been so salt laden that nothing could live in it and the heaviest humans floated in it.

"The water that flows toward the eastern region goes down into the valley," Jesus said, "and when it reaches the sea, its waters are healed. Every living thing that moves, wherever the rivers go, will live. There will be a very great multitude of fish, because these waters go there; for they will be healed, and everything will live wherever the river goes. But its swamps and marshes will not be healed; they will still be given over to salt. Along the bank of the river, on this side and that, will grow all kinds of trees used for food; their leaves will not wither, and they will bear fruit every month, because their water flows from the sanctuary. Their fruit will be for food, and their leaves for medicine."

The idea of so much water in this desert fascinated Cameron. He had spent a lot of time in this region during the Tribulation and had often wondered what it would look like if there had been enough irrigation.

Jesus said, "I will give the rain for seeds sown and bread of the increase of the earth. It will be fat and plentiful. Cattle will feed in large pastures. There will be on every high mountain and on every high hill rivers and streams of waters. Waters shall burst forth in the wilderness, and streams in the desert. The parched ground shall become a pool, and the thirsty land springs of water."

———

Tsion Ben-Judah felt particularly privileged as one of the chosen people and a tribulation martyr. Of most interest to him on this day at the cusp of the Millennium was to try to understand how the Old Testament law would mesh with the work of Christ on the cross. How thrilling to learn that the glory of the Lord would fill the temple and that the Mosaic laws would be observed—even the sacrifices. Every year they would observe both Passover (the seven-day Feast of Unleavened Bread) and the Feast of Tabernacles. No lamb would be slain at Passover, thus making plain and memorializing annually that Jesus had been the perfect and once-for-all sacrifice for the sins of the world. And for these observances, even the Gentile nations would be required to have representatives sojourn to the temple.

Tsion was dizzied when Jesus specified how the land was to be allotted: "These are the borders by which you shall divide the land as an inheritance among the twelve tribes of Israel." He spoke of His having long ago raised His hand in an oath as to who should occupy certain regions. Using the names of the cities of old, he outlined where the Jews should settle. "They will divide it by lot as an inheritance for themselves, and for the strangers who dwell among them and who bear children among them. The strangers shall be as native-born among the children of Israel; they shall have an inheritance among the tribes of Israel. In whatever tribe the stranger dwells, there he shall be given his inheritance."

It seemed strange to Cameron to realize that he, along with all other Gentile believers, was the stranger here. *And yet we worship the same God.*

Jesus said, "The Lord is King over all the peoples of the earth. The Lord is one, and His name one."

And yet it soon became clear that Jesus, while the ultimate sovereign, would not be ruling alone. He began calling out from the multitudes counselors from each tribe who would adjudicate all matters among the citizens. These would serve as judges who would report to

the ultimate judge of each tribe, one of the twelve apostles. Cameron thrilled to see these heroes of his faith take
their places with Jesus in the temple.

Then the Lord explained that the judges would report
to the king of Israel—in this case, Jesus' prince, David
himself.

———

Tsion kept his eyes peeled to see this great biblical hero,
the one who had slain the giant, subdued a lion, con-
quered kingdoms, and been a man after God's own heart.

And yet the plain-looking, medium-sized man who
emerged from the throng at Jesus' beckoning looked nothing like a prince, let alone a king, and certainly not a hero.
His gait was tentative, his posture timid. When he came
within twenty feet of Jesus, he fell prone, hiding his face
and crying out, "Unworthy! I am unworthy! Behold, I am
unclean! Have mercy upon me, O God, according to Your
lovingkindness; according to the multitude of Your tender
mercies, blot out my transgressions. Wash me thoroughly
from my iniquity, and cleanse me from my sin. For I
acknowledge my transgressions, and my sin is always
before me. Against You, You only, have I sinned, and done
evil in Your sight. Purge me with hyssop, and I shall be
clean; wash me, and I shall be whiter than snow. Hide
Your face from my sins, and blot out all my iniquities."

"David, My prince, stand. For I long ago heard your
cries and judged you and created in you a clean heart,
renewing a steadfast spirit within you. I did not cast you

away from My presence, and I did not take My Holy Spirit from you. Your sin is separated from you as far as the east is from the west and will be remembered no more, so delight in the joy of your salvation. I will uphold you by My Spirit that you may teach transgressors My ways, and sinners shall be converted to Me. I have delivered you from the guilt of bloodshed, so sing aloud of My righteousness."

David, standing now, shoulders back, chin raised, reached for Jesus' embrace. "O Lord, open my lips, and my mouth shall show forth Your praise. For You do not desire sacrifice, or else I would give it; you do not delight in burnt offering. The sacrifices of God are a broken spirit, a broken and a contrite heart—these, O God, You will not despise. I praise You for Your good pleasure to Zion and for rebuilding the walls of Jerusalem. Be pleased with the sacrifices of righteousness." David washed and anointed himself and went into the house of the Lord.

Rayford wished he could take notes to remember all that the Lord was imparting this day. It was as if He had waited until all were assembled to explain the wonders and mysteries of the coming thousand-year reign.

"The mountain of My house is established on the top of the mountains," Jesus thundered, "and shall be exalted above the hills; and nations shall flow to it. Many people shall come and say, 'Come, and let us go up to the mountain of the Lord, to the house of the God of Jacob; He will

teach us His ways, and we shall walk in His paths.' For
out of Zion the law shall go forth, and My word from
Jerusalem. I shall judge between many peoples and rebuke
strong nations afar off; they shall beat their swords into
plowshares, and their spears into pruning hooks; nation
shall not lift up sword against nation, neither shall they
learn war anymore.

"The wolf also shall dwell with the lamb, the leopard
shall lie down with the young goat, the calf and the
young lion and the fatling together; and a little child
shall lead them. The cow and the bear shall graze; their
young ones shall lie down together; and the lion shall eat
straw like the ox. The nursing child shall play by the
cobra's hole, and the weaned child shall put his hand in
the viper's den. They shall not hurt nor destroy in all My
holy mountain, for the earth shall be full of the knowledge of the Lord as the waters cover the sea.

"Now the deaf shall hear the words of the book, and
the eyes of the blind shall see out of obscurity and out of
darkness. For I am a Father to Israel, and Ephraim is My
firstborn. Hear My word, O nations, and declare it in
the isles afar off, and say, 'He who scattered Israel has
gathered him, and keeps him as a shepherd does his
flock.' For the Lord has redeemed Jacob, and ransomed
him from the hand of one stronger than he.

"Therefore come and sing in the height of Zion, streaming to the goodness of the Lord—for wheat and new wine
and oil, for the young of the flock and the herd. Your
souls shall be like a well-watered garden, and you shall
sorrow no more at all.

"I have turned your mourning to joy; I will comfort you, and make you rejoice rather than sorrow. I will satiate the soul of the priests with abundance, and My people shall be satisfied with My goodness. Old men and old women shall again sit in the streets of Jerusalem, each one with his staff in his hand because of great age. The streets of the city shall be full of boys and girls playing in its streets."

Just what did it mean, Rayford wondered, that "the child shall die one hundred years old, but the sinner being one hundred years old shall be accursed"? Back on the causeway with Tsion, he sought the older man's opinion.

"No one born during the time of the kingdom will die before age one hundred," Tsion said. "And when one dies, he will be considered young, for everyone else will live for the entire Millennium. And you know, Rayford, the only ones who *will* die will be Gentiles who do not trust Christ for their salvation."

"Only Gentiles? How do you know that, and how can it be?"

"We're living out the prophecies now, friend. And Jeremiah wrote, 'Behold, the days are coming, says the Lord, when I will make a new covenant with the house of Israel and with the house of Judah—not according to the covenant that I made with their fathers in the day that I took them by the hand to lead them out of the land of Egypt, My covenant which they broke, though I was a husband to them.

"'But this is the covenant that I will make with the

house of Israel after those days, says the Lord: I will put My law in their minds, and write it on their hearts; and I will be their God, and they shall be My people. No more shall every man teach his neighbor, and every man his brother, saying, "Know the Lord," for they all shall know Me, from the least of them to the greatest of them, says the Lord. For I will forgive their iniquity, and their sin I will remember no more.'"

"Amazing. But then, even among us Gentiles, how could a child born into this new world ever choose not to trust Christ?"

"It's a mystery," Tsion said. "Imagine—children of the Tribulation, when they reach an age of understanding and, thus, accountability, become the only unregenerate persons alive. And each one born here—without birth pangs, according to the prophecies—still must come to a place of repentance and a decision to become a follower of Christ."

"Then that person would be raised in the nurture and admonition of the Lord, would live in the physical presence of Christ, and would be influenced not only by his immediate family but also by every other person with whom he comes into contact."

Tsion nodded. "And yet the Scriptures are clear that at the end of all this, Satan is loosed again for a little while to tempt the nations, and the army he amasses is as numerous as the sand on the seashores. So not only will there be those who choose their own ways, there will be countless numbers of them."

"Hard to imagine."

"Especially now, when everyone you see is either a believer or too young to be accountable."

All Rayford could think of was how ominously important was Chloe and Cameron's ministry to children. And yet if children lived to a hundred without becoming born again, they would die. How could any rebellion against Jesus be sustained through the generations until that final conflict when Satan was loosed?

On the one hand, Rayford was grateful that such a return to the hatred and rebellion of his former life would not occur for a thousand years. On the other, he shuddered to realize that very soon, this idyllic kingdom would begin to become populated by those who—against all odds and all reason—would eventually spawn the fire of war that the evil one would fuel.

FOUR

"I'M NOT gloating, Rayford," Tsion said. "I am just smiling."

They walked leisurely from the vast Temple Mount on the long paved causeway back to the valley where they lodged. Irene and Raymie and many of their friends strolled nearby, everyone seeming to radiate the wonder of Christ.

"So you like that we Gentiles are low on the totem pole now, huh?"

"It amuses me. But it is simply another fulfillment of prophecy. The government now starts with the Christ and extends through His prince and king of Israel, David; the apostles, who are now judges over the twelve tribes; their princes; local judges under them; counselors; and finally you foreigners. Oh, don't look that way, friend. You know we will not make you suffer. Think of how different is this society, this whole world, compared to what we came from."

Rayford could only shake his head. He always found Tsion engaging and interesting, but now he could barely take his eyes from the beauty of the new creation. The landscaping that lined the causeway was breathtaking.

Tsion must have noticed. "You rightly admire this handiwork," he said, "because this road—if I may be so pedestrian as to call it that—is yet another reflection of the sinless beginning to the kingdom. I dare say it will be many years before we suffer the blights of war, abortion, murder, robbery, drugs, pornography—you name it."

"And does this causeway reflect that?" Rayford said.

"Isaiah the prophet foretold this: 'The parched ground shall become a pool, and the thirsty land springs of water; in the habitation of jackals, where each lay, there shall be grass with reeds and rushes. A highway shall be there, and a road, and it shall be called the Highway of Holiness. The unclean shall not pass over it, but it shall be for others. Whoever walks the road, although a fool, shall not go astray. No lion shall be there, nor shall any ravenous beast go up on it; it shall not be found there. But the redeemed shall walk there, and the ransomed of the Lord shall return, and come to Zion with singing, with everlasting joy on their heads. They shall obtain joy and gladness, and sorrow and sighing shall flee away.'"

The next morning, as Cameron Williams lay on his back in his bedchamber, hands behind his head, he eagerly

anticipated another day of service to his King. Beyond
the heavy draperies that had been fashioned to keep out
the glare of the sunlike moon through the night, not to
mention the irrepressible morning sun, lay a delightful
day to serve the Lord.

Today was the day of the celebration in honor of the
wedding of the Lamb. All were invited to the marriage
supper, and as Cameron showered and dressed, he was
compelled to return to the new temple by way of the
Highway of Holiness. When he rushed to the front door,
Chloe and Kenny waited, appearing barely able to control
themselves. From outside came the cacophony of millions
already on foot, talking, laughing, singing, dressed in
their finest.

Millions were on their way as part of the bride of
Christ. The rest were companions of the bride or friends
of the Bridegroom. The bride, of course, consisted of all
born-again believers from the time of Pentecost until the
Rapture. Tsion had explained that John the Baptist, for
instance, was not part of the bride, for he died before
the church was founded. John had referred to himself
as a friend of the Bridegroom: "You yourselves bear me
witness, that I said, 'I am not the Christ,' but, 'I have
been sent before Him.' He who has the bride is the bridegroom; but the friend of the bridegroom, who stands and
hears him, rejoices greatly because of the bridegroom's
voice. Therefore this joy of mine is fulfilled. He must
increase, but I must decrease."

Jesus Himself had said, speaking of His forerunner,
"Assuredly, I say to you, among those born of women

there has not risen one greater than John the Baptist; but he who is least in the kingdom of heaven is greater than he." Finally that confusing verse made sense to Cameron. For the Kingdom of Heaven was finally at hand, and even the least here was a member of the bride of Christ, while John the Baptist himself was merely invited to the celebratory supper as a friend of the Bridegroom.

The vast throng that eventually filed again into the temple courtyard spilled into the holy neighborhood created for the priests and Levites. They found miles of tables lined end to end, convenient for sitting or even reclining, laden with bowls and goblets to receive a feast unlike anything Cameron had ever seen or imagined. The aroma alone from near the throne seemed to transport him to heavenly places. Here he had lost his taste for meat and craved the fresh fruits and vegetables that weighed down every branch and vine in the kingdom, yet arrayed before him and the multitudes was that and more.

Stretched from sky to sky were spectators, the angels, who in no way qualified as guests. In their bright robes they sang out praise and glory to the Lamb who was slain, now the Bridegroom who was honoring His own bride.

Apparently the edict that men and women would find their sustenance somewhere other than in the flesh of animals had been lifted for this occasion, for as soon as Cameron found his place, the Lord Jesus Himself announced, "On this mountain I have provided a feast of choice pieces, a feast of wines on the lees, of fat things full of marrow, of well-refined wines on the lees. See, I have prepared my dinner; my oxen and fatted cattle are killed, and all things are ready. I have girded Myself and bid you sit to eat, and I will come and serve you."

Cameron had learned to stop using phrases that limited time, such as, "For as long as I live, I'll remember . . ." because he was slowly coming to grips with the fact that he was now destined to live forever. Even with that caveat, he knew he would never forget this day, this feast, this celebration. For as Jesus had fed five thousand men and their families with a young boy's small lunch more than two millennia before, now He served a sumptuous meal to millions, all at the same time. They sat or reclined and ate and drank and worshiped and sang and celebrated the introduction of the bride, her companions, and the friends of the Groom—including all of Israel who had been redeemed by their faith before the time of the church or who had become tribulation saints.

Cameron ate his fill and closed his eyes, knowing that even without seeing he was always aware of the ever-present Savior, the Bridegroom, who had wooed him to Himself and loved him with an everlasting love.

Rayford felt no sense of loss that both Chaim and Tsion had been assigned to build their own homes with their respective tribes, north of the valley where he had been directed. Many of his Gentile friends and family would be close by, and anyway, his dear mentors were only a few miles away.

Already friends and acquaintances expert in the knowledge of technology had begun trying to find the resources necessary to rebuild infrastructures. And from all over the world came reports that citizens were determined to rebuild mass communications methods, airplanes, and computers, restoring all the modern conveniences.

As for Rayford, he wondered how he was to build his own dwelling. Was he to hew newly created trees? It seemed a desecration. But when the day dawned that he felt compelled to begin his work, everything he needed was there, including the strength and knowledge to work with dispatch. Within days, toiling with dozens of like-minded men and women, he helped create lodging for hundreds of thousands of people in their lush valley alone, assembling the beautiful dwellings from raw materials.

Meanwhile Rayford believed that one day his abilities as a leader and organizer would again be employed. For now he was to aid Chloe and Cameron in their ministry to children. At first this took the form of more building, constructing huge recreation and teaching centers to accommodate the hundreds upon hundreds that began showing up every day. There was no telling how large this number would swell to, as it seemed word of mouth brought more each day, and there appeared to be no competition. Rayford was delighted with the endless sea of young faces of all colors.

They clearly loved Chloe and Cameron, and naturally Rayford had never seen his daughter and son-in-law happier. Daily, it seemed, children on the older end of the age range—around seven—were putting their faith in Christ. Irene shared Rayford's wonder at how any child born during the Tribulation or the kingdom could make any other choice.

But of course, those who did choose the alternative were not public about their intentions. Their fate and their true loyalties would be revealed only in time.

Meanwhile, Abdullah and Yasmine and Bahira and Zaki seemed as deeply immersed in COT as Raymie and Irene were. Rayford would have been content to remain in an assisting role for the whole of the Millennium, but he was just as happy to do his Lord's bidding, regardless.

And so it transpired that he and Irene felt compelled by God to head a team that would supervise growth and development in Indonesia. It seemed that the goal and the task of such teams were to ensure that no nation fell behind but that all would enjoy the full complement of blessing and benefits extended in the Holy Land. Raymie was to remain to aid in Chloe and Cameron's ministry.

Representatives of all nations would make their annual sojourns to the temple, and it seemed apparent that Jesus wanted all the citizens of the world to enjoy the bounty of His new creation.

Ninety-Three Years into
the Millennium

FIVE

BACK FROM Indonesia for a week, Rayford sat in a rocking chair on the rear deck of Tsion Ben-Judah's tidy estate in northern Israel. "I had always wondered what that prophecy meant, about God's people moving about with walking sticks by the end of the millennial kingdom. But I'm over 140 years old now, and I'm beginning to feel it."

"Oh, go on!" Tsion said. "A man is still a child at one hundred here, so you're just a young teen."

"I'm telling you, I'm not the man I once was. I can't imagine what it'll be like for me hundreds of years from now."

"Look at Dr. Rosenzweig, Rayford. He's twenty-five years older than you."

"And you, Tsion, with your glorified body. You look younger than ever. Irene looks like she's stuck at thirty-five and Raymie at twenty-five."

"Well, we had our chances at glorified bodies, didn't we?"

"Don't remind me."

"And how goes the work?"

"We're almost finished, Tsion. The Lord put us together with some of the brightest minds I've ever worked with, and because we're in charge, we haven't had to do much but equip them, encourage them, and let them go."

"I hear wonderful reports out of Indonesia. Their technology rivals that of any nation, and you must take credit for that."

"It's the Lord's doing, of course," Rayford said. "I believe that more every day. I just wonder what He has for us next."

"What is He telling you?"

Rayford stopped rocking and sat forward. "It's strange, but He has been impressing upon my heart an old passage from Matthew. It was one of the last things He told His disciples. 'All authority has been given to Me in heaven and on earth. Go therefore and make disciples of all the nations, baptizing them in the name of the Father and of the Son and of the Holy Spirit, teaching them to observe all things that I have commanded you; and lo, I am with you always, even to the end of the age.' What do you make of that, Tsion?"

"More importantly, friend, what do *you* make of it?"

"If I didn't know better, I'd pray about becoming a missionary."

"But you know better?"

"Well, sure. I mean, here, Tsion? Now? In the kingdom? There have to be precious few to evangelize or baptize or even teach. We work with Chloe and Cameron in COT when we're around. That's where the real need is, of course. And it's been most rewarding. Do you think He's leading me to similar works elsewhere in the world?"

"Have you asked Him?"

"Of course, but you know how sometimes He doesn't tell you everything—"

"Because it should be obvious, sure," Tsion said. "So you're asking questions to which He implies you should know the answers."

"But I don't feel led to children in other countries."

"Do you feel led at all? Or is He just bringing that verse to mind for no reason?"

"Surely not. But if I feel a nudge, it's toward adults."

"Remember, Rayford, anyone under a hundred is a child now."

"Excuse me, Tsion." Rayford stood and moved away as the cellular implant in his inner ear sounded and Chloe spoke.

"Dad?"

She sounded sad. How long had it been since he could say that about anyone? "Hey, Chlo'!"

"Could you come? Bring Tsion if you want. We have an issue here."

"An issue?"

"We've been rocked, I have to say."

"Tell me."

"In person, Dad. Please."

Rayford asked Tsion if he wanted to come along.

"Not unless you need me. Go and assess the situation."

Rayford soon sat in Cameron Williams's great room surrounded by Irene, Chloe, Cameron, Kenny, and Abdullah and Yasmine Ababneh.

They all looked staggered.

"Who died?" Rayford said, thinking he was being rhetorical.

"Cendrillon Jospin," Cameron said.

"The French girl? She was a leader, with you since the beginning."

Chloe sat shaking her head. "You could knock me over with a fig, Dad. If I'm not mistaken, she had actually led others to faith."

"I'm not sure about that anymore, Chloe," Cameron said. "She taught, yes, and she counseled. And it seemed she was an enthusiastic saint. But as I think back, I can't say I ever knew of someone coming to Christ specifically through her leading. Can you?"

Chloe fell silent.

"The Jospins want me to speak at her funeral, Rayford," Cameron said. "They know the truth, and yet still that's what they want. Whatever would I say? She seemed a wonderful girl, and had her death been the result of an accident back in previous years, I'd have been able to rhapsodize about her. She was a dear friend, a valued coworker."

"And an unbeliever," Chloe said.

"How did the conversation go with her parents?" Rayford said. "What are they suggesting you say?"

"They just want a simple eulogy," Cameron said. "But a funeral is no place for me to tell the awful truth. Cendrillon is in hell, no longer with us because she never trusted Christ for salvation. Is that what I tell people? And would her parents forgive me? Perhaps they're in denial, desperate to find some loophole, some reason why a believer might die at one hundred."

"Ask them, Cam," Rayford said. "Because if they don't permit you to be honest, there's no point in doing anything but declining their request. The only benefit I see coming from this is if they allow you to warn other young people of the consequences of putting off the transaction with Jesus. I could go with you to see them and—"

Rayford paused when he noticed Yasmine nudge Abdullah. "Tell them," she whispered. "You know you should."

"What is it, Smitty?" Rayford said.

"Well, it is most troubling. Our daughter—you all know Bahira—when she heard the news she was most distraught, as we all were. But she perhaps a bit more. Not that they were all that close. Cendrillon had wanted to be her friend, but our daughter rebuffed her."

"Because?"

"Because of what we are talking about now. In front of Cameron and Chloe and the others, Cendrillon was a model leader. Behind their backs she was critical, a scoffer, a doubter at best."

"How long has Bahira known this?"

"Just a few weeks, and she feels horrible for not telling us sooner. She worries that she is responsible, because she knew Cendrillon's birthday was coming and that it was possible she was not a believer."

Rayford stood. "We need to visit the Jospins. Perhaps it should be only the three of us—Cam, Abdullah, and me. Is that all right with everyone? We'll go to see about funeral arrangements and try to determine how much they knew and what they are thinking now. You know the saddest part about this, don't you?"

Irene nodded. "Of course, Rafe. She is only the first. Maybe some who follow will be less surprising, but as the children of the Tribulation come of age, this is only the beginning of death during the Millennium."

Raymie Steele knew that had it not been for the Rapture, he would have been long since dead. He had been twelve years old when Jesus shouted from the clouds and the trumpet sounded and he and his mother disappeared from their beds in the twinkling of an eye. He would have been nineteen at the Glorious Appearing, but his glorified body made him look more like a man in his midtwenties, and there he had stayed despite having now lived for 112 years.

He retained a crisp memory of his childhood despite the intervening aeon. Simple, believing, trusting, naïve— that's how he would have described his prepubescent self. He loved his family, adored his mother, and worried about and prayed for his father and sister. How he rejoiced with the angels when Rayford and Chloe Steele became believers.

It was no stretch for Raymie to understand why one-hundred-year-olds would still be referred to as children now. People aged slowly and time seemed to pass quickly. Things he hadn't given much thought to as a child—war, pestilence, disease, violence, crime—were virtually nonexistent, and he realized that this largely accounted for the longevity of the population. He had to chuckle. *That and the promise of almighty God.*

How bizarre it had been to enjoy long, rambling, interesting conversations with his parents. He had gone from an obedient, sometimes challenging—especially to his irresponsible, promise-breaking father—youngster to an adult overnight, and most striking was that he suddenly enjoyed an adult's intellect as well. It had been new to him to realize that practically every subject of discussion had intricate layers of meaning, things that had to be examined and ferreted out in order to under-stand.

He enjoyed having become a favorite among the children who visited what he had come to refer to as Chloe and Cameron's Cosmic Day Care Center. COT was a handy acronym for Children of the Tribulation, of course, but Raymie enjoyed teasing his sister about her recompense from the Lord turning into full-time babysitting.

Plainly, it was more than that. Because these kids

showed up as blank slates and the only convert prospects in the world, Raymie considered his work as important as any in the kingdom. Nothing gave him greater joy than explaining to children old enough to understand that despite being born and raised in homes of believers and in a society where every adult was a follower of Christ, still they had to come to faith in Jesus on their own and for themselves.

In his dwelling, not far from where his parents frequently returned from their efforts in Indonesia, Raymie portrayed on his walls photos of the hundreds of children he had prayed with as they trusted Christ for salvation over the years. He thought about also pinning up his prime targets, but he needn't be reminded of them. God kept them at the forefront of his mind daily.

While Raymie wondered what a normal life might have been like, with dating and love and marriage and parenthood, he found it convenient to not be distracted by such things while immersed in a life of service to Christ. As he prayed for the children under his charge, the Lord gave him the assurance that his efforts would nearly always be successful.

So now, for the first time in nearly a century, Raymie was confused. Had life been way too easy? Certainly. Was this tragedy—the death of a former colleague—a glimpse of how things would be as the kingdom became gradually infiltrated by sin?

Raymie was sad. He was shaken. He had been duped by a girl not much younger than he. And he knew the reason all too well. Nothing was automatic; nothing was guaranteed. While Satan was bound and thus could not tempt people to sin, could not fill their hearts with doubt and fear and questions, clearly the other two legs of the three-legged stool of evil—the world, the flesh, and the devil—were enough to lead one astray.

Raymie had stayed away from the impromptu meeting at Chloe's when the news had spread, for he knew instinctively that his dear friend Bahira—daughter of his parents' friends the Ababnehs—would need him. He met her near a favorite brook that skirted the foothills to the west, and they strolled in the cool early evening air despite the brightness of the sun.

He embraced her, and she wept on his shoulder. Raymie had not seen tears since before the Rapture. It felt strange to console a vibrant woman whose usual countenance was one of sheer joy. Bahira had a chiseled face, gleaming teeth, and huge dark eyes normally full of wonder and humor. Raymie led her to a rock, where they sat.

"I have discovered the reason for the Lord's silence," she said.

"You've experienced it too?"

"Of course."

"Usually it's because we should know the answer to what we're asking."

"But that's not it this time, Raymie. I was asking Him for nothing but comfort. He granted a measure, but His silence scared me. Then it came to me. He too is grieving. As He rejoices whenever a soul chooses Him, the time has come again when some will go the other way."

"But He is all-knowing, Bahira. Cendrillon could not have been a surprise to Him."

She shrugged. "But still it must grieve Him. You know, I have only distant memories of fear and sadness from when my father turned hateful toward my mother because of her faith. Zaki and I worried and hid and cried and prayed. It was way too much for people our age. And then, like you and your mother, we were all suddenly in heaven and soon rejoicing at our father's conversion. Our reunion with him at the Glorious Appearing remains one of my favorite memories. I tell you all that to say how foreign are the emotions I suffer now."

"But you and Cendrillon were not close."

"No, but until recently I had no concerns about her either. There are so many brothers and sisters in the Lord here; one can't be close to all of them. You've been a cherished friend for many years, and I hope you know how much I treasure that. And I have others. Your sister has been special to me, and many of the children I've prayed with have remained close for decades. But how could I have missed what was going on with Cendrillon? I had no inkling until just recently. . . ."

"But you did get a hint?"

Bahira nodded and moved to the brook, where she knelt and cupped her hands to capture a drink. "She had always been mischievous and a kidder, but she was so involved in all our ministries that I thought I knew her heart. She sang; she told stories; she was wonderful with the little ones, playing with them, looking after them. I had no reason to believe she was not one of us."

"Me either."

Bahira dried her hands on the skirt of her robe and sat again. "Not long ago she said something strange, and I didn't know what to make of it. She said that as her childhood was coming to an end, there were times when she wished that for just one night she had pagan parents."

"Pagan?"

"The word hit me as strangely as it does you, Raymie. I hadn't heard it for so long. Cendrillon acted as if she were teasing, but she talked of visiting France or Turkey to see for herself if the nightlife rumors were true."

"They are true, Bahira. My dad checked it out. It basically consists of kids in their eighties and nineties who crow about having not yet become followers of Christ. They call themselves the Other Light and say their study of the ancient Scriptures makes them fans of Lucifer and not Jesus."

"But they're just doing this for attention, aren't they? Jesus lives beyond the Scriptures. He's the Living Word. Surely they can't claim not to believe in a God who has again limited Himself to human form and lives and reigns among us."

"Dad says they seem for real. Yes, it may be for attention, and perhaps they know better and are planning to change their minds and their courses in time to avoid death at one hundred. I'm surprised the Lord doesn't squash them like bugs."

"His mercy is everlasting," Bahira said quietly. "I know that sounds like a cliché, but He promised longevity, and Jehovah will not judge them as accursed until they reach that age. What did your dad say? Did he see them? hear them?"

"Oh yes. He says they have left the homes of their parents—who grieve them noisily and cry out in pain for others to pray for their children—and have begun enterprises that must be a stench in the Lord's nostrils. Brothels, nightclubs, black markets."

"But what have the judges done about such things?"

"Penalties have been handed down. Both France and Turkey have had to reestablish law enforcement agencies and even jails and prisons. But all this has seemed to accomplish is to make these infidels more attractive to other young people. Even with the evil one neutralized for now, the heart of man is deceitful above all things and desperately wicked."

"I worry about the next generation. The world is no longer pristine as it was when the Millennium began. And people are still born into sin. How long will it be before the awfulness of the earth returns, the way our parents knew it, and we have murder and other crimes?"

Raymie shook his head. "I just don't get it. I suppose because you and I have glorified bodies and minds, it's hard for us to empathize with people who want to go their own way. To me this *is* heaven, with Jesus here. What worries me is that by merely giving themselves— their movement—a name, they become organized and somehow legitimatized. The Other Light could become something that young people idealize or even idolize and want to join. You didn't get the impression Cendrillon was a member, did you?"

"No, but how would I know? To my knowledge she had not yet visited France or Turkey, even though she is French. She did tell me that her cousins had told her of another pocket of TOL in Amman."

"That's news to me."

"Again, Raymie, I hoped she was teasing, but I soon realized she was not. She pleaded with me to go with her to check it out. It would be our secret, and her cousins wouldn't tell. We wouldn't have to do anything, she said. Just watch and imagine, pretend our parents weren't followers of Christ. I reminded her, 'Cendrillon, I was raptured. I came from heaven. I am more than a follower of Christ. I have been redeemed and sealed. I don't even have the desire to dabble in this.'

"That's when she turned on me, Raymie. She accused me of being superior, holier-than-thou. I actually apologized. I certainly didn't want to lord anything over her. I hadn't been bragging, just explaining why the temporary pleasures of sin had no hold on me. She said, 'They don't have a hold on me either. I just want to see what I'm missing.' Well, I guess she knows now."

"Excuse me," Raymie said, turning away to get a message from his father. When he turned back, he told Bahira of the plan for the three men to visit Cendrillon's parents. "Should I tell my father what you told me?"

Bahira nodded. "Never fear the truth. The Jospins

may not want to hear it, but they must be told. Her funeral can be a warning that saves countless lives."

As they walked back to their dwellings, Raymie said, "I don't envy the men this task. How would you like to have to tell parents such truth about their child?"

SIX

RAYFORD HOPED never again to have to face an ordeal like talking with Cendrillon Jospin's parents. It might have been easier if they *had* become defensive and moved into denial mode. But these were devout believers who knew the truth. "She's gone because she was lost," her father managed, shoulders heaving.

Rayford asked carefully whether they would allow Cameron to make clear at the funeral that there was a way for all Cendrillon's friends and acquaintances to avoid her fate. The Jospins nodded miserably. "We will have relatives here," her mother said, "our siblings and Cendrillon's cousins. I would have assumed they were all believers, but I'm not sure of anything anymore. Oh, it's all such a hardship on our family. They were here not so long ago. Maybe six weeks. We had an early birthday party for Cendrillon."

———————

Raymie sat with his nephew, Kenny, and Bahira and Zaki at the funeral a few days later. It was held in one of the recreation centers on Chloe and Cameron's property and drew thousands, mostly children who knew Cendrillon from COT.

Strange, Raymie thought, but this would spur the return of an entire industry. As children began reaching the age of one hundred all over the world, many would die. Cendrillon's body had had to be kept in a wine cellar at her parents' home until the service. And because cemeteries were nonexistent, she would also be buried on their land.

Zaki, Bahira's younger brother and always more serious than most, seemed unusually quiet and focused. He was apparently studying many in the crowd. Having been raptured along with his mother and sister, he always seemed happy, if not enthusiastically joyous.

Cendrillon's extended family filed into the front rows just before the service began, and her father was the first to take the podium. "We praise Jesus, the author and finisher of our faith," he began, laboring. "But this is neither the memorial of a life nor the celebration of a home going, for as you all know, there is only one place for the dead now, and it is not heaven. Cendrillon's mother and I covet your prayers for our healing. We loved our daughter as much as parents could love a child, and we are in pain—deep, inexplicable pain. We have asked her friend and ministry supervisor, Cameron Williams, to say a few words."

Cameron felt the presence of the grieving Lord with him and believed He gave him utterance. All he could do was present the unvarnished truth: that Cendrillon had seemed a wonderful person and had accomplished many good deeds. "But the sad fact is that either she never saw her personal need for a Savior, or she chose to ignore that need."

While the Jospins had okayed this, it was apparent the extended family was caught off guard. Cameron caught the glares of some and the seeming distraction of others. "You may think this is hardly the time and place for a message like this, but Cendrillon's parents agree that there may be no more appropriate venue. I have a challenge and a warning to everyone who has not yet reached the age of one hundred and who has not received Christ as Savior. The one common denominator throughout all ages, from the creation of Adam to the present kingdom, is that all have a choice to make about God: will you or will you not accept what the Scriptures call 'so great a salvation'? Those who choose Him will enjoy His entire thousand-year reign and enter the heaven He has prepared for His own. Those who do not will be judged, die in their sins, and spend eternity in the lake of fire.

"This is without question the most important decision you will ever make. I ask you directly: have you personally received Jesus the Christ and acknowledged Him as your only Lord and Savior? If you have not, I urge you to do so right now by telling God, 'Thank You for sending Your Son, Jesus, to die on the cross for my sins. I confess I am a sinner and ask Your forgiveness. I receive Jesus as my Lord and Savior and surrender my life and future to Him.'

"Now let me close by saying, your choice in this matter is easier than it has ever been. There may have been times in eras past when it took a great deal of faith to believe that Jesus was the sinless Son of God. But after all that has transpired, all the prophecy that has been fulfilled, all the attention-getting events that have occurred—including the Rapture of the church, the twenty-one judgments from heaven over the following seven years, and now this, the millennial kingdom with Jesus Himself presiding as King—you would be lying to say that the Christ is anything or anyone else than who He says He is. If you have hardened your heart against Him, it is not because you don't believe. It is not because you don't know. It is because you choose to go your own way rather than His, to indulge in a life centered on your own pleasures and wishes rather than dedicated to the One you know is creator of the universe.

"Should you leave here today without acknowledging Jesus, do not say you haven't been warned that you will not survive your hundredth birthday and that you will suffer needlessly for eternity."

Raymie knew it only seemed unique to have a nephew well over ninety years old. As he sat admiring Cameron's boldness and passion, he couldn't help but put his arm around Kenny and pull him close. Kenny was the only one of the four young people who sat there without a glorified body and memories of seven years in heaven with Jesus. He had come into the Millennium as an almost-five-year-old and even now still looked like a teenager, aging ever so slowly in this idyllic utopia, but Raymie prided himself on being able to tell who had glorified bodies and who didn't. Those who did appeared, of course, to not age an iota. The slow effects of time had an impact on the others.

"How about you, buddy?" Raymie said. "You set with Jesus for the future?"

The truth was, Kenny had been taken aback by his own father's message. Cameron Williams had been a writer, never a preacher or even a speaker. But his decades of ministry to kids had given him an ease and a conviction that made him bold in this context.

"Are you kidding?" Kenny said, smiling. "With parents like mine, do you think I had a choice?"

"Everybody has a choice. Now I want to know."

"I was kidding, Uncle Raymie. Come on; you know this story just like I know yours. We have something in common."

"Our mothers led us to Christ."

"Exactly."

"And it's for real with you, right? I mean, I'm not

going to be sitting here stunned again in a few years with my own nephew lying in a box up there?"

"Not a chance."

"Attaboy."

Zaki leaned over and whispered, "Look at this."

From all over the building, people were streaming toward Cameron, many weeping. Hundreds knelt as he led them in prayer. Kenny would not have guessed there were this many holdouts in the world, let alone right here in Israel.

"Get a load of these guys," Zaki said, nodding toward some young men in the family section. They stood and milled about, looking bored at best, distracted at worst. "I wish I looked like Kenny. I'd infiltrate and find out where they stand. But I've got that GB look."

"Glorified body?" Kenny said, smiling. "That *is* your curse. I suppose I look ancient?"

"You've just got some miles on you, that's all," Bahira said. "You've heard your dad's Tribulation Force stories. Do something for the cause. Find out if those characters are the cousins who tried to influence Cendrillon. They don't know who you are. Be circumspect. You may be an old guy, but you still look like a kid."

Circumspect. That was a new one for Kenny Bruce Williams. He'd never had to be anything other than transparent. Even before he had received Christ, he had not been deceptive. All his life he had been around people who knew and loved Jesus and served Him with their whole hearts. His parents had been martyred, after all, and had been in heaven with God. There was no denying their fervor or what they were about.

Kenny had been ten and living in the kingdom a few years when his mother led him to Christ and prayed with him while putting him to bed one night. "I don't feel like a sinner," he had told her. "I hardly remember doing anything wrong."

"Sin isn't necessarily just things we do," she had said. "It's what we are and who we are. We're all born in sin and need forgiveness."

It hadn't taken much persuasion. Kenny had seen Jesus. If He wasn't God, nobody was. To Kenny, the decision seemed easy. And while he had heard all the stories of his parents' and his grandfather's exploits during the Tribulation, he found living "the life," as his parents called it, easy during the millennial kingdom. When he was younger, Kenny had actually wished there were more opposition so he'd have something exciting to do. But once he had become a believer himself, working with COT had been all the excitement he needed. Almost every day he had either led a child to Christ or known of someone who had.

Be circumspect. Now there was a concept. A tingle went through him as he separated himself from his uncle and his friends and began casually milling about, edging toward the young people from France who might actually be devotees of the Other Light.

As he reached the family, he noticed two young men about his age who looked a lot alike. He reached for one's hand. "You a relative of Cendrillon's?" he said.

The bushy-haired young man shook Kenny's hand. "Depends," he said. "She owe you money?"

Kenny couldn't help but grimace. What a thing to say at time like this.

"Yeah, she was my cousin. Name's Ignace. This is my little brother, Lothair."

"Nice to meet you both. Sorry about your loss."

Lothair, a redhead, was the thinner and taller of the two. He snorted. "That crackpot sure made her sound like a loser. Don't know who he thinks he is."

Kenny flinched and hoped it didn't show. He had never heard people this age talk that way. Little kids, sure, roughhousing, fighting, squabbling over toys, not sharing—that was common. But for almost-adults to be so negative, to talk so mean? That was new to Kenny.

Still, he had to be guarded. "Yeah, well, I don't know what else he could have said."

Lothair chested his way close to Kenny. "You're saying she *was* a loser?"

"No, I—"

"Did you even know her?"

"Yeah, sure. Not well, but she was from my area."

"Then you know she wasn't some big sinner. She hadn't even been outside Israel since she was a little kid. We couldn't even talk her into having a little fun."

"Fun?"

"Yeah, you know. Fun. Something other than singing songs to Jesus to make sure you live past a hundred."

"I wouldn't mind living past a hundred," Kenny said.

"Then you'd better get saved, don't you think? According to this guy, that's the only way to make it. Unless you got a pass by coming straight here from heaven. You didn't, did you?"

"Me? Nah. Do I look like it?"

"You don't, actually; no offense. Those glorified people all look the same, like porcelain dolls. Hey, anywhere to have fun around here?"

"Such as?"

"You know what I mean. Somewhere where people like this nursery guy won't condemn you to hell if you do anything but worship."

"Remember where you are, guys. There's hardly what you'd call nightlife in Israel."

Ignace laughed. "No dances at the temple, eh? No shows? No strong drink? Lothair here makes his own. Takes it right out of the foothills. Speeds up the fermentation process. Gives it a real kick."

"You don't worry about messing with God's wine?"

"Lothair only makes it better, friend."

Kenny was too new at this. He could think of little else to say. He admired the young men's suits.

"Thanks. Custom-made."

"Nice."

But as he looked closely at the pinstripes, he noticed they were made up of a nearly microscopic pattern. Tiny letters. Row after row of LTO, LTO, LTO. The letters ran together, forming the distinctive pattern LTOLTOLTOLTOLTOLTOLTO that from even two feet away just looked like normal striping.

The three were trading contact information when it struck Kenny that maybe it wasn't LTO at all. Maybe it was TOL.

SEVEN

In MANY ways, Rayford decided, what had become known as the Cendrillon Jospin tragedy became a catalyst for good. Good that most in the kingdom did not even know was needed. Somehow, over the first century of the Millennium, the citizenry had taken for granted that what they were experiencing was merely a picture of heaven. Every adult was part of the fold, and the precious children who weren't soon would be, largely due to the ministry of COT. People had begun sending their offspring there daily.

Outside Israel, no similar ministries had sprung up—at least ones of that magnitude. So to learn that Cendrillon was only the first of many to die at age one hundred—and such deaths began the day after her funeral—spread alarm through Eden. If in the very capital of the world, where Jesus Himself ruled from the throne through David

and where the greatest outreach to children was head-
quartered, there could be hundreds—yea, thousands—
dying lost, what did that say about the rest of the world?

"It certainly adds urgency to my call of God, Tsion,"
Rayford said.

"And Irene—how does she feel about all this?"

"The same. We're ready to go. But this will hardly be
anything akin to what we used to see and hear from
missionaries back in the day."

"No, I daresay it will not. I am intrigued, however,
Rayford, as you do not qualify as a 'son of Israel.' You
see, Isaiah writes of you as a stranger and the sons of
Israel as priests and ministers of God." Tsion opened his
Bible. "The prophet is writing to Israel, not to Gentiles,
when he says, 'Strangers shall stand and feed your flocks,
and the sons of the foreigner shall be your plowmen and
your vinedressers. But *you*—' emphasis mine—'shall be
named the priests of the Lord, they shall call you the
servants of our God.'"

"So I'm not qualified?"

"Well, I don't know, especially if it *is* God putting this
on your heart. As you know, as a Gentile you are an
adopted child of God. I don't suppose the Lord would
preclude your doing missionary work, especially now.
Zechariah prophesied that missionaries of the kingdom
would find eager ears among the nations. He wrote:
'Thus says the Lord of hosts: "Peoples shall yet come,
inhabitants of many cities; the inhabitants of one city
shall go to another, saying, 'Let us continue to go and
pray before the Lord, and seek the Lord of hosts. I myself

will go also.' Yes, many peoples and strong nations shall
come to seek the Lord of hosts in Jerusalem, and to pray
before the Lord." Thus says the Lord of hosts: "In those
days ten men from every language of the nations shall
grasp the sleeve of a Jewish man, saying, 'Let us go with
you, for we have heard that God is with you.'"'"

"Well, again, Tsion, I am not a Jewish man. Perhaps
I've intercepted a call that was intended for you."

"You know better than that. Seek the Lord with all
your heart, and I know you will do what He asks."

———————

Raymie, Kenny, Bahira, and Zaki met near the brook
where Raymie and Bahira had walked and talked. They
knelt by the rock, and Raymie prayed, "Lord Jesus, we
sense that You are in this and that there is a great task
ahead of us. Tell us each and all if we have misunder-
stood or if we ever stray from Your instruction."

He waited to see if any of the others spoke up.

When they didn't, he said, "I want to be cautious,
but I'm struck by the makeup of our little band here,
compared to the original Tribulation Force. You've all
heard the stories. There were three men and a woman
when they started too. My father and my sister and
her husband were three of the original members." He
glanced at Bahira and Zaki. "Your father came along
later and served several years. Who would have dreamed
another effort like that might be needed during these
times?"

"The Millennium Force," Bahira whispered.

"Times have changed," Raymie said, "but our mission would be no less important. It wouldn't be as dangerous for us, because God has promised to preserve us until heaven. But still the souls of men and women are at stake."

———

Kenny bore the only nonglorified body among the four, and that had given him entrée to a world in which the others would never be welcomed without suspicion. "Ignace and Lothair Jospin are deep into the Other Light," he reported, "but the underground nightclubs in Paris and elsewhere are merely a front. They are frequently raided and revelers arrested and imprisoned. Those who commit actual crimes have been known to be put to death by lightning, God dealing with them immediately as He did to Ananias and Sapphira of old."

"A front for what?" Zaki said.

"The Other Light is, in essence, a secret society within our own. It is spreading worldwide, largely through computer technology and encrypted messages. The bushy-haired one, Ignace, and the redhead, Lothair, are slowly bringing me into their confidences. I feared at first they would make me prove myself by coming to Paris and engaging in some debauchery, but that—so they claim—is beneath them. Their current deal is a missive called 'If It's True . . . ,' which they send to carefully selected dissidents. The gist of it is that if it's true that the opponents of Jesus die at age one hundred, the efforts of all must be redoubled before they die off, in effect martyring themselves for the sake of the final effort at the end of the Millennium."

"That makes no sense," Bahira said. "If it's true that unbelievers die at one hundred—and we know it is—it proves everything we believe about Jesus, everything that is obvious. I don't understand why this doesn't spur them to repent and save themselves."

"I know what you're saying, Bahira," Raymie said. "But like my brother-in-law said at Cendrillon's funeral, these people already know who Jesus is. They don't doubt His deity. They don't like it. They oppose it. That their comrades are dying at one hundred only convinces them of the rightness of their cause. So, Kenny, how do they plan to overcome the ultimate prophecy, the final reward for their leader at the end of the Millennium?"

"Naturally, their biggest fear is losing all their forces at the end of every century. Eight more of their generations will die out before the final one, and that one will not even be born until nine hundred years into the millennial kingdom. They're the only ones who will be alive to join Satan in waging his war against Christ. These people aren't stupid, though. They recognize that each succeeding generation is way more populous. They expect billions of potential adherents to their cause by the end of the Millennium."

"This goes without saying, I know," Zaki said, "but they don't have a chance. And the deaths of their kind every hundred years should prove that over and over."

"Their plan," Kenny said, "is to keep passing down their doctrines and arguments and plans and hopes so that the newborns become well versed and ready by the time of the final conflict. It's lunacy, I know, and it's destined to end as the prophets have foretold. I mean, we wouldn't have to do anything. We could sit on our hands and watch, and the result would be the same. But what about those who might otherwise have chosen Christ and are instead influenced by these monsters? That has to be the reason we still have work to do, even in the kingdom."

———

Rayford bolted upright in the night, the Lord speaking to him. "You are to be My witness," He said.

"Here am I, Lord. Send me."

"I would that you send others."

"I'm listening, Lord." Rayford slid from his bed to his knees on the floor as Jesus laid out for him a plan to continue spreading the gospel throughout the world. He knew it was foreordained that Satan fail, but still the battle must be waged for the souls of men and women. The population was exploding exponentially, and it was clear that Jesus coveted every soul for heaven.

The plan seemed to roll out before Rayford on a scroll in his mind. All the believers in his orbit were to redouble their efforts and mobilize. Irene, Cameron, Chloe, Kenny, Raymie, Abdullah, Yasmine, Bahira, and Zaki were to become proactive and aggressive with every child that came under their care through COT, for this was the future of the church.

———

"We need another natural," Kenny told the others. "Those of the Other Light can tell one of you GBers a mile away."

"Ideas?" Raymie said. "Anyone? Surely we all know plenty of naturals."

Zaki raised a hand. "I have a close friend," he said.

"How close? You trust him?"

"I do. We discovered we are from the same area of Jordan, so we hit it off."

"Qasim Marid?" Bahira said. "I'm glad you trust him; I don't."

"Qasim, yes. What's wrong with him? I met him at COT when he was very young. Now that I have not aged in all this time, like Kenny he has grown up and caught me. Some ask if we are brothers."

"He is a brother in Christ?" Raymie said.

"I think so."

"You *think* so? That should be easy enough to tell."

"He is full of mischief," Bahira said. "That's what troubles me. He reminds me of Cendrillon."

"He is streetwise; that's all," Zaki said. "But he is one of us."

"You don't know that," his sister said.

"Sure I do."

"You waffled when first Raymie asked."

"Well, we don't talk about it."

"That should make it obvious enough."

"But he often works at COT."

"Have you seen him ministering to the children?" Kenny said. "Has he led any of them to the Lord?"

"I don't know. I think so."

Raymie sighed and stretched. "You're not making me feel comfortable about him. Kenny is saying we need another natural to be an infiltrator; aren't you, Kenny?"

Kenny nodded. "And it has to be someone strong in faith, who knows who he is and where he stands. The day may come when the people of the Other Light put us to the test. We have to be able to stand. I would hate to see an unbeliever or a weak brother try to face the worst wiles of the enemy."

Zaki shrugged. "We'll know soon enough. He's not far from his hundredth birthday."

"How far?" Raymie said.

"A couple of years."

"We can't wait that long. We need somebody who's ready to go right away."

"I'm telling you he's your man," Zaki said. "He's adventurous and brave. He'd love this kind of thing."

"Then you have to ask him flat out, find out where he is with Christ."

It was the fall of the year, and the Feast of Tabernacles had seen millions from all over the world descend upon

Israel and the temple yet again. Jerusalem had been
stretched to its limits for housing, and the Highway of
Holiness had been packed daily as supplicants made
their way to the ceremonies.

The buzz throughout the Holy Land now, with the
foreigners headed back to their homelands, was that
Egypt had, for some reason, sent not one representative.
That's what Rayford was thinking about when he arose
the next morning.

Rayford was stunned when he emerged from his
chamber for breakfast to find Bruce Barnes and Mac
McCullum leaping from their chairs to embrace him.

Irene watched with a smile. "We're already caught up,
Rafe. Nearly a hundred years in ten minutes. It's your
turn."

Bruce, who had been the first martyr from the Tribulation Force, told of his experiences in heaven, many of
which naturally coincided with Irene's and Raymie's,
though from his unique perspective. And since he and
Rayford had briefly greeted each other after the sheep-
and-goats judgment in the Valley of Jehoshaphat nearly
a hundred years before? "I was immediately assigned to
Africa, serving on a development team. It's as rewarding
a task as I've ever enjoyed. I worked myself to a state of
refreshed exhaustion every day, if you know what I mean.
The Lord gave me gifts I never would have expected, and
He helped me exercise them to the fullest from day one.
I built roads, helped construct buildings, even worked
on power grids and helped neutralize and dismantle
weapons. I can't wait to see where He assigns me next."

"Me either," Mac said. "I've been toiling away in my area of expertise all these years, living in what used to be Russia. We're working on building airliners for the whole world."

"Excuse me, Rafe," Irene said, "but a priest is at the door, looking for you three."

They looked at each other. "Send him in," Rayford said. "By all means."

EIGHT

THE SHORT and stocky priest wore a linen garment and trousers. When he bowed and introduced himself as Yerik from the line of Zadok, neatly trimmed hair showed from beneath his turban.

"We are honored, sir," Rayford said. "Would you join us for fried vegetables and fresh fruit?"

"Thank you, no. Ma'am, have you ground your meal yet today?"

Irene shook her head. "I'm sorry."

"No matter. You did not expect me. Nonetheless, I pray the Lord's blessing on your house."

"Thank you," Irene said.

"To what do we owe the privilege?" Rayford said.

"I bring you greetings from and an invitation to an audience with the prince at midday."

"King David?" Rayford said, the words catching in his throat.

"You are to inform no one else, and you are to bring your two associates from the tribes. They are being summoned as we speak and shall meet you three on the causeway."

"Forgive me, sir," Rayford said, "but there is another. Abdullah Ababneh?"

"Hmm. You may take that up with the prince. To my knowledge, you and Dr. Rosenzweig and Mr. McCullum are the only naturals invited. May I inform the prince of your acceptance?"

"With our highest regards."

Raymie didn't know what to think of Qasim Marid at first, but it did strike him as strange that Zaki brought the young man without Bahira along and knowing that Kenny was already busy at COT. The three met at Raymie's home.

Qasim had a long, pointy face with a scraggly black beard, and while he was thin and of only average height, his robe was too short. It hung just above his knees, and the sleeves barely reached his elbows. He spoke quickly and explained that he liked it that way because it allowed him to move easier. "Especially when I have to run, which is often." This was followed by a rollicking laugh. "So, how can I help you fellas?"

Raymie cocked his head and studied the man. "We are a close-knit group," he began slowly. "And we don't apologize for being devout followers of—"

"It's not like I'm a stranger," Qasim said. "Me and Zaki here have been buddies for ninety years."

"I must have seen you around COT. Why don't I recognize you?"

"The beard's new. Plus I work in a different area. I'm in recreation."

"So you play with the children."

"Thousands of 'em."

"Have you ministered to them?"

"Well, sure, yeah." He looked to Zaki, who nodded. "I know all the songs and all the stories and all the prayers."

"The prayers?"

"You know, I pray with the kids, know what to say— that kind of thing."

"He does," Zaki said.

"Pardon my saying so," Raymie said, "but so did Cendrillon."

"This guy's for real, Raymie. Trust me. We've been friends for—"

"A long time, right. I got that. Let's let Qasim speak for himself, shall we? Have you led children to Christ?"

"Have I led them?"

"Surely you know what I mean. Often we debrief late in the afternoon, and workers tell of children who saw their need for the Lord."

"Well, I've sure told them about Jesus. I mean, that's what we do. Whether any have actually prayed with me or in front of me, I couldn't say. Some people are better at that than others, you know."

"I know."

"But a lot of the kids I've worked with became believers, and a whole bunch of 'em are fellow workers now."

"That's something," Zaki said, and Raymie gave him a look.

"Tell me about your own faith," Raymie said.

"My own?"

Is there an echo in here? "How did you come to Christ?"

Qasim shrugged and pursed his lips. "I hardly remember; it's been so long. I mean, I don't recall my life at all before I was a believer. You know, with Jesus being here and in charge and all that since I was a baby, that made it easy."

"But at some point you had to have—"

"Seen my need, as my dad calls it? Sure. Born in sin. Separated from God. Needed a bridge. Prayed the prayer. Got saved."

That sure seemed to Raymie a passionless recitation of the steps to reconciliation with almighty God. "I'm going to have to pray about this, Qasim," he said. "And the rest of us will discuss it. We'll get back to you."

"Great! Because I'd love to become part of your little band and find out what those French guys are up to."

At COT later in the morning, Chloe told Cameron what her mother had told her of the royal invitation. Cameron sought out his mother-in-law.

"So I guess there *is* sin in the kingdom," he said, "even among us glorified ones. I have to confess, I'm feeling left out. Jealousy? Almost. I mean, I'm thrilled for Rayford and the others, especially Chaim and Tsion. But I'd give anything to be there."

"Now *I* need to confess," Irene said. "I just realized why the priest told Rayford not to tell anyone else. Clearly that had to go for me, too. But listen, Cam, this has to have something to do with the Lord putting some mission on your father-in-law's heart the last several days. And you already have your calling. You're not losing your enthusiasm for COT, are you?"

"Never. But one of these days I'm going to take a day off and talk to some of my Old Testament heroes."

Rayford was so excited he could barely contain himself. When he and Bruce and Mac met Chaim and Tsion on the Highway of Holiness, they chattered like classmates at a milestone reunion. And yet Rayford kept finding himself striding far ahead of his comrades.

Presently Yerik appeared and walked with them. "Foreigner," the priest said, "I beg you to match my pace, and we will arrive at the appointed hour."

"Foreigner!" Mac said, laughing, making Chaim and Tsion smile.

"Indeed," Tsion said. "And yet it is this Gentile's coattails we ride merely to sit in on the conversation."

The majestic towers on three sides of the foursquare

Temple Mount loomed on the horizon, and soon the outside walls came into view. Yerik held up a hand and stopped just before the fifty cubits of open space between the causeway and the northern gateway to the outer court. "I know you have been here before," he said, "but indulge me as I rehearse the requirements for entrance. I have brought you to the northern gate because, as the Scriptures tell us, 'the glory of the God of Israel came from the way of the east . . . and the earth shone with His glory.' The eastern gate 'shall be shut; it shall not be opened, and no man shall enter by it, because the Lord God of Israel has entered by it. As for the prince, because he is the prince, he may sit in it to eat bread before the Lord,' but even then 'he shall enter by way of the vestibule of the gateway, and go out the same way.'

"Now, whoever enters by way of this north gate shall go out by way of the south gate, just as whoever enters by way of the south gate shall go out by way of the north gate. No one shall return by way of the gate through which he came. 'Thus says the Lord God: "No foreigner, uncircumcised in heart or uncircumcised in flesh, shall enter My sanctuary, including any foreigner who is among the children of Israel."' You brethren, of course, are either children of Israel or circumcised in heart.

"The prince himself, whom today you shall visit, has said, 'Who may ascend into the hill of the Lord? Or who may stand in His holy place? He who has clean hands and a pure heart, who has not lifted up his soul to an idol, nor sworn deceitfully. He shall receive blessing from the Lord, and righteousness from the God of his salvation.' I would urge you to take a moment and humble yourselves before God to make certain you are worthy."

Rayford immediately fell on his face and heard his friends do the same. "O Lord, search me and cleanse me of any wicked way."

As the men rose, Yerik quoted Revelation 20:6: "'Blessed and holy is he who has part in the first resurrection. Over such the second death has no power, but they shall be priests of God and of Christ, and shall reign with Him a thousand years.' So you see, even if you are a foreigner, you also are a priest who reigns with Christ."

Yerik led them to the gate, pausing again. "Hear now the words of the Lord: 'They shall serve the Lord their God, and David their king, whom I will raise up for them. David My servant shall be king over them, and they shall all have one shepherd; they shall also walk in My judgments and observe My statutes, and do them. And I, the Lord, will be their God, and My servant David a prince among them; I, the Lord, have spoken.' And now if you would silently follow me."

Yerik led them through the great gate and past a three-storied gallery he pointed out as the quarters he shared with several other priests. Soon they reached the inner northern gateway, where eight tables stood in the sun. Rayford recalled that these had been described by the Lord Himself as where the burnt offerings would be slain.

Rayford and the others followed Yerik up seven steps and past the tables to the portico outside the inner entrance. There Yerik instructed them to sit and wait. Rayford was glad for relief from the sun.

———————

Kenny Bruce Williams found himself distracted as he worked at COT that day. He was intrigued to see that Qasim and Raymie and Zaki had arrived a little late, soon going their separate ways and finding their stations to help the rest of the staff with yet another record turnout. Kenny wondered whether COT had a capacity limit. Even now as additional buildings were being finished, more were in the works.

This day Kenny and six subordinates had charge of just under two hundred kids. They would play games, then hear a story, then sing before napping. He was making assignments and trying to keep the children corralled when an aide nudged him and pointed.

It always warmed Kenny's heart to see his mother approach. Though in this new world both had lived so long that the difference in their ages was hardly significant anymore, he would always see her as his elder. And despite that he was nearing one hundred years old, she still seemed to look upon him as her child.

Now she had in tow a black-haired, dark-eyed, olive-skinned young woman whose white robe made her seem to radiate. She would not meet his eye at first but shyly shook his hand. "Ekaterina Risto," she said quietly. "From Greece."

"Ekaterina is an applicant, sweetheart."

"Mom!"

"Sorry. Kenneth."

This made Ekaterina smile and wink at Kenny, and for the first time in his life, something fluttered inside. Perhaps it was that he had never been winked at by anyone but his parents. And he had to face it: like most young people, he hadn't yet become interested in the opposite sex. Well, this one seemed interesting, and he didn't know the first thing about her.

"Just let her observe until you have time to interview her . . . Kenneth. Your father . . . uh, Mr. Williams . . . has already screened her, as I have. We'll look forward to your evaluation."

"Will do. Thanks, Mrs. Williams."

And Ekaterina laughed again.

"Well, come along, plebe. If all these kids don't scare you off first, at nap time we'll get a chance to talk."

NINE

RAYFORD, TSION, Chaim, Mac, and Bruce were sitting at the top of the steps when Yerik appeared below and discreetly signaled them to rise. Passing the priest from behind and taking the steps two at a time was the Lord's prince, King David of Israel. Rayford felt awkward, struggling to his feet, and he sensed the others did too. He wondered if he would find his voice as David began greeting each of the men by name, embracing and kissing them on both cheeks.

"Tsion, the celebrated scholar whose courage sacrificed his own family . . .

"Chaim, also known as Micah, leader of the remnant. Welcome.

"Montgomery Cleburn, also known as Mac, a loyal friend . . .

"Bruce, one of the first to wear a blood-washed robe. Welcome, welcome."

Rayford had seen David only from afar but was struck again by how human and normal he seemed. After having admired the man and his exploits for so long, he wouldn't have been surprised to discover him the size of Goliath. David too had apparently been restored to his ideal age, appearing perhaps in his late twenties with sinewy arm and leg muscles, large hands, bronzed skin, and a trim dark beard that set off prominent features. He wore a purple robe with gold fringe, but a simple gold crown with a small silver frontispiece bearing a diamond was pushed back on his head, almost as an afterthought.

"Rayford Steele," David said, reaching for him, "he of the changed mind and heart."

Rayford, nearly overcome, took a step back after the embrace and bowed. "Your Majesty."

"Oh, we don't concern ourselves with such formalities here," David said. "Unless we're dealing with some reprobate subject, which you plainly are not. We all know who the real Sovereign is. Sit, sit, please."

As the men sat again, Yerik disappeared and David settled a few steps below them. Rayford had the feeling they should switch places, especially after having assumed they would meet somewhere below David's throne.

"Forgive me, sir, but it doesn't seem right to be looking down on you."

"Well," David said with a laugh, "it's all right with me, provided your view of me is only physical."

"I assure you it is."

"I know. Your faithfulness to the Lord is well established, all of you."

Rayford was amused that the others were still obeying the priest's admonition of silence. They did not acknowledge even this compliment.

David spoke with an earnest passion and direct gaze. "Presiding over Israel has been simple during this era," he said. "The counselors, judges, and I have adjudicated minor disputes, mostly over land or possessions. The Lord has given us His wisdom so that the opponents leave happy and usually friends. This is the result when the Lord is the King. Another benefit is that most nations have had the foresight to keep children out of places of authority. Unfortunately, Egypt failed to see the wisdom in that, and she elevated two to her elder council who had not even yet reached a majority. I imagine you have heard the result."

Rayford nodded. "Tongues are wagging all over Israel regarding Egypt's failure to attend the Feast of Tabernacles."

"It should be no surprise that this has kindled the wrath of the Lord," David said. "One of the reasons He decreed mandatory involvement in these observances was that these nations had reviled His chosen people in generations past. The Feast of Tabernacles allows all nations to pay homage to the Lord, in His house, for the annual harvest and provisions. The Lord has been faithful. Egypt has proven unfaithful. Thus says the Lord God: 'My eyes shall be on the faithful of the land, that they may dwell with me; he who walks in a perfect way, he shall serve me. He who works deceit shall not dwell within my house; he who tells lies shall not continue in my presence. Early I will destroy all the wicked of the land, that I may cut off all the evildoers from the city of the Lord.'

"That, gentlemen, is why it behooves all kings to be wise and be instructed. They should serve the Lord with fear and rejoice with trembling. Kiss the Son, lest He be angry and they perish in the way, when His wrath is kindled but a little. Blessed are all those who put their trust in Him. And it shall come to pass that everyone who is left of all the nations which came against Jerusalem shall go up from year to year to worship the King, the Lord of hosts, and to keep the Feast of Tabernacles. And it shall be that whichever of the families of the earth do not come up to Jerusalem to worship the King, the Lord of hosts, on them there will be no rain. They shall receive the plague with which the Lord strikes the nations who do not come up to keep the Feast of Tabernacles.'

"Sir, I summoned you and your associates today because I need your help. I am but king of Israel, prince to Jehovah. Egypt is beyond my jurisdiction. He will deal with her as has been prophesied in His Word. However, the Lord has assigned me to see to the healing of that land after the accursed are slain and the land has suffered drought."

"Slain?"

"Do you marvel that the Lord keeps His word?"

"No, but—"

"You assumed that those responsible for leading astray the rest of Egypt's leaders would not be judged until they reached their hundredth years."

"I suppose I did."

"By their actions they have cursed themselves. Still viewed as children because of their youth, they have become an affront to the Almighty, and they shall surely die. The Lord shall mete out justice, but He also seeks to heal their land. Egypt will require rebuilding and growth and development. You and your men are His choices to carry that out. With your labor shall come the responsibility and the privilege of telling the good news of His salvation to the remainder of Egypt's young unregenerate."

Rayford fell prone and his friends with him. "We are at the Lord's service. May we be found worthy."

And Rayford's next century of effort was fixed.

"We traveled from Greece for the Feast of Tabernacles, as we do every year," Ekaterina Risto told Kenny as they sat at a table fifty feet from hundreds of napping children. "And now we want to stay where the Lord Himself sits on the throne, although we will miss our homeland."

"Tell me of your life there."

"My parents met in an underground church that was once ministered to by your grandfather and your parents, as I understand it. The congregation feared for their lives every day, hiding from Global Community

Peacekeeping Forces. My mother was pregnant with me when Jesus returned at the Glorious Appearing."

"So, like me, you are in your nineties."

"A child," she said, smiling. "Of course, this is all I have known, but I have seen pictures of my mother when she looked much as I do now. She tells me she had just turned sixteen."

Kenny nodded. "This time is as the days of Noah, when people lived for centuries."

"I only wish I could stop aging at a youthful year, as your mother and grandmother have."

"I didn't know my grandmother before the Glorious Appearing," Kenny said. "But pictures of her from before the Rapture show her older than she looks now."

Kenny found Ekaterina easy to talk to, and he felt more comfortable with her than he had almost anyone else he had ever encountered.

"How did you become a believer?" she said.

He smiled. "That's what I'm supposed to be asking you."

"Oh, my story is not so dramatic. You first."

"Mine is less," he said. "For as long as I can remember, our house has been filled with stories of the Rapture, the Tribulation, the Glorious Appearing, the millennial kingdom. I grew up in it, and I was the first child in COT."

"Indeed?"

"They tell me I am the reason for this ministry, that because my mother was martyred first and my father was killed on the last day of the Tribulation, God promised to repay them a hundredfold for losing me. Only they didn't really lose me. My grandfather took care of me until they returned from heaven. Regardless, God keeps His promises, and look at what their hundredfold has become. And it was my mother who led me to Christ, just as is true of my uncle, who also works here."

"Raymie Steele? His mother is Irene?"

"Exactly."

She shook her head. "What a heritage. As I said, my story is not so colorful. Sad to say, however, I was eighty before I became a believer."

"Really? You were actually an unbeliever that long, with the background you had?"

She nodded. "It might be more precise to say I was undecided. I could not doubt that Jesus was the Lord and the Son of God and God. I just didn't know what I wanted do about it."

"Surely your parents raised you to understand the faith."

"And my need, yes. I felt terrible about my indecision. But there was a stubborn, selfish, prideful side of me that would not give in."

"Did you fake it, or did your parents know?"

"They knew. I never hid my feelings. I had a huge problem with my free will. I didn't want to *not* have a choice, and so I vowed I would choose on my own in my own timing."

"Did you know you had only until you turned one hundred?"

"Of course. That was my parents' biggest fear—that I would remain resolute too long."

"What changed your mind?"

"Friends. A few felt the same way I did, or at least I thought they did. They took their resolve further than I did. I was sincere in wanting to decide for myself, to not just inherit my parents' faith. I was not a scoffer. I didn't criticize or turn against Jesus. I just wanted my own way, to live for myself. And I thought I understood the consequences. How this terrified my parents. They tried everything, reminding me that it had been their hard hearts that had caused them to miss the Rapture and have to endure the Tribulation. It was only by the grace of God that they survived till the Glorious Appearing."

"But your friends . . ."

"They were hostile. They didn't study or investigate or even think about it after a while. They made fun of the devout, and they refused to acknowledge Jesus at all. Have you heard of the Other Light?"

"Oh yes."

"Some of them moved to other parts of Europe so they could join that. They not only chose against Christ, but they also chose for Lucifer. It was as if he became their hero, like a martyr who wasn't dead but only temporarily bound."

"But don't they know his destiny?"

Ekaterina stood and paced. "That's just it, Mr. Williams."

"Kenny."

"Oh, I don't know about that. If I'm going to work

for you . . . I mean, not that I'm saying I know I'll get the job . . ."

"It's all right. Call me what you wish."

"I'll tell you what: if you call me Kat, I'll call you whatever you wish."

"You're on, Kat."

"Anyway, that's just it. They have delusions of grandeur. They actually believe they can become so organized and widespread and strong that they can change the course of history."

"Even if they die hundreds of years before the final conflict."

"Imagine that," she said. "But again, this is where they've become so idealistic. They *want* to be martyrs to their cause. They find that glamorous. One told me she believed that if they did their jobs and passed down through the generations their doctrines and their war plans, Satan would actually win and have the power to resurrect them so they could rule with him."

Kenny stood and leaned against the table. "That's a new one for me. I suppose they'd have to sincerely believe that to continue in their lunacy."

Ekaterina nodded. "Eventually that's what changed my mind. I found that the more of my friends who found the Other Light attractive, the more repulsed I was by it. My hesitation over Jesus was all about me, myself, my pride, my ego. I didn't want to give up the reins of my life. For my friends, it was that they had actually become the Lord's enemy. They read the same Scriptures I did, heard the same stories, and came to opposite conclusions. They came to believe that Lucifer got a raw deal, that he hadn't really done anything bad enough to be treated the way God treated him. They actually started praying to him. None of them ever claimed to hear from him, but the very idea terrified me. To be casting your lot with and praying to the enemy of God, locked away somewhere in the bowels of the earth for a thousand years . . . like you say, it's lunacy."

"So that changed your mind?"

"Well, sort of. That's the best part."

TEN

"Now RISE, BRETHREN," David said, "and let me bless
you." He mounted the steps and gathered the men in an
embrace. "God be merciful to us and bless us, and cause
His face to shine upon us, so His way may be known on
earth, His salvation among all nations. Let the peoples
praise You, O God; let all the peoples praise You. Oh, let
the nations be glad and sing for joy! For You shall judge
the people righteously, and govern the nations on earth.

"Behold, He who keeps Israel shall neither slumber
nor sleep. The Lord is your keeper; the Lord is your
shade at your right hand. The sun shall not strike you by
day, nor the moon by night. The Lord shall preserve you
from all evil; He shall preserve your soul. The Lord shall
preserve your going out and your coming in from this
time forth, and even forevermore. Amen."

"Amen," Rayford said. "And thank you."

"And now is there anything I can do for you, sir?"

"For me?"

David chuckled. "The king of Israel is speaking to you, servant of God."

"Forgive me. I do have a question about another close friend and confidant of ours."

"The Jordanian."

"Yes."

"As a natural, he will be of tremendous value to the efforts against the Other Light. He and his wife will be relocated to their homeland."

"I hate to lose them."

"Only temporarily. There are many centuries to go, you know. And I'm sure you've already learned to trust the Lord's wisdom."

"Of course."

"That request was easy. Anything else I can do for you?"

"Yes, actually, there is something."

"Name it."

Rayford began to tell David of the Children of the Tribulation ministry.

"I know it well," David said. "How can I help?"

Rayford told him how the daily highlights were the stories from the Bible. "The children plead for these above refreshments, above games, above singing."

"Indeed?"

"They love the stories and demand to hear them again and again."

"And . . . ?"

"I can't help but think what an unspeakable thrill it would be for them, for us, for everyone involved, if . . . oh, I can't give it utterance. It's too much to hope for."

"You of little faith," David said. "You have not because you ask not."

"Very well. Just imagine if their heroes were there in person to tell their own stories one day."

"Who?"

"Noah."

"Done."

"Really? Seriously? I—"

"I have spoken. Who else?"

"How many dare I ask for?"

"Test the limit of your faith."

"Joshua."

"Done, and I shall send Caleb with him. Who else?"

"You."

"With pleasure. I wonder what story of mine they might ask for. . . ."

The men laughed.

"I am more than grateful," Rayford said.

"Go in peace."

———

"Tell me, Kat," Kenny said. "You've brought me this far."

"I found myself in my room, sitting on my bed, praying for my friends."

"And you were not yet a believer yourself."

"Not really, no. Ironic, isn't it, to pretend to be still

holding out, all the while knowing whom to plead with for the well-being of my friends? Funny thing was, Jesus, as close and ever-present as He had always been, wouldn't speak to me. I had learned verses as a child. How could I not? So I knew the problem. The Scriptures say that "the effective, fervent prayer of a righteous man avails much." I was hardly righteous, and so regardless how fervent, my prayers were anything but effective. So—"

"They didn't avail much."

She smiled. "They availed nothing. But the exercise was good for me, because while Jesus wasn't speaking to me, He was impressing something deep within me. I was suddenly overwhelmed with the fact that I was no better than my friends, regardless the reason for their disbelief. In fact, I was no better than Lucifer himself. I can see by your look that you feel I've overstated it, Kenny. But think about it. I was guilty of the very thing that got Lucifer cast out of heaven. I wanted my own way. I may not have said I wanted to be God or imagined myself bigger or better than He is. But I wanted to be the god of my own life, and that usurped His right and His authority."

Kenny was moved. "Only God could have taught you that."

"My feeling exactly. I came to the conclusion that He may have been silent, but He was still communicating. I suddenly saw myself for what I was—a self-possessed sinner in desperate need of forgiveness and salvation. I knelt on the floor, and you know, that didn't seem low enough. For my whole life I had held Jesus at bay. I lay flat on the floor, weeping, pleading for forgiveness, and committing myself to the Lord forever. He has been with me ever since, and I have never looked back or regretted it."

"And your friends?"

"Two actually became believers. Three others I am still praying for, but they are totally enmeshed in TOL. I know God is sovereign, but in the flesh, I am nearly out of hope."

"He allows them to make their choices."

"And it seems they have."

Kenny was tempted to tell her of his and his friends' plans to try to infiltrate and thwart TOL at some level. But for the same reason Raymie and the others were slow to embrace the idea of Zaki's bringing in a new face, he decided to wait.

———————

Rayford couldn't quit talking as he rushed up the causeway back toward his home. "Irene thought she would miss Indonesia, and of course she misses many people, but she has so quickly found a home helping with COT, which she just loves. Now to have to tell her that we have a new assignment—"

"Closer to home than Indonesia, anyway," Chaim said.

"Well, that's true, but then when I tell her that our heroes of the faith will be coming to share with the kids their own stories in person, well, she'll want to be here for that and—"

FLO

"Rayford," Chaim said, "slow down. I am not 150 anymore. And could one of us get a word in? We were silent long enough in the presence of the prince."

"Yeah," Rayford said, "sorry. Could you believe that? An audience with King David himself?"

"We were there, partner," Mac said. "Now just stop a minute and take a breath. We're gonna scoot a mile past our valley and have to backtrack."

At the end of the day, Kenny found it hard to concentrate on what Raymie wanted. He had called the Millennium Force together at one end of the property, and all Kenny wanted was to report to his mother his enthusiasm for the new recruit.

Zaki actually asked whether he should bring Qasim.

"Are you serious?" Raymie said. "He's who we're discussing."

"We're going to vote then? Because you know what I'll say. He's ready. He's perfect for the assignment."

Raymie held up a hand. "Zaki, let's use a little discernment here and remember that you and I were the only ones among us who chatted with him."

"I know, but Bahira and Kenny trust us, don't you? We liked him. I mean, if there are more formalities, let's get him in here so everybody can be as sold on him as we are, and—"

"I'm not sold on him, Zaki," Raymie said.

"Neither am I," his sister said.

"You weren't even here, Bahira."

"I wish I had been. Then we *could* vote. And it would be two to one against. What was your concern, Raymie?"

"Everything. He's young, immature; he doesn't look right, doesn't comport himself appropriately. He talks too fast and too much. And frankly, I don't like what he has to say. He didn't do himself any good talking about his own conversion. He used all the right words, but they seem just rote to him. And he didn't do himself any favors trying to summarize his own ministry. I don't think he's led one child to Christ in all the time he's been here."

"To be fair," Kenny said, still wishing they could wrap this up so he could make sure his mother hired Ekaterina, "he has been confined to the recreational division."

"Even rec counselors lead kids to the Lord occasionally," Bahira said. "You'd almost have to work at it not to."

Zaki sat shaking his head. "You're going to blackball this guy. I can't believe it. How am I going to tell him?"

"You shouldn't have invited him in the first place," Bahira said. "Then you wouldn't have to tell him anything. You should have just suggested we get to know him and check him out without suggesting or implying anything. If he's disappointed or offended, it's only because you overpromised."

"Okay, I'm sorry if I thought he would be perfect for us. Guess he can call off his trip."

Kenny stole a glance at Raymie.

"What are you talking about?" Raymie said.

"He's going to France in a few days, determined to infiltrate and bring us a report. Don't you want that?"

"He won't be going under our auspices," Raymie said. "And you'd better be sure he says nothing about us. Kenny has made some inroads with the Jospin brothers, and we have to be careful not to compromise that."

Zaki looked embarrassed.

"What?" his sister said. "I know you. Tell me you didn't mention the Jospins to Qasim."

"Well, I didn't know! Who else was he supposed to try to observe there? If he's not looking for someone, how would he even get in?"

"Stop him," Raymie said. "He mustn't go. If he's determined to infiltrate some TOL cell, there are plenty of others."

"You want to brief him first?" Zaki said. "Make sure he doesn't give us away?"

"No! I want him not to even think he's going on our behalf, because he's not."

Zaki sighed. "He's not going to be happy."

"That makes two of us," Bahira said.

Kenny's mother was preparing to leave when he finally reached her.

"I need to hurry," she said. "You're invited to your grandfather's to hear of his audience with King David today."

"What?"

"If you don't know about it, you may be the only one. Grandma wasn't supposed to say anything, but, well . . . it's getting around. Can you come?"

"Wouldn't miss it. But I need to give you my impression of Miss Risto."

"No, you don't."

"I'm sorry?"

"I hired her," his mother said.

"Just like that?"

"Yes. Is there a problem? We all loved her."

"So my interview with her was just a formality?"

Chloe laughed. "Your interview? You think I couldn't see how you two connected? Your report was a foregone conclusion."

"Then I can expect her tomorrow?"

"Oh, she'll be here. But *you* shouldn't expect her. She's been assigned to recreation."

"You're not serious."

"Of course I am. Admit it, Kenny; she'd be a distraction for you. Don't worry. She'll still be in the vicinity. You can get to know her if you wish. Now, come on. Your grandparents are waiting."

ELEVEN

IN HIS PAST, Rayford would have said he couldn't believe his luck. But this was more than fortune; this assignment proved he was continually blessed by God. His leadership skills had been tapped and his muscles stretched by the decades he'd spent leading a development team in Indonesia. And now it became his charge not only to rebuild and develop Egypt but to lead the spiritual effort as well.

That was not his strength, of course, certainly not his specialty. But he could not have done better selecting the team if it had been left to him alone. Admittedly, he would have wanted Chloe and Cameron on board, even Raymie and Kenny. But that would have crippled the COT effort.

Rayford hadn't worked with Bruce since just after the Rapture a hundred years before, but he knew him to be an excellent preacher and student of the Bible. And who better to teach and mentor Bruce than Tsion Ben-Judah and Chaim Rosenzweig?

Bruce's wife, who had been raptured, had a gift for organization like Irene's. They would be of tremendous help to Mac, who would be in charge of technology, transportation, and logistics.

It was clear to Rayford that Irene had mixed emotions about the move and the new mission. She loved the kids of COT and especially getting to work alongside her immediate family. "But I am happiest in the service of Christ and will go wherever He sends me."

As for Rayford, he couldn't move fast enough. He was eager to hear of Abdullah's assignment and would miss working with him. But the idea of seeing the ravages left on a nation from which the Lord had removed His hand and then having the resources to bring it back to productivity under His authority made Rayford feel one hundred again.

Abdullah came by to help with packing. He explained that he soon had to get back to help Yasmine with their own. "I suppose you know we're headed back to Amman. That will seem very strange. I cannot imagine how it must have changed in a century. Somehow I think that despite the passage of time, painful memories will be dredged up."

"I pray the Lord will use them to show you how far He has brought you."

"Even though I will miss all the children, and of course Bahira and Zaki, I like the idea of my new role."

"Tell me about it."

"The Lord appeared to me in the night, apparently just before He deposited Mac and your former pastor—"

"Bruce."

"—right, on your doorstep. He told me sin was spreading, encroaching on my own homeland, and that He knew I would want to play a part in thwarting it. Rayford, I would have dug ditches if that's what He'd asked. When the Creator God visits you, you tend to want to do what He says. One of my questions was whether I could take my family along. It has been so strange to work with Yasmine as a sister rather than a wife. And to have my children—it is bizarre to call them that at their ages—as colleagues rather than as dependants, well, that has been a joy. Alas, the children are to stay here and work with Chloe and Cameron. But Yasmine was free to choose."

"Really? It seems that would be a difficult decision for a wife, of sorts, and a mother. Plus, like most everyone involved with COT, she seems to love it here."

"She did not make her decision lightly. As she has always done, she sought the Lord. Within days, she told me that she and He had come to an agreement. It was all I could do to stifle a laugh. It was as if they had been negotiating. I wouldn't dare negotiate with Him, but she has been to His Father's house and has a glorified mind as well as body, and so I expect they are on different speaking terms than He and I. Anyway, they apparently agreed that I need looking after. And He told her before He told me that my assignment would be dangerous. I suppose He worries that I have grown soft since the Tribulation."

"Haven't you?"

Abdullah laughed. "From flying you Trib Force crazies all over the planet for seven years to working at a children's day camp? They seem equally demanding to me."

"Dangerous, eh?" Rayford said. "Surely the Lord doesn't expect a man your age to pose as a member of TOL."

"Captain Steele," Abdullah said solemnly, laughter dancing in his eyes, "I recall the days when a comment like that to a person of ethnicity was punishable as a hate crime."

Within a few days, Mac had flown everyone and their belongings about 270 miles west to the city of Al Jizah, south of Cairo, where the Lord had directed Rayford to a tract of land on which he was to build living quarters for the team.

"You should have asked David to hit up Noah for the ark blueprints," Chaim said as he watched the younger men do most of the work. In truth, much of it fell to Rayford and Mac as the other three met during the day and evening studying and planning their ministry attack.

As soon as they had landed in Al Jizah, it became clear the area was wounded. Since the Feast of Tabernacles in Israel several days before, no rain had fallen in the entire nation of Egypt. Worse, it was obvious that God had shut off even the underground springs—deadly to a desert climate. Rivers had stopped flowing, and rapidly evaporating water lay stagnant everywhere. Citizens filled containers as fast as they could, trying to collect the last of the good water.

———

Kenny Williams had begun looking for Ekaterina Risto after work every afternoon. They often sat together in the staff debriefing sessions. Today she was beaming, and when it came time for workers and volunteers to tell of anything interesting that had happened that day, Ekaterina was the first on her feet.

"Kat Risto," she said. "I know a lot of you, but for you others, obviously, I'm new here. I've been working in rec, and at first I was afraid I wouldn't get a chance to do as much ministry as you guys who teach or lead worship. But today I told the story of Jonah, and a little girl—she said she was ten—asked me to pray with her for salvation."

The staff erupted in applause, but Kat wasn't finished. "It was the sweetest thing. When she prayed, she told Jesus that, like Jonah, she had been running from Him. She said, 'I kept trying to give myself to You, but I would borrow myself back. Now I want to be Yours for good.'"

Later, as Kenny walked her home, Ekaterina said, "I had no idea how thrilling and rewarding this was going to be. In Greece we worked with the kids where we worshiped. We knew they were the only ones who still had to make decisions. But we pretty much left that responsibility in the laps of their parents, forgetting, I guess, how kids look up to their teachers. Often they'll listen more to us than to Mom or Dad. In all the years I worked with kids, I never prayed with one to become a believer. That was a huge failure, and I didn't even know it. Someday I need to take this COT idea back home."

"I think it would work anywhere," Kenny said. "I'm surprised there aren't more ministries like it around the world."

A neighbor man about Rayford's age wandered over to the Al Jizah construction site one afternoon. "You the ones the Lord sent?" he said.

"That would be us, sir."

"Can you do anything about getting Him to turn the water back on?"

"That's why we're here, but as you can imagine, the leadership of this nation is going to have to get in line."

"I hope you're not expecting a warm welcome in Cairo. Those young men who talked the other leaders out of going to the feast are dead, slain by lightning in the very presence of their colleagues."

Rayford stretched. "The Lord's justice is swift, friend. He clearly made an example of those two, as His Word warned. When their ends came, there could have been no question why. And I believe we'll be seen as the messengers we are. We're praying the whole ordeal will give us a hearing among the young people here, show them there's no trifling with God."

"Well, know that every other believer is praying the same thing. Why must we suffer for the actions of a few?"

The Millennium Force met in a semiprivate back room at the Valley Bistro just south of the Valley of Jehoshaphat. "So, we're still looking for a natural to try to infiltrate the Other Light?" Bahira said.

Raymie nodded, but—no surprise—Zaki jumped in. "Qasim's already done it, and he has a report for us."

"Zaki, we've been over this," Raymie said. "He's probably already given us away."

"No, and he's prepared to debrief us. Trust me; there's stuff you're going to want to hear."

"I'll let you know."

"He's probably outside by now, waiting for me to bring him in."

"You told him where we were meeting?"

"Well, yeah. It was no secret, was it?"

"Zaki, if we're going to do this, be this force, we don't want a lot of people knowing about it. I'm not afraid of the young people of the Other Light, because they can't hurt us. But they can sure hurt a lot of other people, so we have to stay under the radar."

"Fine, but can I bring him in?"

Raymie looked to Bahira, who rolled her eyes and shook her head.

"I guess there's no harm in hearing what he has to say," Raymie said.

That was clearly all Zaki needed to hear. He rushed out and returned seconds later with Qasim, who pulled out a notebook and appeared to be waiting for his cue.

"Before you start," Raymie said, "I need to be clear. You realize you're not part of this group and you don't work under our auspices."

"Granted. But it's in your best interest to know what the competition is up to, wouldn't you say? And they're up to a lot. Those so-called nightclubs of theirs, at least the one in Paris, are so underground hardly anybody even knows about them."

"Well, that makes sense," Kenny said. "No matter what they're doing in there, they're breaking every law on the books, and if they flaunted it, they'd be in deep trouble."

"Rumors say they have these dances and orgies and do a bunch of drugs, but unless they were just putting on a show for me, none of that was going on. They just meet there and talk and scheme and plan."

"How'd you get in?" Kenny said.

Qasim looked self-conscious. "I said I was a friend of a friend of Ignace and Lothair Jospin. The younger one, the redhead, met me at a prearranged spot. He was pretty circumspect, I have to say, wanting to know who I knew and how I knew you."

"*You* meaning *me*, right?" Kenny said.

"Of course."

"Brilliant. How hard do you think it'll be for them to find out I'm a believer, working in a ministry?"

"I covered all that."

"Do I want to hear this?"

"Sure. I was good. I told him you were a subversive, infiltrating the enemy. Little did he know that that's really what I was doing."

Raymie feared Qasim would come off to TOL the way he appeared here—totally amateurish. He sighed. "So, what did you learn?"

"Well, for one thing, these people are serious."

"Come on," Bahira said. "That goes without saying. They're in the minuscule minority, what they're doing violates the law of almighty God, and they know it! Some of their people have died, and while they revere Satan—"

"They like to say Lucifer; they say Satan is a pejorative label the believers gave to a poor guy who got a raw deal."

"Regardless, while they revere him, he's powerless and can't even be planting these ideas in their heads. These people are totally making this stuff up as they go along, and it's entirely in the flesh. They've been seduced by the world and by their own pride. They can't even blame it on the devil!"

"That doesn't make them any less passionate, Bahira," Qasim said. "They trust me, though. I know that."

"How do you know?"

"They gave me a copy of their 'If It's True' manifesto."

"Really?" Kenny said. "They haven't even sent me one."

"That's because they don't trust you yet. But I won 'em over. They'll be sending you one."

"You see why we needed another guy?" Zaki said. "I told you Qasim could pull this off."

Bahira scowled. "Don't be so sure. For one thing, he's not working for us. And for all we know, all he's done is expose us."

"Well, you're wrong," Qasim said. "But thanks for the gratitude. Now, you want to see this manifesto or not?"

TWELVE

Without so much as a call or an official invitation, Rayford Steele's small band entered the Egyptian parliament building that had been rebuilt in Cairo during the first year of the millennial kingdom. Whatever had been going on, the entire place fell mute, and all heads turned to watch the men approach the dais.

The man presiding immediately said, "We've been expecting you," and several members of the government stood to applaud. Others glared at them until the ovation petered out.

Tsion strode to the microphone with the others forming a half circle behind him. "Excuse me," he said as the presiding official moved away and took his seat.

"Micah!" someone shouted, and it seemed to Rayford that many who began clapping again recognized Chaim, the famed leader of the Jewish remnant at Petra during the Great Tribulation, standing behind Tsion. But again, the applause was short-lived.

Rayford had seen Tsion Ben-Judah in countless situations, but never had he seen him carry himself with such authority and—clearly—anger. "On your knees!" he shouted, and immediately the assembled slid from their chairs to the floor.

"Woe to you, says the Lord God of Israel, for helping to scatter His people throughout the generations. He healed your land and reestablished you, populating you solely with believers until your offspring were born. Yet you kept the name of your nation, a stench in the nostrils of God. Egypt: 'temple of the soul of Ptah,' indeed! Ptah a pagan deity from generations past. Where is he in your time of need?

"You deigned to rebuild this structure after the global earthquake, somehow believing God would be pleased by an edifice that looks nothing like a temple dedicated to Him but rather harks back to your days worshiping patron deities? Still, all He required of you was to observe the sacrifices and feasts, and you thumbed your noses at Him. Is it any wonder He has cursed your land?

"Where was your backbone, your leadership, when unbelievers persuaded you to commit the affront of absenting yourself from the Feast of Tabernacles?"

A man looking not much younger than Kenny stood. "Sir, if I may argue our side of the issue—"

"*Your* side? You are accursed! Or are you a believer, confident you shall live past your hundredth birthday?"

"It merely happens that I respectfully disagree—"

"Respectfully? You are fortunate you remain on this earth, for God willed that your young compatriots become examples for the rest of this nation."

"But, sir, that is precisely our point. What kind of a loving God is so capricious that He would—"

"Demolish this building!" Tsion roared. "Rebuild it as a temple to the Lord. Delight in His ways. Seek His face. Follow His statutes. Never again disobey His commands. And henceforth this land shall be known as Osaze, 'loved by God.' Lest you fear that His wrath evidences something other than His love, imagine what He could have done in the face of this ultimate insult.

"Now we His servants shall travel throughout Osaze, teaching the whole counsel of God to the wicked and the undecided and the unbelieving. Woe to anyone who attempts to hamper this effort! While the Lord has not told us when He will restore the life-giving waters, He hereby confirms His immediate judgment of sin. There shall be no more even temporary tolerance of disbelief. Those who choose their own way will continue to perish by their hundredth birthdays, and anyone who dares blaspheme before that shall immediately surely die."

As Rayford followed Tsion and the others out, the entire auditorium was filled with weeping and men and women pleading for forgiveness and mercy.

———————

Raymie was intrigued as Qasim pulled the document from his robe. The others huddled close to read over one another's shoulders. It read:

> To the thinking members of the global society: Use your brains! You are capable of rational thought. We of the Other Light acknowledge that everyone who entered this period of history was a believer in God, either surviving the last seven years on earth as they knew it or returning from heaven with Him.
>
> We do not deny that God was the Creator and that Jesus is His Son. We deny that He ever came to earth in the flesh or that He died and was resurrected. We aver that He unfairly treated one of His own creations, an angel, and summarily cast him out of His presence, forever besmirching his name and reputation.
>
> Worse, He has left men and women no choice but to believe in Him and serve Him, denying our free will. We have no quarrel with those who believe and follow Him and consider themselves devout. We simply insist on the right to decide for ourselves.
>
> And now we come to the crux of our manifesto: If it's true that we, as His opponents, are not allowed to live past the age of one hundred, this merely proves our point: He will not countenance an alternate point of view. Critics and even some of our most loyal members have suggested that if it's

true, we should have abandoned our ill-fated cause when the first wave of deaths hit.

We, however, insist on our right to rebel, even in the face of seemingly insurmountable odds. Because of the new world, the population is exploding as never before. Literally billions more souls will be born with every generation, and therein lies our hope. Even if it's true, our progeny, properly informed and coached, will—by the end of the Millennium—amass an innumerable force. God's own prophecies indicate this.

Even if it's true that we will continue to die out every hundred years, if we remain committed to our cause against the vengeful, bloodthirsty God of the Old Testament, we have hope. If we can equip the eventual mega-army of dissidents to where they can actually emerge victorious in the end, perhaps the new ruler will resurrect us and allow us to reign with him.

The biggest mistake God makes will be to loose our leader for a season at the end of this Millennium, for that shall truly signal the end of His kingdom. Let us not be deterred by intermittent defeats. Watch our ranks grow with every generation, and we will in the end prove that God is anything but gracious and loving and forgiving.

Our hope and wish and instruction to the future torchbearers of the Other Light is that they continue to add to and refine this manifesto until—by the last generation—it becomes the most motivational and strategic call to arms the world has ever known.

And be encouraged. Even if it's true that we die out every generation, it stands to reason that our progeny will become more numerous each time. And if *that's* true, it should be exponentially encouraging to each new wave that carries on our message.

So, what if it's true? Add to this document. Refine it. Improve it. Pass it on. And we'll see you on the victory stand in the end.

The Other Light

Abdullah Ababneh had not been in Amman an hour before he was engaged by a neighbor curious to know what he thought of the most recent judgment from God.

"I did not know we even had people of the Other Light within our borders," the neighbor said. "But God exterminated one this morning."

"TOL is spreading quickly," Abdullah said, unwilling, of course, to reveal that he was in Jordan for the express purpose of infiltrating them. "Tell me what happened."

"If possible," the man said, "there is a faction within TOL that is even more radical than their mainstream. They believe that if they can somehow impregnate women with glorified bodies, they can create a super mongrel race of potential converts to their side who would be partially glorified and perhaps able to live past one hundred. Imagine if they are right."

"They are wrong," Abdullah said. "Simply wrong."

"How can you say that?"

"It only stands to reason, friend. Why do you think that among the glorified there is no marrying or giving in marriage? The glorified bodies of women must have no childbearing capabilities, because they are not even interested in reproductive activity."

"You may be right, and I hope you are, but that didn't stop a TOLer from attempting to rape a glorified woman this morning."

"And . . . ?"

"Her story is that she fought him off, but he subdued her. However, before he could proceed, he died in her arms. When she reported it to authorities, they found his ashes in her bedroom."

"He had been struck by lightning, and she was not affected?"

"She may have been immune anyway, because of the nature of her body, but her account is that he merely died. The incineration had to have happened while she was running for help."

"But her dwelling was not damaged?"

"Not even the blanket on her bed. It reminds me of those strange stories from the past. Spontaneous combustion."

"We must spread this story far and wide," Abdullah said. "Does anyone know how old the perpetrator was? The younger the better, for it will convince these people that such acts will cost them even the few years they have."

"DNA tests identified him as a local eighty-six-year-old."

"Perfect," Abdullah said. "I grieve for anyone lost in their sin, but this will be a lesson for others."

That evening Abdullah and Yasmine strolled familiar streets. "How I wish," she said, "that we had been friends like this when we were husband and wife."

"I'm sorry."

"We're way past regrets, Abdullah. I rejoice that you became a believer, and the past must remain the past. We share a blessing not everyone can claim: children who follow the Lord and serve Him."

"Um-hmm."

"Are you listening to me, Abdullah?"

"Hm? Sure. Sorry."

"You're distracted. About what?"

"I need to find Zeke."

"Mr. Zuckermandel? You've told me of him—the one who was so helpful with disguises for the Trib Force?"

"He's going to have to work some magic. How am I, a natural, supposed to look younger than one hundred? Maybe we missed God's instruction. Perhaps it's you who are to infiltrate the Other Light. You don't look a day over ninety-five."

Kenny visited Ekaterina that evening, hoping to muster the courage to tell her how affectionate he had become toward her. He could never quite seem to find the words, and she kept changing the subject. She moved from exulting anew over what had happened with the little girl that day to asking how well he knew the Jordanian. "You know, the one who's been working at COT for years but was gone the last several days."

"Qasim?"

"That's it. Where's he been?"

"I understand he was visiting France."

"Whatever for? Does he have people there?"

Kenny shrugged, feeling guilty about being evasive but also knowing that it was too early in their relationship—in fact, it was not even a friendship yet; merely an acquaintance—for him to be telling Ekaterina anything about the Millennium Force or Qasim and his self-motivated infiltrations of the Other Light.

And then it hit him. Ekaterina would be the perfect infiltrator! The right age. The right gender. No baggage. And she was a ton more mature than Qasim. She could do whatever the Millennium Force needed, and she would know how to keep confidences.

Ah, what was he thinking? He barely knew her and wanted to be more than friends, and he was already thinking of recruiting her for a clandestine operation with a Force she wasn't even aware of? What was wrong with him?

THIRTEEN

"YOU LOOK wonderful for your age, Abdullah,"
Yasmine said. "But if I may be frank, not even your
friend Zeke—"

"I know, I know," Abdullah said. "He's a miracle
worker, but how do you camouflage the aging of more
than a century? Imagine what I would have looked like
had I lived this long before the Millennium."

That made Yasmine laugh, but she quickly covered
her mouth when Abdullah feigned offense. "What
would Zeke do with you, and what would be the plan
if you were made to look like a young person?"

Abdullah shrugged. "This was the Lord's idea. He's
going to have to tell me what to do."

"The Lord really is a miracle worker, of course.
But those young people will know, if it's obvious

you've survived your hundredth birthday, that you're an interloper. And while I don't worry that they can do you harm when you belong to Jesus, even finding you out couldn't be good for our cause."

———————

"Anyway," Ekaterina said, "I think he likes me."

"Pardon?"

"Qasim, the Jord—"

"I know who you're talking about. Why do you think he likes you? Has he said so? Have you spent any time together?"

"Not really. We were in charge of relays the other day, and he asked me all about my background. Then he started teasing me. It seemed like flirting, and while I was not rude, I didn't engage him in the banter. Later he told me he would like to see me."

"See you? As in go out with you?"

She nodded. "And I agreed."

"What? Tell me you didn't!"

"Kenny! What's the matter? I didn't want to be rude. He just wants to take me to dinner Friday night. What can be the harm? You know him better than I. Is there some reason I should not accept an invitation from a brother?"

A brother? Kenny wasn't so sure. Raymie was suspicious of Qasim, and his personality grated on Kenny. But that wasn't enough to make him bad-mouth the guy to Ekaterina. Kenny knew full well why he had a prob-

lem with Qasim's interest in Kat. He had merely beaten
Kenny to the punch.

"Well?" she said. "No warnings? No dire stories?"

Kenny shook his head. He wanted to blurt out that he
cared for her and would rather date her himself, but it
was too late. He had missed his window of opportunity.
He would look jealous and desperate. Would he have to
compete with Qasim to see her at all now?

———

Three days later, on Friday afternoon, Cameron and
Chloe had just bidden farewell to the last straggler at
COT and were sitting down to a heaping bowl of fresh
fruit when the priest Yerik appeared at their back door.
As he began to introduce himself, Cameron said, "We
know who you are, sir. May we offer you anything?"

"Thank you, no," Yerik said. "I come bearing news.
You know of the arrangement between your father-in-
law and King David regarding the men—"

"Of the Bible who are to come, yes."

"I am here to inform you that if you can avail some
time tomorrow, Noah is prepared to be here."

"Oh, certainly! Of course, we had hoped for more
notice so we could let our people know and ensure the
largest crowd possible. And we'd also like to prepare the
children by reminding them of his story."

Yerik smiled. "The children don't know his story?"

"Well, sure, but . . ."

"Just so you're aware, he'll be here alone. He will

require nothing. No food, no drink, no introduction. And while there may be no way to preclude this, neither is he comfortable with praise. No doubt the children will want to cheer him, but there's no need to encourage it. And as for drawing a large crowd, allow me to ask you, sir: have you already thought of whom you might inform as soon as I leave?"

Chloe laughed. "I don't know about Cam, but *I* have! Starting with our staff, of course."

"Then I daresay," Yerik said, "that news will spread quickly. There will not likely be a family associated with your ministry who will not be aware of tomorrow's visitor. And you should probably plan for a crowd that extends beyond your ministry families as well."

"Sir?"

"Your families will tell their friends, and people will arrive who have no children in COT."

News of the new name of Egypt spread quickly through that nation, and as Rayford, Irene, Chaim, Tsion, Mac, Bruce, and his wife visited the various cities, the people would cry out, "Long live Osaze, 'loved by God,' and long live our King, the Lord Christ!"

But after one of the team preached and young people under one hundred streamed forward to commit their lives to Christ, someone was always bound to demand to know when God would lift His curse.

"That is up to you!" Bruce or Tsion would boom.

"We believe the Lord is waiting to bless repentant hearts and minds and spirits."

"But we have seen our sin and confessed!" the people would yell. "And ours was a sin of omission! We allowed others to sway us, but we did not choose to oppose the Lord!"

Rayford's team never left an area without constructing, developing, advising, counseling, and even initiating technological advances. But even Rayford himself wondered how long it would be before God lifted His hand of discipline from the land.

It was all Kenny could do to contain himself Friday evening, knowing that Qasim was at dinner with Ekaterina. He had got Kat to agree to come and see him later to tell him everything, and she had chuckled that it would be like "telling everything to a girlfriend, but of course you're not a girl at all—I didn't mean to imply that. But we're chums, aren't we? I should be able to tell a friend everything, especially about a date, shouldn't I?"

All Kenny could do was nod. He'd rather not know her or even be her enemy than be her chum, but he would take what he could get. He had to talk himself out of praying that Qasim would make a bad impression on her.

"You're not really going to go down that road, are you, Kenneth?" the Lord said.

"No, Lord."

———————

"Albania?" Yasmine said. "What is Zeke doing there?"

"A little of everything, I guess," Abdullah said. "Farming and teaching young people."

"I can't imagine he's still in the forgery and disguise business."

"I plan to find out. Will you fly with me?"

"Tonight?"

"Right now."

"How far is it?"

"A thousand miles or so. Maybe eleven hundred. An hour's flight."

———————

It was very late, but Kenny knew Kat wouldn't forget to call. He wouldn't sleep until he heard from her, but when his implanted cell phone sounded, it was Raymie.

"You sound disappointed," Raymie said.

"No, sorry. Just had my mind elsewhere."

"Well, it's good to know you weren't thinking about me," Raymie said, laughing. "Listen, I just got the strangest call from my sister, and she wanted me to call a few people for her. You're one of them."

"I'm listening."

"You'll never guess who's coming to speak to the kids tomorrow."

Kenny decided Raymie had been right: he wouldn't have guessed Noah in a million years. Much as he

wanted a full rundown of the evening from Kat,
now he had something even more dramatic to share
with her.

"Needless to say," he told Raymie, "I'll be there."

"Somehow I guessed that. You'll want to be early.
I have a feeling the place will be overrun."

To Abdullah it appeared that Gustaf Zuckermandel Jr.
hadn't changed in a hundred years. He was still large
and baby faced, though he did seem to have a smile that
wouldn't quit. The big man greeted Yasmine with a bear
hug. "I heard all about you, ma'am," he said. "I sure
did. Tell you what—I'da been your husband, you'd have
changed *my* mind." As soon as he said it he appeared to
realize how it sounded, blushed, and apologized. "I just
meant . . . you know . . . never mind."

Abdullah and Yasmine had entered Zeke's humble
dwelling and found him listening to music at the end
of what he said was "yet another long, satisfying day. I
haven't said anything different about a day for a century,
but this is going to be one to remember with you guys
here."

It turned out that Zeke was primarily farming,
but he had started a ministry he called For the Undecided. He advertised to "anyone honestly still seeking
answers about the Lord. If you're a genuine seeker,
let's talk."

He said he had led "probably thousands" to Christ,

"mostly people in their seventies and eighties. They all
have the same story, pretty much. Raised by believers,
of course, they just have a lot of questions and worry
that they're just inheriting their parents' faith. I get a few
scoffers or even potential TOLers, but I just tell 'em up
front, 'If you're not open and honest about your search,
you're probably talking to the wrong guy. I'm not here
to argue and fight or defend the Lord. He sure doesn't
need that, especially from me.' These young people sure
like to hear Tribulation stories, though, and I've got a
million of 'em, as you know."

When Abdullah told Zeke of his assignment from
the Lord, the younger man recoiled. "Sorry, man, but
nobody in TOL is going to believe you're under a
hundred."

"That's why I'm here. You're the best."

"Yeah, but I'm no plastic surgeon, man. Hey, sorry,
I don't mean to be rude. I mean, for one thing, I
haven't been in the craft for decades. With technology
the way it is now, I could make you a killer new ID,
but it's only as good as the disguise, and unless you
were wearing a mask, I mean, come on. Now don't
look at me that way, Smitty. You know I'd do it if I
could. I'm not trying to be a wise guy, but you ought
to tell the Lord that if He really wants you playing a
young guy, He's going to have to work a miracle. Now
Yasmine here—you don't mind if I use your first name,
do you, ma'am?"

"Not at all."

"I could make her look eighty, maybe even seventy.

She doesn't look older than twenty-five or so in the kind of years we used to live. Making up a glorified face would be a trick, though, and I don't think I'd want to even try it. Seems sacrilegious, you know? But then that's not what you're asking."

"Don't think I haven't thought of checking to be sure I wasn't getting her assignment," Abdullah said. "I just thought you might have an idea, other than reminding me how ancient I look."

"You know I didn't mean anything by it. . . ."

"I'm teasing you, my friend. I don't know what I was hoping for. If the best I get is reconnecting with you, it was worth the trip."

"You gotta promise me something though, Smitty. You've got to tell me what comes of all this. God must have something in mind, and if He does, it's going to be special."

It was well after midnight when Kat called Kenny, suggesting it was too late to visit.

"Are you kidding? I've been waiting. I need to hear everything."

"You *are* just like a girlfriend," she said, obviously delighted. But she must have been able to tell from his silence that that was the last thing he wanted to hear. "Oops," she said. "Sorry."

"Just come over," he said. "Unless you don't want to."

"I want to."

Before retiring to their respective chambers, Chloe said, "Cam, I'm wondering whether the Lord has let Dad know that his request is going to be honored, starting tomorrow. I know he'd want to be here."

"Ask him."

"Really? You think I should?"

"Of course. Find out if he knows, and if he doesn't, tell him. And invite him."

"But he's got such important work going there in Egypt."

"Osaze."

"My mistake."

"Still, Chlo', if I were him, I'd at least want to be given the option. You know your mom would want to be here."

"Here's hoping their . . . um . . . Boss gives them some time off."

FOURTEEN

"I FOUND Qasim hilarious," Ekaterina reported, plopping herself on Kenny's couch and declining his offer of grapes. "I'm stuffed. He took me to the Valley Bistro, where you had your meeting."

"Our meeting?"

"Your Millennium Force meeting. Anyway, it was great. Did you just love it? I did. And Qasim was chivalrous, full of stories, talked a mile a minute—in fact, I feel like I've just now caught that from him. Have I? Am I just talking incessantly? Stop me if I am. I don't mean to be. He wants to see me again. I probably will let him, but I didn't promise."

Kenny's mind was whirling. He liked the quiet and shy Kat better, and he hated that she seemed so intrigued by Qasim. But her knowing about the Millennium Force troubled him most.

"The Millennium Force?"

"Yes! Don't play dumb, Kenny. I'm surprised you hadn't told me about it, all clandestine and skulduggery. He told me how you're pretending to be a TOLer, telling them that you're working undercover at COT, playing both ends against the middle. It sounds so exciting. And Qasim infiltrating in Paris? Wow."

Kenny looked away and popped three grapes into his mouth, tucking them into his cheek. "So, he didn't leave me anything to tell you."

"He doesn't even know we know each other!"

"And still he told you my business?"

"It's his business too, Kenny. He admits he's not an official member of the Millennium Force, but he's your primary outside contractor."

"Contractor?"

"Well, not for money, but who knows what might come of it now that he's delivered the goods."

"The goods."

"The TOL manifesto."

"He didn't leave a thing out."

"Don't worry; he swore me to secrecy. Hush-hush."

"Yeah, that Qasim. Real tight-lipped."

"He thinks I would make a good undercover infiltrator too."

"He does?"

"Because I look young for my age, I could tell them I'm ten or twenty years younger and stay on the inside a lot longer."

"Um-hmm."

"You don't think so?"

Kenny strode to the window and pulled the drapes apart, letting in the bright moonlight. "I think you're most valuable and productive right where you are. I mean, I'd rather you were working directly with me, but don't you feel as if you're where God wants you?"

He heard Ekaterina lean forward. "Look at me, Kenny."

He turned.

"You're upset. You're taking this way too seriously. I'm not considering anything Qasim mentioned tonight. All that stuff is just fantasy. I mean, I'm impressed that he does it and that you and your friends are trying to figure ways to thwart TOL. But you're right. The best way to do that, at least for me, is to keep doing what I'm doing. I would rather lead one child to Christ than expose a dozen TOL cells. If their dying off doesn't convince them they're destined to lose in the end, nothing I say or you say or Qasim says is going to change their minds."

"I worry that they're affecting young people, though, Kat. Kids like you were—honest seekers. Those types could be swayed."

"True. So let's get kids saved early; then these characters won't have any impact on them. But again, Kenny, you're overreacting to this. Why so troubled?"

Kenny sighed. This was Qasim's fault. He had put everything on the table, proving again that he was a loose cannon, impossible to trust, the quintessentially wrong person for the job. Kenny sat again, picking a handful of grapes from the bunch and swirling them in his palm. "I need to tell you about Qasim, but I don't want you to take it the wrong way."

"What would be the wrong way to take it?"

"I don't know. Maybe that instead of giving you a brotherly warning about a guy, I was just being jealous."

"Jealous of what?"

"Your attention."

That seemed to stop her. She looked genuinely surprised. "Don't tease me, Kenny."

"Tease you?"

"You needn't be jealous of anyone seeming to have my attention. I've wanted your attention since the day we met."

"Seriously? I've been afraid to—"

"I just figured you saw me as too young, too new in the faith, a little flaky because it took me so long to become a believer. I don't know; maybe you thought I was too immature, hadn't had enough real ministry experience. Or maybe you just didn't think of me in, you know, those terms. Attention terms."

Kenny tried to put the grapes in his mouth, but one missed and rolled down his front, bouncing off his belt buckle and rolling across the floor. Ekaterina made a move to retrieve it, which embarrassed him. He said, "I'll get it," but with his mouth full, his words sounded mushy, which made him laugh, and another grape came shooting out.

Now Ekaterina was laughing, and they were on their

hands and knees, gathering the errant grapes. "At least let me get the one that's been in my mouth," Kenny said, and she howled all the more.

Once they were both seated again and Kenny felt the color receding from his face, Ekaterina reached for his hand. He wiped it on his pants to be sure it wasn't sticky with grape juice and extended it. No one but his parents had ever held his hand.

"Now, you're going to tell me about Qasim. And then I'm going to tell you how innocently I view him regardless. And then we're going to tell each other why we're so interested in each other's attention."

"It's always good to hear from you, sweetheart," Rayford said. "How's Cam?"

When Chloe finished bringing her father up to date on everything and everyone, she asked if he knew Noah was on the COT schedule the next day.

"I didn't know. But isn't that just like David or the Lord or whoever arranged this? Scheduling him on the Sabbath."

"I hadn't thought of that. Maybe that's to keep the crowd down."

"Or up. If it's all right for a patriarch like that to be there, it's certainly all right for everyone else. I'd sure like to be there, and we both know your mother would. We're scheduled for Siwa tomorrow, which is more than six hundred miles from you."

"And we don't know when he's going to show up, Dad. In his own time, I suppose. We'll sure be ready."

"Well, we'll be thinking of you regardless."

———

Kenny searched himself for any ill motive in telling Ekaterina his misgivings about Qasim. She fell silent and seemed to cloud over as he spoke.

"Do you wonder about him spiritually?" she said finally.

"I don't know what to think. Raymie is dubious because Qasim's conversion story is so cut-and-dried. And he doesn't seem to have been successful in ministering to kids at COT—actually leading them to Jesus, I mean—despite all the years he's worked there."

"I wasn't going to say anything," she said, "but now that you mention it, he never initiates conversation about the Lord. It's always about him. And when there's work to be done—I mean real work, not playing with the kids—he always seems to disappear. Carrying stuff, putting equipment away, preparing a field . . . you just can't find him. He always has some alibi. Like tomorrow even. I said something innocuous about seeing him tomorrow, and he said no, he was taking the day off because some special speaker is coming and he's sure it's going to be crowded. He said, 'There'll be enough parents to help. The staff wouldn't even have to be there.'"

"Special speaker? That's what he said?"

She nodded. "I'm not even sure he's right; is he? Do you know of a guest coming tomorrow?"

"You didn't hear?"

"No."

"He didn't tell you?"

She shook her head.

"You seriously don't know."

"Can you think of one more way to ask me, Kenny? Just tell me."

He did.

"No! Not *the* Noah."

"Do you know another?"

"Qasim had to know that, right?"

"We tried reaching everyone. I'm amazed he didn't tell you. And I'm shocked he could stay away. How could he?"

The entire Rayford Steele development team was traveling in a huge motor coach currently encamped just outside Siwa in the west of what had been known for aeons as Egypt. It was now Osaze, of course. Rayford had taken the call from Chloe late, making sleep impossible. He didn't want to awaken the others, so he tiptoed out, slipping on his sunglasses against the moon, the light from which reminded him of noon sunshine from his former days.

Rayford was strolling near the Siwa oasis when it was as if God turned the water back on. He felt the rumble in the ground and heard the movement of the springs and even a small waterfall. "What is it, Lord?" he said. "The last holdout repented? What?"

But God was silent. Rayford knew well that the Creator took His own counsel, had His own schedule and agenda and clock. If it was time, it was time, and no one else had to know or understand.

"Thank You, Jesus," Rayford said. "This will certainly make our work easier. Dare I ask for the freedom to return to Israel for the day tomorrow?"

The sound of the motor coach door slamming made Rayford turn.

Tsion approached. "Ah," the professor said, "I hoped that rumble meant what it did. Look at that water."

Rayford told him what was happening at COT the next day.

"We're going, are we not? Surely the prince expected that when he acceded to your requests."

"The Lord is not saying," Rayford said. "Should I take your interest as His blessing?"

"That's on you," Tsion said. "But you can be sure the rest will want to go. How about we put out a fleece? See if Mac can get us there by the crack of dawn and back as soon as it's over, and if he can, we'll take that as divine permission."

"Works for me," Rayford said.

"All right," Ekaterina said slowly, "I have lost my enthusiasm for the unique personality of Qasim Marid. I suppose I know what to say when he asks to take me out again. But whatever will I do with my spare time now?"

"I have some ideas," Kenny said, smiling.

"I thought you might. Would you start by walking me home? I don't want to be late to work tomorrow."

Ekaterina's parents' place was about three-quarters of a mile from Kenny's, giving them more time to chat.

Kenny took her elbow as they walked. "I was struck from the first by your obvious passion for the Lord," he said.

"Me too," she said. "I mean about you."

"It's something I have to work on," he said. "How bad is that? I'm living in the millennial kingdom with Jesus right here on the throne and ever-present, and still I struggle with the flesh."

"We're not in heaven yet. The glorified-mind-and-body people seem to have no distractions to their devotion."

"The undecideds trouble me more."

"Tell me about it, Kenny. I *was* one for way too long."

"If it's hard for me to be as devout and consistent as I want to be—with my heritage and my work—I can't imagine what it's like for those who stubbornly want to insist on their own way."

"They're easy targets for the Other Light," she said. "What a name for the resistance, huh? They really worship the Lesser Light. The *Way* Lesser Light."

They fell silent as they neared Ekaterina's home. She reached up and intertwined her fingers with his. "So is it my turn?" she whispered at last.

"Your turn?"

"To tell you my first impression of you."

"That's your call."

"I found you courtly."

"That's a quaint term. And you liked that?"

"I quickly became infatuated," she said. "Is that too forward?"

"Not for me. But I don't understand. We hardly saw each other after that first day."

"That was all it took for me. I was so glad you didn't ignore me after that, even though we worked in different areas."

"Ignore you? If you were infatuated, I don't know what to call what I was. What I am. I just know I want to spend a lot more time with you, Kat. I want to really get to know you."

"Well," she said, gazing at him, "it seems we have plenty of time for that. For one thing, I am going to be putting in for a transfer to a more direct-ministry-oriented department. I mean, I like rec and I've had my ministry opportunities. But I'd feel more comfortable now in an area that doesn't have Qasim in it."

"It's unlikely my parents would put you in my area. My mother was on to us from the first day."

"Oh, how embarrassing! It showed?"

"According to her."

"Mothers know these things. But I want to learn from you how to make reaching these kids an everyday thing."

"Well," Kenny said, "if our relationship is going to be educational, we ought to start on the way to work tomorrow, wouldn't you say?"

"Just tell me when to be ready, Professor Williams."

FIFTEEN

CAMERON WILLIAMS was up two hours before anyone was
expected on his property, which now covered eighty
acres and was threatening to have to expand yet again.
Daily he and Chloe and Kenny and a couple hundred
other staffers hosted the children at what had become
known as the biggest day care center in the world.

But of course it was more than that. Besides that the
kids all seemed to revere and, yes, love him and Chloe—
which he accepted gratefully from Jesus as recompense
for their giving up their small family in service to Him
during the Tribulation—COT had become the most
effective salvation ministry anyone was aware of.

Cameron sang and prayed as he strolled the grounds,
checking on everything from parking areas and gates to
buildings and open areas. Everything seemed in order for
their special visitor. Predicting within a few thousand

how many might show up was another thing. Only one staffer had informed him and Chloe that he wouldn't be there, giving no reason, just asking for the day off. Who knew? Maybe he wanted to be there as a spectator. Why else would a person not want to be working today?

"Lord, may this be more than a spectacle. May children come to You because Your servant is here."

Cameron turned at the sound of an engine and saw a van pulling onto the property a hundred yards away. As he squinted into the rising sun, he followed the cloud of dust until the vehicle skidded up next to him and the tinted driver's window lowered.

"We're lookin' for the circus, buddy," Mac McCullum said. "We in the right place?"

"Hush, Mac," Irene called out from a backseat. "Cam, I called Chloe on the way in, and she's already started on breakfast. She said we'd find you out here, but I've got to get back and help her. Hop in."

———

Things were different between Kenny and Ekaterina by the time he arrived at her place that morning. He was struck that they seemed to look at each other differently. She looked him full in the face, her eyes not wavering from his.

"Let me introduce you to my parents," she said.

"They're up already?"

"They've got places to go today," she said. "A celebrity is in town, in case you didn't know."

She led him inside, where Mr. and Mrs. Risto immediately rose, smiling, from their places at the table. After introductions, Mr. Risto said, "I hope it's okay that we come today. We haven't asked anyone."

"I'm sure you won't be alone. But you realize we don't know when he's coming."

"We'll just stand by and wait for Ekaterina's call. Now please join us for breakfast."

"Oh, thanks, but I can't. I'm sorry, but my grandparents and their friends have just arrived from Egy—Osaze. They've asked me to join them."

"Oh," Ekaterina said, "you'd better hurry then. I'll be along."

"No, they've invited you, too. You haven't eaten yet, have you?"

"Are you sure?"

"Absolutely. Please. They're waiting for us."

The Ristos smiled their blessing, and Kenny and Ekaterina were off.

"So this relationship is new just since we've left?" Rayford said, leaning past Chloe to taste her baked vegetable casserole.

"It's not even a relationship, Dad, as far as I know. They barely know each other, though I think Kenny could be sweet on her if given the chance. When I called him, he said she was walking with him to work this morning, that's all. I told him to bring her along."

"Tell me about her," Irene said.

"All I know are the basics, Mom," Chloe said. "She's Greek, was kind of a late convert, and she's fit in well here in a short time."

"And Kenny's got designs on her?"

"That's a quaint way to put it, but yes, he and most other naturals his age. She actually went out with one of the other guys on staff."

"Yeah?" Cameron said. "Who's that?"

"Abdullah's boy Zaki's friend. Qasim something."

"Marid?"

"That's it."

"He's the one who's not working today."

"What? He sick or something?"

"Just asked for the day off."

"Does he know what he's missing?"

"I told him, Chlo'."

––––––

When Kenny and Ekaterina walked in, everyone's response was Kenny's worst nightmare. It was painfully plain that they had been talking about whom he was bringing to breakfast. Everyone had gone mute and studied Kat, reading way more into this than it was worth— at least yet.

"Sorry," he whispered, but Ekaterina immediately took the initiative and introduced herself to everyone. Of course, she knew Kenny's parents and grandparents, but she was most solicitous of Tsion, Chaim, Bruce and his wife, and Mac.

"You don't got an older sister, do ya?" Mac said, eyes dancing. "Like about eighty years older?"

Ekaterina threw her head back and laughed. "I'll keep an eye out."

"Kenny," Bruce said, "I haven't seen you in forever. You know you're named after me, don't you?"

"Yes, sir."

"And that I performed your parents' wedding?"

"I know that too, sir. Good to see you."

"You don't need to blush, Kenny Bruce," Bruce said. "I'm not suggesting anything."

"Bruce!" his wife said.

"I'm just saying, you know where to reach me."

Fortunately Ekaterina was elsewhere and hadn't heard this exchange. While Bruce's wife was scolding him, Kenny added, "We're just friends."

"Yeah," Bruce said, chuckling. "That's some radiant friend. You two couldn't look more enamored with each other if you were posing for wedding pictures."

More than ninety minutes before COT was scheduled to open, the crowds began to arrive. Cameron pressed into service everyone available—including his father-in-law and all his friends—helping people park and find places to sit. He hadn't thought of grandstands, but most families brought blankets and began spreading them all over the athletic field. Crowd control was going to be Cameron's biggest headache. On the other hand, only the children had been invited; he didn't feel obligated to the rest. They were on their own.

So far, with the first few thousand, people seemed in wonderful moods. They apparently knew there had been no announcement of the patriarch's schedule, and they appeared content to wait as long as necessary. Cameron decided to start the children's ministries as usual, breaking whenever their guest arrived. It wouldn't pay to just have everything held in abeyance for who knew how long.

He and Chloe had discussed whether to try to arrange for food for the multitudes, but that didn't seem their responsibility either. Chloe had wondered aloud whether the Lord would feed them as He had at least twice done during his first-century ministry. But it was obvious He had acted in another way. Every family had brought baskets of vegetables, fruit, cheese, and bread with them.

Cameron announced to the staff that they should head for their respective areas and start the day as usual. "We'll let you know if and when we're reconvening."

Before Ekaterina headed for the rec center, Kenny said, "When Noah gets here, save me a seat and I'll find you."

He felt self-conscious as he began teaching his lesson for the day, because while a parent or two often looked on during a normal day, he had never entertained this many. There seemed as many adults as children. Well, at least they would find out what went on at COT every day. Maybe it would give them even more confidence to keep sending their kids.

But the children were as distracted as the adults, including Kenny. It had been a long time since he last felt this disorganized and scattered, and he found himself continually praying silently that the Lord would speak through him in spite of himself.

That settled Kenny, and the kids started paying better attention too. He led them in songs and choruses before preparing them to shift to the recreation area for games. But just as he and his aides were getting them lined up, it became clear that the very atmosphere had changed.

Where there had been a loud hum of activity throughout the Williams acreage, now silence pervaded. No one spoke; no one moved. Everybody turned as one and stared toward the main entrance, where a lone figure strode purposefully onto the grounds.

He wore a colorful robe with a wide blue sash, and his white hair and beard contrasted with his robust appearance.

———

Cameron was struck that there wasn't a hint of danger to Noah despite his having no entourage or even security. Noah looked like a man on a mission who knew why he was here. How Cameron wished there had been no proscription against introducing the man. He had instructed the entire staff to teach a New Testament passage about Noah to the children that morning. He only hoped they'd already gotten to it, because here came the man about whom the Scriptures said, "By faith Noah, being divinely warned of things not yet seen, moved with godly fear, prepared an ark for the saving of his household, by which he condemned the world and became heir of the righteousness which is according to faith."

On cue, the staff led the children to the athletic field, and when the crowds intersected the path of the most famous sea captain in history, he merely looked down, kept walking, and repeated, "Excuse me. Good morning. Excuse me. Excuse me. Thank you."

SIXTEEN

RAYFORD DIDN'T know if the man's natural voice was so powerful he didn't need amplification or if the Lord merely allowed everyone to hear Noah as if he were standing next to them. But Rayford assumed the latter. Noah didn't even seem to raise his voice, and yet every throaty, raspy syllable was crystal clear.

"Greetings to you," he began, "my young and old and glorified brothers and sisters in the faith. And if you are a youngster who has not yet committed your life to the Messiah, I pray that my story will aid you on your journey. To those of you who have not spoken Hebrew all your lives, it may interest you to know that my name in the now universal language is Noach. If that jangles in your ear, think of me by whatever name you have been familiar with relating to my story from the Scriptures.

"I have been called a hero, but as you will see, I was

but a man, frail and weak if, I pray, faithful. Now, children, I may not look like I lived 950 years. That is because, when God granted me my glorified body, he set me back to midlife and the relatively spry age of just five hundred, when I was married and the father of three sons. Why did we live so long back then? For the same reason you will live long. The world actually exists now, as it did then, under a canopy of water that blocks the most harmful effects of the sun. When that condition no longer existed, life spans were greatly reduced, as history shows.

"Now, I am most known for what?"

"The boat!" someone cried out.

The old man laughed. "Yes, the ark and the animals and the flood. But did you know that many revere me for something else? No? No one? I was the first to appreciate the juice of the grape as much as the meat, the fruit, of it, and devised a way to pull the liquid from it and make a drink of it. You are too young for wine just yet, and one of my great regrets is that I embarrassed myself because of it as well. Worse, I sinned against God and humiliated myself, and this was after proving my faithfulness through obedience. Guard your hearts that you do not stumble the same way.

"Well, let me get to the real story, what actually happened behind all the tales you may have heard about me and my wife and my sons and their wives and all those pairs of animals.

"Like me, men began to have many children, especially because we were all living so long. The earth was growing with more and more people. This may be hard for some of you to understand, but during that time disobedient, fallen angels were banished from heaven and lived among men on the earth. They married human women against the will and law of God. God saw that most of the world was filled with wicked men and women, and He decided to give them only 120 years to see their need for Him, or He would wipe them off the face of the earth. The Lord said, 'My Spirit shall not strive with man forever, for he is indeed flesh.'

"Soon the Lord saw that the wickedness of man was great in the earth, and that every intent of the thoughts of his heart was only evil continually. It actually got to the place where the Lord was sorry that He had made man, and He was grieved in His heart. Imagine it! The creation had shaken its fist in the face of the Creator.

"So the Lord said, 'I will destroy man whom I have created from the face of the earth, both man and beast, creeping thing and birds of the air, for I am sorry that I have made them.' But, children, somehow I, Noah, found grace in the eyes of the Lord. Now notice that I did not say that God found in me any good thing that made me worthy. I believed in Him, that He was the Creator and my Sovereign and my only Savior from sin. I humbled myself before Him and pledged faithfulness and obedience. That is all we can do.

"You must understand—I did not see myself as an extraordinary man. I was like anyone else. I toiled. I worried. I raised my family and kept them close to me— all three sons, even after they married. We were not perfect. We sometimes argued and squabbled, wanted our own ways. But for the most part we respected and honored each other and our wives. They deferred to me as their senior and as their father. And as much as was within me, I sought to serve the Lord.

"Somehow God saw me as just, and I walked with Him. But the earth was corrupt and filled with violence. One day He said to me, 'The end of all flesh has come before Me, for the earth is filled with violence through them; and behold, I will destroy them with the earth. Make yourself an ark of gopherwood; make rooms in the ark, and cover it inside and outside with pitch.'"

A girl raised her hand. "What is gopherwood and pitch?"

"Good question, young lady. Gopherwood trees don't grow anymore, but they are similar to cedar or cypress. All right? And pitch is like tar, a sticky black liquid that kept water from seeping through the cracks in the wood."

The girl nodded and Noah continued. "And the Lord told me how to make the ark. He said its length should be three hundred cubits, its width fifty cubits, and its height thirty cubits. Who knows what a cubit is?"

Several children tried to answer at once, convincing Rayford that they had recently been taught. Noah singled one out, who said, "The distance from the tip of the middle finger to the elbow of a grown man."

"Exactly! About eighteen inches. And God told me, 'You shall make a window for the ark, and you shall finish it to a cubit from above; and set the door of the ark in its side. You shall make it with lower, second, and third decks.' Are you getting an idea how big this structure was? It was boxy and wide, and that's why it never capsized or sank. And just wait until you hear how many creatures we carried!

"God said, 'Behold, I Myself am bringing floodwaters on the earth, to destroy from under heaven all flesh in which is the breath of life; everything that is on the earth shall die.'

"Can you imagine how that made me feel? I was grateful that I had found grace in His eyes, but it is a fearful thing to see almighty God at the end of His patience and mercy with all of mankind. It soon became clear that I and my family were to be the only humans left. God said, 'But I will establish My covenant with you; and you shall go into the ark—you, your sons, your wife, and your sons' wives with you.

"'And of every living thing of all flesh you shall bring two of every sort into the ark, to keep them alive with you; they shall be male and female. Of the birds after their kind, of animals after their kind, and of every creeping thing of the earth after its kind, two of every kind will come to you to keep them alive.

"'And you shall take for yourself of all food that is eaten, and you shall gather it to yourself; and it shall be food for you and for them.'

"Think of it, children. My sons and I herded more than seventy thousand animals onto that boat! Not to mention millions of insects and enough food for us and for all of those creatures! As you'll see, we needed enough food for a whole year. Well, it took decades just to accomplish this, but I did according to all that God commanded me.

"I was six hundred years old when the Lord said, 'Come into the ark, you and all your household, because I have seen that you are righteous before Me in this generation. For after seven more days I will cause it to rain on the earth forty days and forty nights, and I will destroy from the face of the earth all living things that I have made.'

"And it came to pass after seven days that the waters of the flood were on the earth. You see, God tarried that one more week, I believe, hoping that more would repent of their sins, but none did. Many have retold this story over the generations, leaving the impression that forty days and forty nights of solid rain was enough to cover the entire the earth. But the truth is that all the fountains of the great deep were broken up, besides the windows of heaven being opened. The water came from above *and* below!

"My family and I were on that ark with every beast after its kind, all cattle after their kind, every creeping thing that creeps on the earth after its kind, and every bird after its kind, every bird of every sort, two by two, of all flesh in which was the breath of life, male and female of all flesh.

"The waters increased and lifted up the ark, and it rose high above the earth. The waters prevailed and greatly increased on the earth, and the ark moved about on the surface of the waters. And the waters prevailed exceedingly on the earth, and all the high hills under the whole heaven were covered. The waters prevailed fifteen cubits upward over the highest mountains. Mount Ararat itself, where we would eventually come to rest, was about seventeen thousand feet high, but we needed not worry that we would strike it or any other mountain until the waters began to recede.

"Well, as you might imagine, all flesh died that moved on the earth: birds and cattle and beasts and every creeping thing that creeps on the earth, and every man. All in whose nostrils was the breath of the spirit of life, all that was on the dry land, died. It is no trifle to defy the Lord God. He destroyed all living things which were on the face of the ground: both man and cattle, creeping thing and bird of the air. They were destroyed from the earth. Only I and those with me in the ark remained alive.

"As you might imagine, that was a terrifying and sobering time for us. God was showing His great power and, yes, His anger. While I was relieved and grateful that somehow I had found favor in His eyes, imagine how lonely we felt, knowing that at the end of this, we would be the fathers of all the generations yet to come.

"While you have no doubt heard that it rained for forty days and forty nights, the waters prevailed on the earth one hundred and fifty days. There were times when I wondered if the Lord had left us, but we kept our faith. Finally God made a wind to pass over the earth, and the waters subsided. The fountains of the deep and the windows of heaven were also stopped, and the rain from heaven was restrained. And the waters receded continually from the earth. At the end of the hundred and fifty days, the waters decreased.

"Would you have liked to have been with us, my sons and me and our wives? Think about it before you decide. Imagine the work. Imagine the smell!"

This caused the children to laugh.

"Oh, make no mistake, it was hard work. The ark finally rested in the seventh month, nestling on the mountains of Ararat. It took three more months for the waters to decrease continually until the tops of the mountains were seen.

"And so it came to pass that at the end of forty more days, I opened the window of the ark and sent out a raven, which kept going to and fro until the waters had dried up from the earth. I also sent out a dove, to see if the waters had receded from the face of the ground. But the dove found no resting place for the sole of her foot, and she returned into the ark, for the waters were still covering the face of the whole earth.

"I waited another seven days and again sent the dove out from the ark. That evening the dove returned, and behold, a freshly plucked olive leaf was in her mouth. That told me that the waters had receded from the earth. So I waited yet another seven days and sent out the dove, which did not return again.

"And it came to pass after an entire year since the flood began that the waters were dried up from the earth. I removed the covering of the ark and looked, and indeed the surface of the ground was dry. A month later the whole earth was dry.

Then God spoke to me, saying, 'Go out of the ark, you
and your wife, and your sons and your sons' wives with
you. Bring out with you every living thing of all flesh
that is with you: birds and cattle and every creeping
thing that creeps on the earth, so that they may abound
on the earth, and be fruitful and multiply on the earth.'

"So we went out and led all the creatures out. Then
I built an altar to the Lord and offered burnt offerings
to Him. When He smelled the soothing aroma, He said,
'I will never again curse the ground for man's sake,
although the imagination of man's heart is evil from
his youth; nor will I again destroy every living thing as
I have done. While the earth remains, seedtime and
harvest, cold and heat, winter and summer, and day and
night shall not cease.'

"And children, God has kept His promise. He blessed
me and my sons and said to us, 'Be fruitful and multiply, and fill the earth. And every beast of the earth and
bird of the air, all that move on the earth, and all the
fish of the sea shall fear you. They are given into your
hand. Every moving thing that lives shall be food for
you. I have given you all things, even as the green
herbs.'

"He also told me that 'whoever sheds man's blood,
by man his blood shall be shed; for in My image I made
man. And as for you, be fruitful and multiply; bring
forth abundantly in the earth and multiply in it.'

"You know what that means, children? It means you
are all, each and every one of you, descendants of me
and my sons. God also spoke to me and my sons, saying,

'Behold, I establish My covenant with you and with your descendants after you, and with every living creature that is with you: the birds, the cattle, and every beast of the earth with you, of all that go out of the ark, every beast of the earth. Never again shall all flesh be cut off by the waters of the flood; never again shall there be a flood to destroy the earth. This is the sign of the covenant which I make between Me and you, and every living creature that is with you, for perpetual generations: I set My rainbow in the cloud, and it shall be for the sign of the covenant between Me and the earth. It shall be, when I bring a cloud over the earth, that the rainbow shall be seen in the cloud; and I will remember My covenant which is between Me and you and every living creature of all flesh; the waters shall never again become a flood to destroy all flesh. The rainbow shall be in the cloud, and I will look on it to remember the everlasting covenant between God and every living creature of all flesh that is on the earth.'

"How many of you have seen a rainbow?"

All the children raised their hands.

"Then you have seen the hand of God, still keeping His promise thousands of years since He pledged it to me and my sons and our wives and all the animals.

"Would you believe that after the flood I lived three hundred and fifty more years? I am the oldest man you have ever seen, but if you trust in God and become the Lord's child, you will never die. At the end of this Millennium, these thousand years, we shall enter heaven with God and with His Son, the Messiah. I want you all to be there with me. Will you come? Will you promise me, as God did?

"Who will be there with me? Who?"

And from here and there all over the acreage, children shouted, "I will! I will! Me too! I will!"

They stood and waved and jumped and yelled, and in the midst of it, Noah made his leave. As he walked through the masses back the way he came, the immense crowd seemed to part as the waters of the sea. No one touched him or even approached him. They just smiled and waved and cheered and applauded.

And as Noah left the place, Rayford heard him whisper, "All praise to the God of our fathers, who shares His glory with none other."

SEVENTEEN

KENNY WILLIAMS was not surprised that the rest of the day at COT was a write-off. Half the kids left with their parents, and the other half could do little else than jabber about getting to see the real Noah in the flesh and hear him tell his own story.

Kenny tried to get them to fashion model arks and line up toy animals, but these activities deteriorated into more fun and games. He was as excited as they were and had to wonder when things would get back to normal. And to think that other heroes of the faith were scheduled! Fortunately, no one knew when.

Ekaterina was no less wired as they walked home, unabashedly holding hands now, even in front of others. Kenny knew the news of their being an item would soon get around. When they reached her house, her parents clearly noticed but did not raise a brow or say a word.

He would have to ask Kat the next day if anything was said after he left.

As they parted, Kenny asked Ekaterina whether she was still determined to ask for a transfer within COT.

"Yes," she said, "but I won't even try to get assigned with you. Not now."

Kenny was conflicted all the way home. He had Noah and, of course, Kat on his mind, but he also had an urgent need to talk with Raymie. He called him and set a meeting for later that evening at Raymie's place.

It was time for Abdullah to seriously seek the Lord. It wasn't as if he hadn't done that every day of his life since acknowledging his need of a Savior. But this whole Jordan assignment had him puzzled. He prayed with Yasmine. He prayed without her. He called his children and asked them to pray. No surprise to him, Bahira sympathized and promised to pray; Zaki wanted to counsel him. The boy had all the answers.

"Maybe God will work a miracle and blind them so they don't see you as an old man . . . or, I mean, your age. Or maybe He'll turn you into a shape-shifter so you can look like someone their age. What do you think?"

"I think I am still confused and would ask you again to fervently pray for me. I have to think that those of you who have been with God and Jesus in heaven have at least some sort of an advantage in communicating with Him. Please, for me."

"But, Dad, I am in a little group that calls ourselves the Millennium Force, like you and your friends had in the olden days. We have an infiltrator into the TOL in Paris. Maybe he can be of help to you."

"Maybe."

Kids.

———————

"He told her everything?" Raymie said, clearly piqued.

Kenny nodded solemnly. "I mean, she can be trusted. We're going together now, and I trust her."

"Going together? Since when?"

"Last night."

"You know there are things you won't be able to tell her, just because Qasim seems to have a big mouth."

"I will keep all confidences, but of course the day may come when I would want to nominate her for inclusion into the Force."

"Kenny, please. I've got half a mind to disband the whole thing. It's getting out of control. Qasim is not even part of us, and I couldn't have made that any clearer, yet here he is telling the Jospins that you're some double agent, then telling a virtual stranger—at least to him—all about us and not even getting it right."

"Ekaterina is not really a stranger to him. They have worked together at COT and were out last night when she told him."

"Out where?"

"To dinner. At the bistro."

"Hold on. I thought you said *you* and she were going together."

"Right, well, their date sort of brought things to a head."

"So last night she was out with him, and since last night she's going with you."

"I know how that sounds."

"Apparently you don't. Well, regardless, I'm pulling the plug on Qasim, no matter what Zaki says. We might as well be advertising on billboards if Qasim is going to be blabbing about us to everybody he knows."

"And what if I hear from the Jospins?"

"What if you do?"

"If Qasim can be believed, they think I'm with them and working covertly at COT. Should I try to string them along?"

Raymie shook his head. "I don't know. I don't like it. How hard would it be for them to learn how tight you are with your parents, who run the place? And what are you going to say if they ask about Qasim?"

The Ekaterina Kenny walked to work Monday morning was not the same one he walked home at the end of the day. The first was her bubbly, affectionate self who said her parents had noticed their affection for each other and were most excited. The latter Ekaterina was glum.

"I rarely see you this way, Kat," he said. "Talk to me. Was your transfer request turned down?"

"No, it's not that. I haven't heard about that since I left it in your mother's box."

"Then what?"

"Oh, it's just Qasim. I teased him about missing the biggest day COT ever had, and all he wanted was to keep bugging me about going out with him again."

"What did you tell him? Or do I want to know?"

"I told him about us, of course. He couldn't believe that could have happened so fast. He accused you of moving in on him, undercutting him as soon as you heard about our date. I assured him I had been friends with you before him and that we hadn't even realized how we felt about each other until later."

"I can't blame him for being disappointed, Kat. I was too, when I heard you were going out with him."

"I've never even had a boyfriend, and now I've got two fighting over me."

"I'm not fighting. And I won't. It seems to me you've made your choice."

"Of course I have, but I didn't expect it to become an issue with him. I guess I hoped he was a friend and would understand. Apparently not."

"Well, when my mother talks to you about the transfer, that might be a good thing to mention. You can't be trying to work with someone who's upset with you."

They reached her house and sat out front.

"That's just it, Kenny. I can't remember the last time I was out of sorts with a brother in Christ. I mean, really, it's been around twenty years. I thought we were old enough to be past all that now."

"Does it make you question his faith?"

"Of course it does, and I don't want to feel that way. I just wish the transfer thing was over and done with so I wouldn't have to face him tomorrow."

"You want me to talk to my mother?"

"No! Kenny! How would that look?"

"Just asking. Offering."

"I know, and thanks. But please don't."

"I wouldn't without your permission." He wanted to tell her that perhaps Raymie had already talked to Qasim and laid down the law about separating himself from the Millennium Force, but Kenny didn't want to be guilty of the same loose tongue that had gotten Qasim in trouble.

He arrived home that evening to a computer message from Ignace Jospin. *Oh, great!*

It read: "Glad to hear from our mutual friend of your continuing interest in our cause and your strategic positioning there. Attached is our manifesto, and we would appreciate any reports you can send that would be of value."

How was Kenny supposed to respond to that?

"Good to hear from you," he wrote. "Give me a few days."

"Okay," came the quick response, "but understand what we're looking for: information on key individuals."

He took a call from Bahira.

"Any idea what has Zaki so upset?" she said.

"Yeah, but you should probably talk to Raymie."

"Just tell me, Kenny. We've known each other long

enough, and I know Raymie trusts you and would expect you to tell me."

And so he did.

"Well," she said, "frankly I think dealing with Qasim is overdue. Not that Raymie didn't try to stifle Qasim long ago. This is Zaki's creation, a fiasco he could have fixed early. So do you get the impression that Qasim finally understands he's not associated with us in any way?"

"I have no idea. I'm just guessing that Raymie has had the talk with him and that he's complained to Zaki. Your brother's mad?"

"Something's got him wound up. I can only assume you're right. You're a good friend and brother, Kenny. And I hear good news about you."

"You do?"

"Are you going to play coy or are you going to introduce me?"

"I'd be proud to, sister."

———————

The next day Chloe Williams was perusing her mail when she decided she would have to talk with Ekaterina Risto personally. Conflicting messages made what could have been a rubber-stamp transfer something she would have to examine carefully.

Ekaterina visited the office on her lunch break.

"Did you get a chance to eat?" Chloe said.

"No, but I'm fine."

"Nonsense. I want you fully energized to keep up with these kids this afternoon. Have some bread and cheese."

"Thank you."

They ate together as they spoke. "Ekaterina, tell me in your own words why you want a transfer."

"I guess I just want to be more on the front lines. I get chances to pray with kids in rec, but I'd rather be teaching them and worshiping with them for the whole day like some of the other departments do."

"Like the one Kenny is in."

"Right, but I assume you saw there that I specified I was not asking for or expecting to be working with him."

"You don't want to?"

Ekaterina flushed. "Well, frankly, yes, I'd love that. But I wouldn't permit that if I were you, and I think Kenny and I both are resigned to the fact that that's not going to happen."

Chloe smiled. "You're right. Now, how have things been going in rec, other than that you feel a little stifled on the ministry side?"

"Oh, very well. I did have a little issue with one of the guys who is more interested in me than I am in him. It would be good to be out of that awkward situation, but that's not the real reason I want to be transferred. I've been straightforward with him, so I think he understands."

"That's good. But I do need to talk with you about a work report on you from your supervisor."

"Mattie? She sent a report on me? A good one, I hope. We've gotten along great."

"Actually, it's a troubling one, Ekaterina."

EIGHTEEN

"I AM EMBARRASSED," Abdullah Ababneh told Yasmine. "I believed I heard from the Lord—actually, I know I did—but I jumped to a very wrong conclusion."

"Tell me," she said as they sat down to lunch in their tiny apartment in Amman.

"He clearly called me to work among the people of the Other Light, and naturally I assumed this meant I was to work against them."

"Of course. What are you saying?"

"Well, there is no way to counter them—at least this is what I thought—other than to infiltrate them. The Lord was quite specific that I was to talk to them directly."

"I understand that would be difficult other than under an alias and in disguise."

"Yet everywhere I turned, all I was told was that it was impossible—even from Zeke. If he couldn't make it work, only the Lord could. And He has."

"How long are you going to keep me in suspense, Abdullah? What has changed?"

"I suppose Jesus either got tired of seeing me running around and getting nowhere or was amused by it. Finally He made it plain to me during my morning prayer. Do you know what a chaplain is, Yasmine?"

"Well, certainly, I recall from the old days that some Christian groups or the military had spiritual leaders. We don't have them now, of course, because we have priests and judges and the Lord Himself. . . ."

"And yet He is calling me to be a chaplain."

"A chaplain to what? to whom?"

"To the people of the Other Light."

Yasmine set down her bread and stared at him. "Abdullah, there are two reasons I am stifling my laughter. One, I know you do not like to be laughed at. And two, you say this came from the Lord Himself. How does a non-Christian—even anti-Christian—group have a chaplain? Why would they want one, and what would they do with—or to—him?"

"They will not lay a hand on me; I can assure you of that because the Lord has assured me. He promises to give me everything I need. Wisdom, knowledge, recall, words, and especially courage and confidence."

"I am not following. What will you do?"

"You recall that during the Great Tribulation I became quite a student of prophecy and the Word of God near the end."

"You have told me, yes. I have no doubt of your knowledge."

"I am to use that, much as a pastor would."

"To do what!?"

"I am to find out where TOL meets here in Amman. Frankly, I am not even sure they actually meet here yet. Perhaps the Lord led me here in advance of them simply because He knew they were coming. But once they are here, I am to find them and confront them, but not in a negative way."

"No?"

"The Lord has assured me that He holds their destiny in His hands. They know whom they are opposing, and any criticism or warning will be no surprise to them; neither will it have any impact on their thinking. His new plan is at once both revolutionary and as old as the New Testament. I am to love them and treat them the way I would want to be treated."

Chloe Steele Williams pulled a sheet from the file folder and handed it to Ekaterina Risto, watching carefully for a response. The young woman squinted and seemed to be reading quickly. She appeared unable to speak.

"You know we're fair here," Chloe said. "I would like your side of this."

"I . . . I, uh . . . don't know what to say. Either I'm going crazy or one of us is a liar."

"Mattie Cleveland is one of our best supervisors, Miss Risto."

"Oh, I know! I love her! But this says she has talked with me about these problems. Problems I didn't even know I had. I don't remember her talking with me about them at all. In fact, we haven't talked, except for normal chitchat while working, for days."

"Now, Ekaterina. These are summaries of your discussions. About your being tardy, taking too long of breaks, leaving early, being hard to find when team chores are scheduled, sitting with Kenny at the Noah appearance without permission, disagreeing with her in front of the staff."

"Is it possible for me to talk with her personally?"

"Face your accuser, you mean?"

"I guess."

"But it appears you two have talked quite a bit, and your behavior has not changed."

Ekaterina stood and paced. "I'm not trying to be defensive," she said. "And the Lord knows I'm not perfect. But I'm telling you, I'm not guilty of any of this. Even the sitting with Kenny."

"I saw you two sitting together."

"Yes! With Mattie's permission. I cleared it with her first, made sure she didn't need me to watch any children."

"Hmm."

"So can I meet with her, with you present?"

"I guess. Sure." Chloe had Mattie summoned. "She'll be here in a few minutes."

"I am to speak on Jesus' behalf," Abdullah said. "Say what He would say if He encountered these people."

"But the Bible foretells how Jesus will deal with His enemies at the end of the Millennium," Yasmine said. "There will be no mercy, no patience. There will not even be a battle, though the enemy will plan an attack."

Abdullah opened his hands. "All I know is what He is telling me. I go to them, tell them that I am a chaplain available to them on behalf of the Ruler of this world. I am to tell them not to fear me, that I mean them no harm. I am to speak on behalf of Jesus, and I am to make myself available to them for their spiritual needs—any questions, counseling, teaching, or whatever else they want."

"They will laugh you out of their headquarters, wherever it is. They might even attack you."

"Oh, that is another thing. I am free to warn them about that. I am to say that because I come under the authority of the Son of God, woe to those who would oppose me."

When Yasmine stood to clear the table, Abdullah assisted. "My biggest fear," she said, "would be their ignoring you."

"I am hard to ignore."

"How well I know."

"I am to ask them for an office."

"A Christian chaplain's area within their offices?"

He nodded. "And if they turn me down, I am to set up a table and a chair right outside the entrance."

"For what purpose?"

"To be available to them when they are coming or going—especially, I suppose, when they are recruiting.

Potential recruits will have to get past the chaplain
before they can be enlisted."

"I say this with all due respect, Abdullah, but are you
sure you haven't lost your mind?"

———————

Chloe had long loved Mattie Cleveland. She was tall
with short sandy hair and laughing eyes. She had been
raptured and returned at the Glorious Appearing,
immediately gravitating toward children. She was efficient and thorough, and because of her background in
all kinds of sports, she was loved by the kids who
engaged in her recreation department activities. She
had worked with Cameron and Chloe at COT for well
over ninety years.

"Hey, Chloe," she said as she entered. And as soon as
she noticed Ekaterina, she said, "Kat! How's my favorite
new aide? Why the long face?"

"Your report," Ekaterina said as the three sat.

"Report?"

Chloe handed it to her. Mattie read it with a furrowed
brow, then glanced up at Chloe. "Where'd you get this?"

"It was in my box at the end of the day yesterday."

"Forged."

"I'm sorry?"

"Wholly made up. I've never seen it, didn't write it,
never had these conversations with Kat. Don't know a
thing about it. She sat with Kenny with my permission,
and as for the rest of it, totally fabricated. I've been watch-

ing this one from the first day to make sure she's not too good to be true. I couldn't ask for a better worker."

Chloe sat studying both women. "Then why does she want to be transferred out of your area?"

"Oh!" Ekaterina said. "I haven't mentioned that to Mattie yet."

"Sorry," Chloe said, "but I need this to add up and make sense, and right now, it's doing neither."

"You're wanting to leave me, Kat?" Mattie said. "Whatever for?"

Ekaterina told her.

"I wish you'd said something, hon. I think I can make it work right where you are. I need someone to take the ball and run with it, so to speak, on the spiritual side. It bothers me too that the kids come to us only to play and that they're largely getting their spiritual input elsewhere. What if I put you in charge of that, took you off sports duty, and you were free to roam and talk with kids who look like they have questions or needs?"

"I'd love that, but how does that address the Qasim issue?"

"I noticed he was on your case a lot, but I couldn't tell whether you found it annoying or charming, so I left it alone. He bothers you, I'll put him in his place. How's that?"

Ekaterina shrugged. "Sounds great to me, but don't you agree we still have a major problem?"

"We sure do," Chloe said. "Whoever pulled this prank—and there's no way they thought they could get away with it; I mean, how long did they think it would

take me to check with you, Mattie?—either has a very
poor sense of humor, or they're not even a believer. Unless
someone gets to me very quickly and admits this was
some sort of a joke that didn't work, I have to take it at
face value. It's a lie, it defames someone, and it evidences
someone who is not showing the love of Christ.

"Well, you let me worry about that. Meanwhile, if you
like the role Mattie has outlined for you, how about you
stay put and do it?"

———————

Rayford and his team were seeing a spiritual harvest in
Osaze that had not been seen there in aeons. Everywhere
they went, Rayford led the others in planting and building and developing technology. And when Tsion and
Chaim and Bruce preached, hundreds of thousands of
people turned back to the Lord and young people
became believers.

The preachers pulled no punches. They warned that
God would again strike their land if they chose to ignore
him. But they also thrilled the masses with the promises
of the Lord.

Tsion Ben-Judah was holding forth one cool evening,
telling a crowd of thousands, "Thus says the Lord of
Hosts: 'For I know the thoughts that I think toward you,
thoughts of peace and not of evil, to give you a future and
a hope. Then you will call upon Me and go and pray to
Me, and I will listen to you. And you will seek Me and
find Me, when you search for Me with all your heart.

"'For behold, He who forms mountains, and creates the wind, who declares to man what his thought is, who treads the high places of the earth—the Lord God of hosts is His name.

"'You shall fear the Lord your God and serve Him, and shall take oaths in His name. Seek the Lord while He may be found, call upon Him while He is near. Let the wicked forsake his way, and the unrighteous man his thoughts; let him return to the Lord, and He will have mercy on him, for He will abundantly pardon.'

"Now hear these words of the Most High God: 'For My thoughts are not your thoughts, nor are your ways My ways. For as the heavens are higher than the earth, so are My ways higher than your ways, and My thoughts than your thoughts.

"'For as the rain comes down, and the snow from heaven, and do not return there, but water the earth, and make it bring forth and bud, that it may give seed to the sower and bread to the eater, so shall My word be that goes forth from My mouth; it shall not return to Me void, but it shall accomplish what I please, and it shall prosper.'"

That evening had seen a particularly successful meeting, and Rayford noticed that the team was anything but settled enough to sleep. "Shall we camp out tonight? enjoy a meal over an open fire?"

Everyone agreed, and Irene and Bruce's wife made the assignments. Everyone had something to do, from gathering kindling to erecting a tarpaulin shelter from the blazing moon to helping prepare the meal. They sang and prayed and chatted into the night as they ate.

Finally Tsion said, "Rayford, do you realize where we are?"

"I do, old friend. We're not far from where you came through on your flight from Israel so many years ago. Tell the story. I don't believe Mac and Bruce or the ladies have heard it."

"Okay with you, Chaim?" Tsion said. "You've heard it a million times. You could tell it yourself."

"No, please. It always warms my heart."

"Well, okay. I had made my position clear on international television from Jerusalem that I, a rabbinical scholar, had come to the conclusion that all the prophecies of the Bible that pertained to the coming Messiah were fulfilled in the man Jesus. You can imagine the outcry. My family was slaughtered, and I was chased from the country.

"Cameron helped me escape by driving me across the Negev, not far from this very point, in an ancient bus. We had many dangerous and close calls, and we were pursued all the way. Once, the Lord allowed me to escape detection because nature called just when the security guards were boarding the bus and would have surely found me. But the most dramatic incident happened at a checkpoint where I had no time to exit the bus before the authorities checked it out. Cameron was inside their post, trying to stall them, but I missed the opportunity to slip out. All I could do when I heard footsteps was crawl under a seat and pray. There was no way they would forget to look under the seats and equally no possibility I would not be seen, unless the Lord blinded their eyes.

"As I huddled there, trembling, wondering if it would be the end for me, I could see a flashlight beam darting here and there through the windows. Then a single pair of footsteps boarding the bus. I knew it was not Cameron, as he would have identified himself.

"When the feet came down the aisle, I could see that the man was wearing uniform pants and shoes. Suddenly he knelt and shined the beam right into my eyes. And God did not blind him. He dropped to his elbows and knees, and keeping the flashlight in my face with one hand, he reached with the other to grab my shirt. He pulled me close to him, and I thought my heart would burst. I imagined myself dragged into the building, a trophy for a young officer.

"He whispered hoarsely to me through clenched teeth in Hebrew, 'You had better be who I think you are, or you are a dead man.' What could I do? There was no more hiding, no hope in pretending I wasn't there. I said to him, 'Young man, my name is Tsion Ben-Judah.'

"Still holding my shirt in his fist and with his flash-light blinding me, he said, 'Rabbi Ben-Judah, my name is Anis. Pray as you have never prayed before that my report will be believed. And now may the Lord bless you and keep you. May the Lord make His face shine upon you and give you peace.' As God is my witness, the young man stood and walked out of the bus. I lay there praising God with my tears until Cameron reboarded and drove away."

Tsion, wiping away tears, as were the others, added, "He didn't know what had happened, whether I had been arrested or even killed, until the lights of the border crossing disappeared behind us and he pulled off the road and said, 'Tsion, are you on this bus? Come out now, wherever you are.' Why, I could barely find my voice, I was so overcome. I said, 'I am here. Praise the Lord God Almighty, Maker of heaven and earth.'

"The strange thing was, I never found out whether the young Anis was an angel or a man, but I know he was sent from God."

Chaim said, "I suspect that he was otherworldly, because much later I saw him outside the Garden Tomb—the same young man. Could it have been coincidence that he was assigned twice where our paths would intersect?"

"It was no accident," came a new voice, causing Rayford and the others to jerk around. Standing just outside their shelter, the moon illuminating him and the fire dancing on his cheeks, was a man in silhouette. "I was your rear guard that night," he said, "just as I am on this mission."

And with that his image faded, and Rayford and the others fell on their faces, praising and thanking God.

NINETEEN

AT THE END of the next day, Chloe asked to see Kenny and Ekaterina in her office.

Bahira, Abdullah's daughter, was with them. "I've just met Kenny's Kat," she said. "And I approve."

Ekaterina looked shocked, and Kenny said, "Bahira! First off, she's not *mine*. And second, there's nothing to approve."

"Thank you, Kenny," Kat said.

"You're welcome," Bahira said, winking at Chloe.

"Sit, everyone, please," Chloe said. "Ekaterina, how goes your new role?"

"We're still trying to figure out how it's going to work, and a certain someone seems very jealous that I seem to have my own agenda, but Mattie is keeping him away from me, as promised."

"Qasim?" Bahira said, rolling her eyes.

"You know, Bahira," Chloe said, "it's actually good that you're here for this, because this is an awkward meeting. Back before the millennial kingdom, had Kenny's father and I not gone to heaven, I can imagine having a meeting like this, probably when Kenny reached junior high school or so. I hear all sorts of gossip and talk and who said what about whose boyfriend or girlfriend, and it strikes me that it's so juvenile for such a time as this. Scripture says that you all are to be considered children until you reach age one hundred, but because you're twice as old now as my parents were when I died . . . I don't know; I guess I expect you to be more mature."

Chloe had no idea whether she was getting through to them. They sat there glumly, especially Bahira, perhaps because she felt singled out.

"It's all of you," Chloe said. "Ekaterina is the only one still living with her parents, but you're all old enough to be on your own. It just doesn't seem like you're acting it. Shouldn't we be above all this petty stuff now that we're living in a time when Jesus is reigning over His millennial kingdom?"

"Maybe my brother should be here," Bahira said. "It was his trying to bring Qasim into the Millennium Force that started a lot of this. Everybody knew it was wrong. Raymie hasn't been happy about it."

"Where do you think I've been getting my information?" Chloe said. "I'm grateful my brother trusts me enough to confide in me, but I confess he'd not likely be happy to know that I have taken this into my own hands. He's perfectly capable of fighting his own battles. And Bahira, he thinks the world of you."

"I love him too, you know, in the way that those we met in heaven love each other. Without complication."

"And that's the way it should be. Our lives now should be filled with praising and worshiping Jesus and carrying out His mission on this earth. There are still millions of young people who will not live past their hundredth birthdays unless we stay at the task. That's what COT is all about. And if you're going to have a Millennium Force that mirrors the old Tribulation Force, it needs to be single-minded too. We had one goal, one mission, and that was to thwart Antichrist as best we could by what?"

They all looked blank.

"Come on; did I surprise you with a rhetorical question, or do you really not know? Kenny, I must have bored you to death with this over the last century."

"By adding as many people to the family of God as you could."

"Exactly. That's what the Millennium Force ought to be about, and in talking to Raymie, I know that's his passion. It sounds to me like it has deteriorated into a he-said-she-said free-for-all. And with Satan out of the picture for nine hundred or so more years, this all has to be self-motivated. I can't see what part of the world makes this kind of thing attractive, so that leaves the flesh. Just something to think about. Will you think about it? I'm sorry to come off like the mom here, but you're all coming off like juveniles."

Abdullah was studying one evening and Yasmine was
praying when he was startled by a knock at the door.
Yasmine looked up quickly.

"Does anyone know we're here?" Abdullah said.

"Only those in Israel," she whispered. "But do not fear."

That was easy for her to say, with her glorified mind
and body. Abdullah crept to the door and put his ear
near it. He jumped when someone called from the other
side.

"I am a friend of your son, and I bring you news! May
I come in?"

"What is my son's name?"

"Zaki Ababneh, and his sister is Bahira, also a friend
of mine!"

"And what is your name?"

"Qasim Marid!"

Abdullah looked to Yasmine, who signaled him to
open the door. She immediately rose to get them something to eat and drink.

Qasim embraced Abdullah, who pointed him to a seat.
The young man wasted no time getting to his point as
Yasmine joined them with bread and wine.

"Zaki told me of your mission, and I can only assume
that you will try to infiltrate the Other Light here. I can
tell you who the principals are, where they are headquar-
tered, and I can even help pave the way for them to
somehow believe that someone who looks like you could
be their age. I have infiltrated TOL at the international
level and so can make the introductions."

"I will gratefully accept the information, but persuading them that I am younger than I look will not be necessary because—"

"Oh yes—begging your pardon, sir, but it will be crucial. They will be suspicious from the beginning, and you would be in danger. There is no possibility that you could infiltrate unless we come up with some story of trauma or disease that makes you look forty or so years older than they."

Abdullah laughed aloud. "I have suffered these insults from my own family and old friends, but now even from *their* friends?"

"I don't mean to offend you, sir. I am just being realistic. As a representative of the Millennium Force, I am expert in these things."

"Just tell me who is in charge and where I can find them, Mr. Marid. I will follow the Lord's leading from there. And you would do well to distance yourself from any appearance of knowing me or speaking for me, for if you do not, your own identity within TOL will be compromised."

"Being associated with you would blow *my* cover? How?"

"Because I do not plan to hide who I am. I am a believer, serving the living Christ. They will know from the first instant, and—"

"Your very life will be in danger, sir."

"I rest in the protection of the Lord God."

"If you insist on persisting in this, I am glad to know it so I *can* distance myself from you."

"That would be wise. Are you still willing to give me the information I need?"

"Certainly, but be as circumspect about me as I will be about you."

"On that you have my pledge, young man."

Kenny found himself confiding more and more in Ekaterina. She had taken well his mother's admonitions and proved more than spiritually mature in her response. Nightly now they spent hours together, talking until it was time to go to their respective homes. They told each other every detail of their lives they could remember. Kenny wasn't entirely sure where Ekaterina's heart was, but she had stolen his. He prayed his love for her would not interfere with his devotion to Christ, and that was the subject of his nearly constant prayer.

One night he arrived home late to another message from the Jospins. This time it had been written by the younger brother, and it showed less patience than the previous missive.

> We are at the point where we need solid information. You remain in a strategic place. Don't make us worry or wonder where your true loyalties lie. You can be important to the cause. If you have questions or concerns, raise them now. Otherwise, we will expect tangible results from you soon. Please respond and give us an update.

If it would help you to come to Paris and meet with us, we can make that happen. We are guessing that would be preferable to our visiting you, because it is becoming more and more difficult for us to move about in public, as most people are beginning to understand where we are coming from.

We look forward with great anticipation to hearing from you very soon. Don't let us down. In the memory of our cousin and your friend, Cendrillon, and with loyalty to the Other Light,

Lothair Jospin

TWENTY

Chloe struck out in her efforts to determine who had put the phony employee document in her box. She had begun to interview Ekaterina's coworkers, but after a half dozen painful conversations, she realized her investigation was doing more harm than good. In nearly a century, she had not had to deal with any problem more serious than hurt feelings between employees. With Jesus on the world's throne and King David, the Lord's prince, ruling Israel from the temple, all matters of law and judgment seemed to go smoothly and quickly.

She called in Mattie Cleveland and suggested they just chalk up the crisis, such as it was, to an ill-conceived prank and let it die. "It hasn't caused too much controversy within your staff, has it?"

Mattie shrugged. "Actually, it has. Everyone is talking about it, pointing fingers, the whole bit. I would have loved to have been able to say we found the culprit, dealt with him or her, got an apology, and moved on. But this is all right too."

"You can blame it on me, Mattie. Tell the staff I decided it wasn't worth pursuing."

"Whatever you say, Chloe. I agree we need to get on with what we're here for. I will say this: Qasim has been particularly solicitous ever since this started getting around."

"The one who's been so annoying to Ekaterina?"

"He's really cleaned up his act. He leaves her alone, and he has been much more helpful to me lately. Qasim has even commiserated with me over this mess."

"But I didn't even interview him. What does he know about it?"

"Just what everyone else is saying, I guess. He made the effort to set an appointment with me, counseled me not to take it personally, and reminded me how much esteem he and the rest of the staff had for me. It was really sweet."

Chloe nodded. "A little out of character?"

Mattie cocked her head. "But still sweet. I'd give him the benefit of the doubt."

The day finally arrived when Abdullah knew it was time to act. He told Yasmine he was venturing out to the Other Light's secret headquarters and asked that she pray fervently for him while he was gone.

"I will, and I shall not worry," she said, "because you represent the Most High God."

"True," he said, "but I also want to assure you that I will not be revealing to them that my ministry partner is also here in Amman or giving them any hint as to where I live."

"That is wise, but neither do I fear mere human children, especially those who have chosen to remain outside the kingdom."

Kenny begged off from lunch with Ekaterina to meet briefly with Raymie. He told her he would reconnect with her at the end of the day. Raymie joined him at the far end of the mess hall, where they could talk privately.

"Just a few items," Kenny said. "I want to know where things stand with Qasim. I want to know what you think I should do about the persistence of the Jospins. And we need to talk about Ekaterina."

Raymie, whom Kenny had always found both wise and decisive, did not disappoint. "I don't know what Qasim is telling anyone else, but I have totally distanced myself and the Millennium Force from him. I told him he has no standing with us, and that regardless what he chooses to do in relation to the Other Light, we don't want so much as a report from him, not even a second-hand report through Zaki."

"And he's okay with that?"

"Of course not. He was angry, which showed me his

true colors. And Zaki is not happy either. I had to tell him that he would be next if he couldn't see the wisdom of our totally parting ways with Qasim. I feared offending Bahira if I did that, but she has never trusted Qasim, and I suppose you know we have a sort of mutual admiration society."

Kenny smiled. "Kat and I have speculated on what might have become of you two—as a couple, I mean—if you were naturals."

Raymie shook his head and looked away. "I have wondered the same. As has she. We can talk about it openly because it is so far from the realm of possibility. It's strange that we admire and respect and truly love each other so deeply, and yet the idea of romance never enters the picture. We're simply not wired that way anymore. That allows us to spend a lot of time together, really as brother and sister, worshiping, praying, studying, planning. I can't tell you how rewarding it is."

"And I can't tell you how much fun it is to have someone like that in my life," Kenny said, "plus adding the romance to it."

"I'm happy for you. I really am."

"I can tell. Thanks."

"Let's save TOL for last, then, and tell me or ask me whatever it was you wanted to about Ekaterina."

Kenny wiped his mouth and shifted in his seat. "Well, it's just that our relationship really seems to be headed somewhere. Obviously she's not my wife yet—she's not even my fiancée—but that is certainly in our future. There's little I don't tell her, Raymie, and very little I want to keep from her. I'm not asking that she be made a member of the Force just yet, but I need you to know that I seek her wisdom and counsel about a lot of the stuff we talk about."

Raymie slid his plate aside and leaned on the table. "I guess I can't tell you not to do that. I'd be careful though. You know relationships don't always end up the way we expect. What happens if a year from now you're just friends or acquaintances?"

"I can't imagine it, but I see what you're saying. Still, this pressure from Ignace and now Lothair to, in essence, put up or shut up weighs too heavily on me not to talk about it to the woman I love. She would be able to tell something was on my mind anyway, and it's not fair to her to keep it from her."

"And I gather that you haven't—kept it from her, I mean."

"No, I haven't."

"And what is she saying?"

"Kat thinks I should pursue it, do it right, and—unlike Qasim—act under the authority of the Force. In other words, make sure everybody knows what I'm doing so they can pray for me, keep track of me, and give advice."

Raymie sat back and folded his arms. "I like this girl more all the time. Maybe she *will* make a good Force member someday."

"Do we need a meeting?"

"Of the Force? Sure, if you plan to respond to these guys. What're you thinking, that you would visit them in France?"

"That or start feeding them bogus information. Just enough to keep them on the string."

"I don't know," Raymie said, sighing. "If our goal is not to win them over, what is it?"

"To keep undecideds from being swayed by them."

"And how does misleading TOL accomplish that?"

They rose to start heading back to work. Kenny said, "All I know is that if I don't start playing their game soon, they're going to know I'm not on their side. Maybe that's not all bad. I can stick to what I know and what I believe I'm supposed to be doing—reaching the children right here."

Abdullah knew he needn't be, but he was nervous. He had allowed his beard to grow out, then trimmed it neatly before luxuriating in a long shower. Now he slowly dressed, eschewing the white robe he had worn for years in Israel and opting for more traditional Jordanian civilian wear. He pulled a blousy white top over billowing beige pants, slipped into open sandals, and carefully wrapped a pure white turban around his head.

Yasmine raised her brows when he emerged from the bathroom. "What is the expression?" she said. "All dressed up and nowhere to go?"

"Except today I have somewhere to go. And I couldn't be more excited. Where is my Bible?"

"You are going to show up on their doorstep with the

Scriptures in your hand?" she said. "No subtlety whatsoever? No easing into this?"

"I am going with the confidence of my Redeemer. I am nervous but unafraid."

"I suspect I will be on edge until your return," Yasmine said. "But I too believe that if you are following the leading of the Lord, He will abundantly bless you."

Cameron was tooling around the COT acreage in a golf cart, checking on everything and everybody, when he noticed a man standing near one of the entrances, hands folded in front of him. Cameron slid to a stop and gazed at him from perhaps a hundred yards away. The man was dressed as a priest, and as soon as he noticed Cameron, he discreetly raised a hand.

It looked like Yerik. The priest had either walked the more than eighteen miles from the temple or had somehow been supernaturally translated here. Either way, Cameron felt it would be inappropriate to go skidding up to him in the cart. He parked and walked, hoping all the way that the man brought news of another special visit.

Yerik embraced Cameron. "Brother Williams," he said, "I bring you greetings in the name of the Messiah and of His prince. The Lord bless you in your worthy work for His kingdom."

"Thank you, sir. May I offer you anything?"

"No, thank you. Just a question. Are you able to accommodate Joshua and Caleb on the morrow?"

"Of course! Any idea when?"

Yerik smiled apologetically. "They will come when they will come. Same instructions as last time. No festivities. No introduction."

"And we will never be given more advance knowledge, will we?"

"No, it is likely you will not."

"I will inform the staff."

"And I will pass along your acceptance." Yerik turned away with a shy wave, and as Cameron watched, the man seemed to fade into the horizon after treading several steps toward the Highway of Holiness.

Never a dull moment.

Abdullah felt strangely conspicuous, striding about Amman under the blazing sun in gleaming clothes. Almost everyone he saw was wearing the customary white robe, and his getup elicited double takes and stares but, probably because he was carrying his Bible, always followed by smiles—which he returned. The closer he got to the address in question, the more excited he grew.

Abdullah peeked at the tiny slip of paper to be sure he was in the right neighborhood, and soon he arrived at a square, three-story building topped by towering antennas and satellite dishes. Inside he found a list of offices that included agricultural consultants, hydrologists, computer specialists, and communications experts. Ah, there it was. A downstairs suite was labeled Theological Training Institute. He took the steps.

———

As soon as Cameron had told Chloe, news of the next day's visitors swept COT. Staffers immediately adjusted their plans and schedules. They dug out everything they could find on Joshua and Caleb, and within a couple of hours, the kids knew the stories and were acting out the adventures, building models of collapsible city walls, memorizing verses, and singing "Joshua Fit the Battle of Jericho." And, just like last time, Cameron knew the news had reached parents and everyone else in the surrounding communities.

———

Kenny ducked into the communications center and e-mailed Lothair Jospin. "Interesting things in store. May be able to visit you. Big doings here at COT tomorrow, so may be unreachable. Back to you soon."

On his way back to his post, Kenny ran into Qasim Marid, who pulled him off to the side and whispered, "You keeping in touch with Paris? They're getting antsy."

"Just did. I'll keep them warm. I suppose you heard about tomorrow."

"Who hasn't?" Qasim said. "Can you believe I'm going to have to miss it again? I can't believe it myself."

"You don't want to do that. Change your plans. What's more important than this?"

"Nah, I can't. Wish I could. Tell me all about it, huh? I made a commitment, and I have to follow through. I sure hope there are more of these. I'll make the next one for sure."

TWENTY-ONE

Downstairs Abdullah found several glassed-in suites
with smiling staff moving about. The area for the Theological Training Institute, however, bore nothing transparent. Where the windows should have been were solid
walls and a thick wood door. *TTI* had been painted on it
in huge block letters, but it was locked and there was no
buzzer. A closed-circuit TV camera had been affixed
above it, suspended from the ceiling. Its light glowed red.

Abdullah peered about, hesitant to knock. A woman
from the next office smiled and beckoned him. He pulled
open the glass door to her suite.

"May I help you?" she said.

He brandished his Bible and said, "I'm looking for the
Theological Training Institute people."

"Oh, the Lord bless your heart," she said.

"And yours," Abdullah said. "Do they hold regular
classes or . . . ?"

"Oh no, sir. The only people I've ever seen go in or out of there are the two little guys who run it, I guess."

"Little guys?"

"Well, one's littler that the other, 'cause the one's kinda pudgy, you know."

"No, I don't know. Do you know their names or whether they are present?"

"I'd just knock, hon. Their other visitors knock."

"But I thought you said they were the only—"

"Oh, well, yeah, other than the ones who wear the same kind of clothes."

"Clothes?"

"They don't wear the robes of the righteous, if you know what I mean. I'm convinced they're all naturals, and they wear . . . what do you call 'em?" She snapped her fingers. "Army fatigue things. Just like Mudawar and Sarsour."

"Muda—?"

"You were asking their names. That's their names. Mudawar is the chubby one, and Sarsour is the skinny little guy. Well, I mean, they're both short, but you can sure tell 'em apart."

"I'll knock."

———

"Chloe, you're as excited as anyone," Cameron said.

"Of course!" she said. "What could be better? You know, when I first heard these Old Testament stories, I was a child and loved Sunday school. It wasn't until I got to be a rebellious teenager that I started resenting having to go and fighting with my mother about it all the time. Even when I pulled away from the church and from God, I still enjoyed the memories of those stories. I came to wonder and then to doubt whether they were true, but I couldn't argue that they were great. And I never forgot them.

"There are still times when I regret how much God had to do to bring me to Him, but then He reminds me that He had pursued me the whole time. I didn't want to die, didn't want to leave you and Kenny, but to be with Jesus was, as Paul wrote, far better. This is just icing on the cake. You and I are given this incredible ministry, and now the miraculous stories are brought to life right before our eyes."

"So you'll not be taking the day off tomorrow?"

Chloe smiled and shook her head. "Cam, sometimes I wonder if heaven changed your mind at all."

———

Abdullah wandered back out into the hall and studied the big wood door again. As he glanced about, he became aware of the quiet whine of the TV camera and smiled into it as it seemed to focus on him. He held his Bible up in one hand and opened the palm of the other, as if asking what he should do next. The camera stopped moving, even when Abdullah moved.

He knocked politely. Nothing.

He rapped loudly.

From inside: "May I help you?"

"If you are the Theological Training Institute, you may!"

He listened for any movement inside, and finally, the door was laboriously unlocked—it sounded as if in more than one place—and, like the woman had described, a skinny little man in ancient Jordanian army fatigues poked his nose out. "No classes today."

"Just open the door, Sarsour," Abdullah said with authority.

"What do you want?"

"I want to talk with you and Mudawar."

"He's not here."

"Then I'll talk with you. Open up."

The short, dark man made a face and let go of the door. Abdullah swung it wide and entered a cluttered, claustrophobic space that clearly contained no classrooms. All he saw were three tiny rooms with a few chairs and desks and computers and phones. Papers and books were piled everywhere.

"Mudawar! The authorities are here again!"

"I thought you said Mudawar was not here."

"Ooh, my mistake! You caught me in a lie. Whatever will become of me now?"

"So you are not a man of the truth?" Abdullah said. "Clearly you are a natural."

"I am indeed."

"But you are not a believer, despite what it says on the door."

"What, you're really here for theological classes? None are scheduled currently."

"Another lie, this time of omission. You never teach theology, do you?"

"In a manner of speaking, sometimes we do, actually."

"Antitheology would be more accurate."

Mudawar appeared, also living up to his billing. He was fairer skinned that Sarsour, the same (limited) height, but heavy and oily. Abdullah had the urge to pull out a handkerchief and wipe the man's face.

"This is getting old and boring," Mudawar said. "We have been dragged before the judges before, even threatened to be deported to Israel for an audience with one of the apostles. We pled for the freedom to exercise our own free will and pledged to lie low. Have we not been lying low enough, or have your superiors not kept you up to date on our file?"

"My superior is the Lord Christ Himself."

"Well, aren't we important."

"No, but He is. I come not to arrest or even detain you. I have come to offer my services."

A smile played at Mudawar's lips, and he pointed to a chair, nodding at Sarsour to clear it of a stack of papers. Abdullah sat, and the fat man settled in across from him. "Your services?" Mudawar said.

"I am a chaplain. I minister the Word of God to people's hearts. I teach. I counsel. I pray. I advise."

"And you are offering your services to our Theological Training Institute?"

"No, sir. I am offering them to this cell chapter of the Other Light."

"Aah. I see. So there is no pretense here. You aren't

pretending to not know who we are, and neither are you trying to represent yourself as someone other than who you are."

"Why would I do that? A man my age could never effectively infiltrate your organization, could he?"

Mudawar seemed to study him, squinting. He shook his head. "No, he couldn't. Now tell me, uh . . . I didn't catch your name."

"Abdullah Ababneh."

"Tell me, Khouri Ababneh, what value would your services be to us?"

"That would be up to you, and you may refer to me as Mr. Ababneh or even by my given name."

"Oh! What an honor! I respectfully decline your offer, thank you for dropping in on us, and wish you a good day."

"You will not be providing me office space, then?"

"I beg your pardon."

"I see that you are crowded, but I also understand that you do not hold religious classes here. Perhaps you could clear a little more clutter and find me a space to—how do we say it?—set up shop."

"This has been an amusing interruption, sir, but playtime is over. You may leave now."

"Oh, but I am not leaving. If I am not provided an office here, I shall be forced to bring a portable table from home and establish myself before your door. Do not, however, expect me to double as your receptionist and inform the curious of your comings and goings."

"What would you do out there?"

"Study and read and be available, offering the services I outlined. I will teach, counsel, pray. Whatever anyone wants."

Mudawar laughed while his diminutive cohort stared, plainly puzzled. Whether he was confused by Abdullah or by Mudawar's countenancing this affront, Abdullah could not tell.

"Well," Mudawar said, standing and thrusting out his hand, "I have already clearly told you we are declining your offer."

Abdullah ignored his hand. He pointed into the corner of the next room. "I would be perfectly comfortable right there, and I would be handy to you."

"I am losing patience, friend."

"Oh, I like that you call me friend, as you are the enemy of the One I serve. Would you not find it advantageous to have me in the next room the next time you send out a message to your adherents? You could ask whether you have accurately interpreted something you are criticizing from the Scriptures or even from tradition."

Color began to rise from Mudawar's neck to his moist face. "So the big boss has assigned you to torment us, eh?"

"No, actually to love you."

"To love us. This from the same God who vaporized two earnest, sincere opponents in Egypt, just because they didn't get in line with all the other sheep who trekked to Jerusalem for the—"

"Osaze, you mean."

"You call it what you will. It will always be Egypt to me. And your so-called God of love—is He not the same one who obliterated one of ours who merely deigned to try to make love with one of His 'glorifieds'? This is the same God who slew millions, if the stories of the Old Testament can be believed."

"Mudawar, please sit and let's discuss this."

"There is nothing to discuss!"

"Oh, but there is. My first duty as your chaplain is to correct your view of God, especially if you see Him as merciless and unloving."

"Well, that's the way I see Him!"

"Do you have another moment for me, friend, as I would like to make what I consider a most interesting point?"

Mudawar sat heavily and sighed. "One more minute, but don't call me friend."

"Fair enough, though you may feel free to call me that. Here's what I find intriguing: When I was a young man, younger than you, my problem was that I thought all the dire warnings of God's judgment were wrong, because all I had heard about Jesus was that He was kind and loving and a pacifist, turning the other cheek, preaching the Golden Rule. Then came the end of His patience and mercy, His people were swept off to heaven, and He spent the next seven years trying to get man's attention and persuade him that God was not willing that *any* should perish but that all should come to repentance. And now, here you are, a hundred years later, unable to accept His love."

Mudawar slapped his palms on the table, making both Abdullah and Sarsour jump. "I should have my head examined," he said. "Sarsour, clear the corner of that office."

"What?"

"You heard me! Just do it. This old fool won't be in our way, and who knows? Maybe he'll come in handy. I *will* ask him to defend his God when we have aught against Him. He'll just prove that God is indefensible, that there is neither rhyme nor reason to the maddening two sides of His character."

"Oh, but there is," Abdullah said. "He is loving and full of grace, but he is also perfect and just."

"Yeah, yeah, save it. If you're camping out in here, you'll get plenty of time to spew your platitudes. I've got a newsletter to get out, so you're going to stay out of my hair for the rest of today. Got it?"

"Certainly, but know that I am willing to proofread that for you and make sure you're on track. I mean, you wouldn't want to be guilty of raging against straw men, would you?"

"Sarsour, get him set up in there, and then shut his door."

"Thank you, friend," Abdullah said, offering his hand.

Mudawar gripped it lightly. "Yeah, yeah."

TWENTY-TWO

JOSHUA AND Caleb arrived at COT midmorning the next day, greeting Cameron and striding directly to the spot on the athletic fields where the seemingly endless crowds could see and hear them. Their glorified bodies looked about the same age; Cameron guessed forty. They appeared fit and robust.

Cameron whispered to them, "I will, of course, accede to your wishes, but before you begin, the children would like to recite to you in unison what they memorized from the Scriptures yesterday. Would that be permissible?"

Joshua and Caleb looked at each other and shrugged. "Forgive us," Joshua said, "but you must realize that even after all this time, we remain amazed at what we see in this new world. Life is not at all what it once was, especially in our day."

"Especially the children!" Caleb said. "But yes! By all means, let us hear from them."

Cameron cued the kids, and from thousands of young voices came: " 'The Lord's anger was aroused on that day, and He swore an oath, saying, "Surely none of the men who came up from Egypt, from twenty years old and above, shall see the land of which I swore to Abraham, Isaac, and Jacob, because they have not wholly followed Me, except Caleb the son of Jephunneh, the Kenizzite, and Joshua the son of Nun, for they have wholly followed the Lord." ' "

"Well, yes, amen and amen!" Joshua said, again miraculously able to be heard by all. "Thank you, children! Caleb and I thank you. You are right that the Lord's anger was aroused. He made Israel wander in the wilderness forty years, until all the generation that had done evil in His sight was gone. You know, many people believe the wilderness journey simply took that long, but from the Scriptures you know that the forty years were a punishment for their lack of faith. If you trace our journey on a map, you'll see that we simply wandered around, getting nowhere.

"Now, believe me, I know the story you want me to get to, and I promise I will tell it. But let me ask Caleb here to take you back to when he and I first met and labored together. It may be hard for you to believe, but we were once children, just like you. Now don't laugh. We were!"

Caleb stepped forward. His voice was reedier than Joshua's but just as loud and understandable. "Joshua and I were born in Egypt, while our parents and all the children of Israel were slaves. Even the adults, our parents and aunts and uncles, were called children, because they were the children of God, His chosen people. Joshua and I experienced everything the rest of our tribes went through in the wilderness after escaping. Joshua proved to be a mighty man of valor, serving as a commander in the great war against the Amalekites. He also ministered to our leader, Moses, when he went up Mount Sinai to receive the Ten Commandments from the Lord.

"One day the Lord spoke to Moses, saying, 'Send men to spy out the land of Canaan, which I am giving to the children of Israel; from each tribe of their fathers you shall send a man, every one a leader among them.'

"So Moses sent us from the Wilderness of Paran according to the command of the Lord, all of us men who were heads of the children of Israel. That included Joshua, who was then known as Hoshea until Moses changed his name, and me. He told us, 'Go up this way into the South, and go up to the mountains, and see what the land is like: whether the people who dwell in it are strong or weak, few or many; whether the land they dwell in is good or bad; whether the cities they inhabit are like camps or strongholds; whether the land is rich or poor; and whether there are forests there or not. Be of good courage. And bring some of the fruit of the land.'

"I was glad he added that last, because it was the season of the first ripe grapes. So we went up and spied out the land from one end to the other. When we came

to the Valley of Eshcol—which is not far from Hebron—
we cut down a branch with one cluster of grapes so large
we had to carry it between two of us on a pole. We also
brought some of the pomegranates and figs.

"We finally returned from spying out the land after
forty days, bringing back word to Moses and his brother,
Aaron, and all the congregation of the children of Israel,
and we showed them the fruit of the land. We told
Moses in front of all the others, 'The land where you
sent us truly flows with milk and honey, and this is its
fruit. Nevertheless the people who dwell in the land are
strong; the cities are fortified and very large.'

"Now I could see that this report troubled the people.
And while the report was true, I believed God was in this
and wanted us to proceed. I quieted the people before
Moses and said, 'Let us go up at once and take possession, for we are well able to overcome it.'

"But some of the others who had gone with me said,
'We are not able to go up against the people, for they are
stronger than we.' And they gave the children of Israel a
bad report, saying, 'The land devours its inhabitants, and
all the people are of great stature. We saw giants and we
were like grasshoppers compared to them.'

"Now, children, while this may have been an exagger-
ation, it was close to the truth. Still I believed we were to
trust God for the victory and follow Him into the land.
But all the congregation lifted up their voices and cried,
and the people wept that night. And all the children of
Israel complained against Moses and Aaron, and the
whole congregation said to them, 'If only we had died in

the land of Egypt! Or if only we had died in this wilderness! Why has the Lord brought us to this land to fall by the sword, that our wives and children should become victims? Would it not be better for us to return to Egypt?'

"So they said to one another, 'Let us select a leader and return to Egypt.'

"Moses and Aaron fell on their faces before all the assembly of the congregation of the children of Israel. But Joshua and I tore our clothes and spoke to the children of Israel: 'The land we passed through to spy out is an exceedingly good land. If the Lord delights in us, then He will bring us into this land and give it to us, a land which flows with milk and honey. Only do not rebel against the Lord, nor fear the people of the land, for their protection has departed from them, and the Lord is with us. Do not fear them.'

"But the people wanted to stone us! Then the glory of the Lord appeared in the tabernacle before all the children of Israel."

The children jumped up and cheered, surprising Caleb and making him look to Joshua, who urged him to continue. The children sat again.

"Then the Lord said to Moses: 'How long will these people reject Me? And how long will they not believe Me, with all the signs which I have performed among them? I will strike them with the pestilence and disinherit them, and I will make of you a nation greater and mightier than they.'

"And Moses said to the Lord, 'Then the Egyptians will

hear it, for by Your might You brought these people out from among them, and they will tell it to the inhabitants of this land. They have heard that You, Lord, are among these people; that You, Lord, are seen face to face and Your cloud stands above them, and You go before them in a pillar of cloud by day and in a pillar of fire by night.

" 'Now if You kill these people, then the nations which have heard of Your fame will speak, saying, "Because the Lord was not able to bring this people to the land which He swore to give them, therefore He killed them in the wilderness." '

"And Moses continued, 'I pray, let the power of my Lord be great, just as You have spoken, saying, "The Lord is longsuffering and abundant in mercy, forgiving iniquity and transgression; but He by no means clears the guilty, visiting the iniquity of the fathers on the children to the third and fourth generation." Pardon the iniquity of this people, I pray, according to the greatness of Your mercy, just as You have forgiven this people, from Egypt even until now.'

"Now, children, do you know what God did? He changed His mind. Yes, it happens, and this story proves it. The Lord said, 'I have pardoned, according to your word; but truly, as I live, all the earth shall be filled with the glory of the Lord—because all these men who have seen My glory and the signs which I did in Egypt and in the wilderness, and have put Me to the test now these ten times, and have not heeded My voice, they certainly shall not see the land of which I swore to their fathers, nor shall any of those who rejected Me see it.' "

Joshua stepped forward. "Now let me tell this part, my brother. God continued to speak to Moses, saying, 'But My servant Caleb, because he has a different spirit in him and has followed Me fully, I will bring into the land where he went, and his descendants shall inherit it.'"

Again the children leaped to their feet, clapping and cheering, but now both Joshua and Caleb held up their hands for silence. "There is so much more we want to tell you," Joshua said, smiling. "Please sit."

Caleb spoke again. "Then Moses went up to Mount Nebo, to the top of Pisgah, across from Jericho, and the Lord showed him the land. And the Lord said, 'This is the land of which I swore to give Abraham, Isaac, and Jacob, saying, "I will give it to your descendants." I have caused you to see it with your eyes, but you shall not cross over there.'

"Now, children, Moses the servant of the Lord died there in the land of Moab. He was one hundred and twenty years old, but his eyes were not dim nor his vigor diminished. We children of Israel wept for Moses for thirty days.

"Can you guess whom the Lord chose to be the next leader of the children of Israel?"

Many kids shouted, "You!" and others yelled, "Joshua!"

"Some of you are right," Caleb said. "Joshua was full of the spirit of wisdom. It came to pass that the Lord spoke to Joshua, Moses' assistant, saying: 'Moses My servant is dead. Now therefore, arise, go over this Jordan, you and all these people, to the land which I am giving to them. Every place that the sole of your foot will tread upon I have given you, as I said to Moses. From the wilderness and this Lebanon as far as the great river, the River Euphrates, all the land of the Hittites, and to the Great Sea toward the going down of the sun, shall be your territory. No man shall be able to stand before you all the days of your life; as I was with Moses, so I will be with you. I will not leave you nor forsake you. Be strong and of good courage, for to this people you shall divide as an inheritance the land which I swore to their fathers to give them. Only be strong and very courageous, that you may observe to do according to all the law which Moses My servant commanded you; do not turn from it to the right hand or to the left, that you may prosper wherever you go. This Book of the Law shall not depart from your mouth, but you shall meditate in it day and night, that you may observe to do according to all that is written in it. For then you will make your way prosperous, and then you will have good success.

"'Have I not commanded you? Be strong and of good courage; do not be afraid, nor be dismayed, for the Lord your God is with you wherever you go.'

"Then Joshua commanded the officers of the people, saying, 'Pass through the camp and command the people, saying, "Prepare provisions for yourselves, for within three days you will cross over this Jordan, to go in to possess the land which the Lord your God is giving you to possess."'

"Joshua told the people, 'Remember the word which Moses the servant of the Lord commanded you, saying,

"The Lord your God is giving you rest and is giving you this land." Your wives, your little ones, and your livestock shall remain in the land which Moses gave you on this side of the Jordan. But you shall pass before your brethren armed, all your mighty men of valor, and help them, until the Lord has given your brethren rest, as He gave you, and they also have taken possession of the land which the Lord your God is giving them. Then you shall return to the land of your possession and enjoy it, which Moses the Lord's servant gave you on this side of the Jordan toward the sunrise.'

"They answered Joshua, saying, 'All that you command us we will do, and wherever you send us we will go. Just as we heeded Moses in all things, so we will heed you. Only the Lord your God be with you, as He was with Moses. Whoever rebels against your command and does not heed your words shall be put to death. Only be strong and of good courage.'

"Joshua sent out two men to spy secretly on Jericho. So they went and came to the house of a harlot named Rahab and lodged there. And it was told the king of Jericho, 'Behold, men have come here tonight from the children of Israel to search out the country.'

"So the king of Jericho sent to Rahab, saying, 'Bring out the men who have entered your house, for they have come to search out all the country.'

"But the woman took the two men and hid them and said, 'Yes, they came to me, but I did not know where they were from. And as the gate was being shut, when it was dark, the men went out. Where they went I do not

know; pursue them quickly, for you may overtake them.'
But she had brought them up to the roof and hidden
them with the stalks of flax.

"As soon as those who pursued them had gone out,
they shut the gate. Now before they lay down, she came
up to them on the roof and said, 'I know that the Lord
has given you the land, that the terror of you has fallen
on us, and that all the inhabitants of the land are fainthearted because of you. For we have heard how the
Lord dried up the water of the Red Sea for you when
you came out of Egypt, and what you did to the
Amorites on the other side of the Jordan, whom you
utterly destroyed. Our hearts melted; neither did there
remain any more courage in anyone because of you, for
the Lord your God, He is God in heaven above and on
earth beneath.

"'Now therefore, I beg you, swear to me by the Lord,
since I have shown you kindness, that you also will show
kindness to my father's house, and give me a true token,
and spare my father, my mother, my brothers, my sisters,
and all that they have, and deliver our lives from death.'

"The men answered, 'Our lives for yours, if none of
you tell this business of ours. And it shall be, when the
Lord has given us the land, that we will deal kindly and
truly with you.'

"Then she let them down by a rope through the
window, and the men said, 'When we come into the
land, bind this line of scarlet cord in the window through
which you let us down.'

"When they returned, they said to Joshua, 'Truly the

Lord has delivered all the land into our hands, for indeed all the inhabitants of the country are fainthearted because of us.'

"Then Joshua rose early in the morning, and they set out from Acacia Grove and came to the Jordan, he and all the children of Israel, and lodged there before they crossed over. So it was, after three days, that the officers went through the camp; and they commanded the people, saying, 'When you see the ark of the covenant of the Lord your God, and the priests, the Levites, bearing it, then you shall set out from your place and go after it. Yet there shall be a space between you and it, about two thousand cubits by measure. Do not come near it, that you may know the way by which you must go, for you have not passed this way before.'

"Then Joshua said to the priests, 'Take up the ark of the covenant and cross over before the people.'

"And the Lord said to Joshua, 'This day I will begin to exalt you in the sight of all Israel, that they may know that, as I was with Moses, so I will be with you. Command the priests who bear the ark of the covenant, "When you have come to the edge of the water, you shall stand in the Jordan." '

"So Joshua said to the children of Israel, 'By this you shall know that the living God is among you, and that He will without fail drive out from before you all your enemies: Behold, the ark of the covenant of the Lord of all the earth is crossing over before you into the Jordan. And it shall come to pass, as soon as the soles of the feet of the priests who bear the ark of the Lord of all the earth shall rest in the waters of the Jordan, the waters shall be cut off, and they shall stand as a heap.'

"And, children, so it was. When we set out to cross over the Jordan, and the feet of the priests who bore the ark dipped in the edge of the water, the flow was cut off, and we crossed over opposite Jericho on dry ground."

The children were cheering again, but Joshua held up a hand for silence.

Caleb continued, "The Lord spoke to Joshua, saying, 'Take for yourselves twelve men, one man from every tribe, and command them to take for themselves twelve stones from out of the midst of the Jordan from the place where the priests' feet stood firm.'

"Joshua set up twelve stones in the midst of the Jordan, in the place where the feet of the priests who bore the ark of the covenant stood, and we hurried and crossed over. About forty thousand prepared for war crossed over before the Lord to the plains of Jericho.

"You see, on that day the Lord exalted Joshua in the sight of all Israel, and we feared him as we had Moses. And Joshua commanded the priests, saying, 'Come up from the Jordan,' and when the soles of their feet touched dry land, the waters of the Jordan returned and overflowed all its banks.

"We came up from the Jordan and camped in Gilgal on the east border of Jericho. And those twelve stones we took out of the Jordan, Joshua set up in Gilgal. Then he spoke to the children of Israel, saying, 'When your children ask their fathers in time to come, saying, "What are these stones?" you shall let your children know, saying, "Israel crossed over this Jordan on dry land"; for the Lord your God dried up the waters of the Jordan before you until you had crossed over, just as He did the Red Sea, which He dried up before us until we had crossed over.'

"And, young ones, here is why. Are you listening? 'So all the peoples of the earth may know the hand of the Lord, that it is mighty, that they may fear the Lord their God forever.' Will you vow to do that? Will you? Raise your hand if you will."

All over the athletic field, youngsters raised their hands, and many waved.

"All right, we're getting to the story you've all been waiting for, and I know you want to hear it from the man himself."

More applause as Joshua traded places with Caleb.

"We had been in the wilderness for more than forty years by now, and it was time to possess the land. We camped in Gilgal on the plains of Jericho. We ate of the produce of the land, unleavened bread and parched grain. The manna from the Lord ceased the day after we had eaten of the land, and we ate the food of the land of Canaan that year.

"One day I looked, and behold, a Man stood opposite me with His sword drawn. I went to Him and said, 'Are You for us or for our adversaries?'

"He told me he had come as Commander of the army of the Lord. I knew who He was. Do you? He sits on the throne in the temple even today. I fell on my face and worshiped, and said, 'What does my Lord say to His servant?'

"The Commander of the Lord's army said, 'Take your sandal off your foot, for the place where you stand is holy.' And so I did.

"Now the people of the city of Jericho knew we were nearby, and so it was locked up tight, no one going in or coming out. The Lord said, 'See! I have given Jericho into your hand, its king, and the mighty men of valor. You shall march around the city, all you men of war, once every day for six days. And seven priests shall bear seven trumpets of rams' horns before the ark. But the seventh day you shall march around the city seven times, and the priests shall blow the trumpets.

" 'It shall come to pass, when they make a long blast with the ram's horn, and when you hear the sound of the trumpet, that all the people shall shout with a great shout; then the wall of the city will fall down flat.'

"I called the priests together and told them what the Lord had told me. And I instructed the people, 'Proceed, and march around the city, and let him who is armed advance before the ark of the Lord. You shall not shout, nor shall a word proceed out of your mouth, until the day I say to you, "Shout!" Then you shall shout.'

"So I had the ark of the Lord circle the city, going around it once. Then we came into the camp and lodged. And I rose early in the morning, and the second day did the same thing. We did this every day for six days as the Lord had commanded.

"Well, you know what happened next, so perhaps my friend and I should leave now?"

The children leaped to their feet, crying, "No! No! Stay and tell the rest!"

Joshua smiled broadly and signaled them to sit and be quiet. "All right, you persuaded me. On the seventh day we rose about dawn and marched around the city, only this day we circled it seven times. On the seventh time around, when the priests blew their trumpets, I said to the people, 'Shout, for the Lord has given you the city! The city shall be doomed by the Lord to destruction, it and all who are in it. Only Rahab the harlot shall live, she and all who are with her in the house, because she hid the messengers that we sent. All the silver and gold and vessels of bronze and iron are consecrated to the Lord and shall come into His treasury.'

"So when the people heard the sound of the trumpet, they shouted with a great shout, and the wall fell down flat."

The children were cheering again.

"Then we marched straight in and took the city as the Lord had commanded. We utterly destroyed it and everything in it with the edge of the sword and with fire, protecting only the harlot, who had been faithful to the Lord, and her family."

Caleb stepped forward once again. "So you see, little ones, the Lord was with Joshua, and his fame spread throughout all the country. You too can be blessed of the Lord if you remain strong and have courage, trust in the Lord with all your heart, and remain obedient and faithful."

Joshua closed the time with the children by praying, but when he finished, the children pressed forward. They wanted to touch the men, to ask more questions. For more than an hour, until Cameron could restore order, kids milled about, leaning in, their faces expectant as they clearly longed for their moment with these heroes.

———

Unlike when Noah had visited, for some reason very few of the children left with their parents when it was over. Kenny was overwhelmed with kids who had questions and others who wanted to act out the scenes they had just heard. Some asked if they could build stone monuments, and Kenny promised to try to find stones small enough so everyone who wanted to could do it.

He was most impressed, however, with children who had deduced that the Commander of the Lord's army was Jesus Himself. One little boy said, "Mr. Williams, I want to be in Jesus' army."

"Oh, don't you realize," Kenny said, "He accepts only those who trust Him for forgiveness of their sins and for salvation?"

"I will."

"You will? How will you do that?"

"I'll tell Him."

"Right now?"

"Can I?"

"Yes, and you don't even have to travel to the temple.

Just pray to Him and tell Him that you know you are a sinner and that you want His forgiveness. Then ask Him to be your Savior and thank Him for dying on the cross for your sins. You know that story, don't you?"

"Sure, everybody knows that. At least everybody here."

"Do you understand that Jesus wants you to decide to follow Him?"

The little boy nodded, and Kenny prayed with him. He couldn't wait to tell Ekaterina, and he was sure she would have similar stories.

Abdullah sat in his cramped new office at the back of TOL headquarters in Amman, reading his Bible and making notes for a lesson he was prepared to give if ever asked. He looked up when he realized Sarsour was peering at him from the other room.

"Need anything?" Abdullah said.

The young man, wiry and nimble, shook his head, but his body language gave him away. He seemed drawn to Abdullah.

"Feel free to come in. Anytime. Chat. Or just sit."

Sarsour wandered in as if he could take or leave the invitation. He pretended to study stuff taped to the walls, but it was all old and faded and likely had been affixed there by him, so Abdullah knew he was just self-conscious. Abdullah went back to his reading, keeping an ear open. He began to hum an old hymn and then softly sing.

"Oh, the love that sought me,
Oh, the blood that bought me,
Oh, the grace that brought me to the fold,
Wondrous grace that brought me to the fold."

Finally Sarsour sat. Abdullah slid his Bible and his papers to the side and looked at him expectantly.

"You really believe this stuff, huh?" Sarsour said.

"I do. And you don't?"

"'Course I don't. I'm a TOLer."

"Your parents have to be believers."

"Yeah. But it's not for me. They tried to raise me in it, but as soon as I started reading other stuff and talking to other people, I realized the Bible isn't the only idea."

"What about all the prophecies that have been fulfilled, all the people who have been resurrected, the ones who have already been in heaven? And what about the fact that Jesus is with us now and sits on the throne, judging the nations?"

Sarsour shrugged. "It's like He's head of the occupying army. We're the resistance, that's all. The rebels."

"And you don't feel destined to lose in the end?"

"We're outnumbered. We're the outcasts, the rejects, the dregs. But we won't give up hope until it's all over. And then we'll see who wins."

"Your compatriots, the ones who reach one hundred, are dying every day."

"I know."

"Do you know of any exceptions?"

"No."

"And that doesn't tell you anything?"

"It just proves God isn't who He says He is."

"How do you figure?"

"He's mean and unloving and unforgiving, violent and judgmental. Disagree and you get killed."

"He's not willing that any should perish. Even you, Sarsour."

"Don't start with me."

"How about I tell you my own story? I wasn't always a believer, you know. I was raised in another religion entirely."

Sarsour shrugged again and looked away. "I don't need to hear it."

Abdullah cocked his head. "Sometimes I just need to tell it. How about I talk and you listen only if you care to?"

"I already told you; I don't need to hear it."

"And I told you; I need to tell it. I was married to a beautiful woman and had two precious children. I was a decorated fighter pilot in the Royal Jordanian Air Force."

Sarsour had stood and was moving away, as if he couldn't care less. But that last stopped him. "You were?"

"Yes. I was what some would call a star. I taught. And I was given the best assignments. I considered myself religious because I followed all the tenets of my faith. Keeping away from impure things. Trying to do right. Praying at prescribed times every day. Then something happened to my wife. . . ."

Abdullah fell silent, and Sarsour sat back down.

"What? What happened to her?"

"Oh, you don't want to hear it."

"It's okay. If you need to tell it, you can keep going."

TWENTY-THREE

OVER THE next several days, Kenny vacillated between the thrill of his relationship with Ekaterina—they had both professed their love by now and had begun enjoying brief good-night kisses—and a dread over what he was going to do about communicating with Ignace and Lothair Jospin. There would soon be no more putting them off.

He had an idea, a fun one he thought Ekaterina would love, but also one that might help him find valuable counsel. He wanted to update Bruce Barnes, his parents' old friend, on him and Kat and see if he was willing to officiate at their wedding someday. But maybe Bruce would be a good adviser too. Kenny got Bruce's number from his mother and called him in Osaze. Bruce was in the middle of a project but promised to call him back that evening.

———

Chloe was troubled. She'd thought the phony Ekaterina
Risto personnel report had blown over, and frustrated as
she was to have never gotten a handle on where it came
from, she had been able to put it behind her. And the more
she got to know Kat, the happier she was for Kenny. It
was clear that relationship had developed into love, and
she and Cameron adored Kat. Chloe only hoped Kenny
was calling Bruce for the reason she suspected.

But that day her in-box had brought another upsetting
note. Unsigned, of course. Cameron had told her she
ought to institute a policy that she look first to see if
suggestions or complaints were signed and summarily
trash them if not. "If a person isn't willing to stand by
what he says . . ."

This note read: *Kenneth B. Williams is your culprit in
the Risto personnel matter.*

That made no sense, of course. Ludicrous. And yet
Chloe carried the crumpled note around all morning.
What was she supposed to do with something like that?
Finally she paged Cameron. "It's not urgent," she said.
"But when you have a moment . . ."

———

It felt weird to Abdullah to be strolling to "work" every
day with a portfolio full of papers and his Bible, setting
up shop, as he liked to call it, in the enemy's lair. It
violated every boundary of logic he had ever been aware
of, and yet God knew. *His ways are not our ways,*
Abdullah reminded himself.

236

Abdullah had the strange feeling that he had somehow captivated Sarsour, and from the looks they both got from Mudawar, it was clear he wasn't happy. Every time Mudawar emerged from his office, it seemed, Sarsour was sitting with Abdullah and listening to some tale. "Back to work, bug," Mudawar would bark.

On the other hand, Mudawar himself had actually been consulting Abdullah almost daily. Despite Mudawar's appearing to take out his impatience and frustration on Sarsour, he seemed to treat Abdullah with more and more deference. Gone was the sarcastic tone and the ridicule. Often he would ask earnestly, "If I wrote something like this about God, would believers say I was wrong or unfair, or would they just be bothered because they don't understand Him either?"

Abdullah would study the paragraph and at times even feel led to advise Mudawar how to better frame his argument *against* God. When the fleshy little man would retreat to his office, Abdullah would seek the Lord. "Is this really what You want from me? I feel as if I am aiding and abetting."

But Abdullah felt God compel him to love the man as Jesus would. No argument of man could besmirch the name of the Lord.

Down deep Abdullah had an inkling of what seemed to be changing these men's minds about him. He really was loving them and caring for them and praying for them. Mudawar had a favorite drink, an especially thick, rich, and dark coffee available only from a certain street vendor. Every day he arrived nursing one of those drinks.

And every day, Abdullah would slip away late in the morning and bring him another.

To win over Sarsour while stringing him along daily with snippets of his own story of his raptured wife, Abdullah discovered Sarsour's love for a particular kind of hummus, a mash of chickpeas and sesame seeds flavored with garlic and lemon. When he ducked out for Mudawar's drink, he would also bring back that treat for Sarsour.

It was clear the young men did not know what to make of Abdullah, but they were growing more civil to him every day.

On his break, Sarsour glanced at Mudawar's closed door and slid a chair next to Abdullah's desk. "So you divorced your wife when she became a believer, and you turned against your own faith, drinking and carousing. When she and your children were taken in the Rapture, you dug out her old letters. And what did they say?"

Abdullah sat back and studied the young man. "Now we are getting very personal."

Sarsour threw up his hands. "Oh, I don't mean to pry. But you began this story. I merely want to hear the end of it."

"I'll tell you what," Abdullah said. "On Monday I will bring the most potent of the letters and let you read it."

———

"You know how I feel about garbage like that," Cameron said. "Toss it."

"I know, hon," Chloe said, having expected that response. "But we haven't had this kind of mischief, and I don't want it now. Isn't there a way to find out who's doing this?"

Cameron sighed. "Before the Rapture, I would have blamed it on the wiles of the devil, devising time wasters to keep us from what's important. It's almost worse to know he has nothing to do with it. This is the flesh. Why don't you ask Kenny if he knows of any enemies who might have some motive for getting him into trouble?"

"I hate to even show him this."

"Then toss it and forget it."

But Chloe knew she couldn't.

Kenny was walking Ekaterina home when Bruce called back. "Oh, hello, Pastor," he said. "Actually now *I* can't talk."

"Oh, she's right there?" Bruce said.

"How'd you know?"

"Why else would you have called me in the first place?"

"A couple of reasons, actually. I'll call you later, Pastor."

"Pastor?" Ekaterina said as Kenny finished. "What pastor?"

"Oh, just an old friend of my parents."

"Bruce?"

Kenny blushed and nodded. "I want to get an outside opinion on what I should do about the Jospins."

That seemed to satisfy Kat, and they spent the dinner hour with her parents, talking openly about their future. Nothing was official yet, of course, but their conversations had progressed even to the logistics of where they would live. Kenny wanted to make his actual proposal something dramatic and special.

That night Raymie called a meeting of the Millennium Force, and it was clear Zaki was not happy. "You still pining over your buddy?" Raymie said. "I don't get it. All of us except Kenny here have glorified minds, and you're still obsessing over what I had to say to Qasim."

Zaki shook his head. "I felt ganged up on, and I know Qasim did. I want to go on record that you overreacted and that you had no right to ban him from our meetings."

"He didn't belong here!" Bahira said. "He was never a member, and Raymie made it clear he was not to even pretend to represent us, but still he did just that! He called himself our TOL infiltration expert!"

"He was just trying to help."

Kenny remembered when these meetings had been positive and consisted mostly of prayer for the undecideds they so longed to reach. "I can't stay long tonight," he said. "I have a call I need to make."

"But you suggested this meeting," Raymie said.

"I know, and I appreciate it. I just think we need to get off the subject of Qasim and talk about what you all think I should do about the Jospins."

"It's time to act," Zaki said. "You've got a chance here to really get next to them and find out what's going on.

One more delay or misstep and you lose all credibility with them."

"I can't argue with that," Raymie said. "Bahira?"

"Much as I hate to agree with my brother—"

"Hey!"

"Kidding! I agree it's time to act."

"Guess that means a green light from us," Raymie said. "Be careful and keep us posted."

"Of course," Bruce said. "Kenny, I would be honored. And I agree it's a nice touch, tying your wedding to that of your parents. But you must get Ekaterina on board. She may have another idea. It has to be her call. I won't be offended either way."

While they were connected by their implanted cellular phones, Kenny filled Bruce in on the situation with the Other Light in Paris.

"What's the benefit compared to the risk, Kenny? What is the upside for the Millennium Force?"

"Knowing what they're up to. Being able to counter what they say before they say it. We're not afraid of them. They're not going to hurt us or any other believers. Our mission, our target, is the undecided."

"As long as it helps accomplish your mission, I'd say go for it."

Monday morning, after Abdullah had stepped out to fetch the treats for the two young men, he asked

Mudawar if it was all right for him to chat with Sarsour
on his break.

"Why are you asking me? He spends a lot of his work
time with you anyway. But sure, fine. You know this is a
joke—a believer, a member of the opposition, officing
here. It's silly when you think about it, but I'm not
amused. Fact is, really, I'm taking advantage of you.
Besides learning a few things and being able to better
articulate our position, I am keeping you from more
important duties, keeping you from the very hearts and
minds we are trying to reach. But don't expect me to let
you sit there in all your glory when we have visitors."

"I am surprised I haven't seen any yet. For what
purpose *do* they come here, and why have there been
none?"

"They come for monthly strategy sessions, and sometimes we get visitors from chapters in other parts of the
world. Your presence when they arrive will be verboten."

"And when will that be?"

"Nothing is currently planned, but believe me, it'll
happen."

"Kenny," Chloe said, "I decided to call both of you in
because I know you'll tell Ekaterina anyway."

He and Kat looked at each other. "Tell her what?"

Chloe spun the note on her desk so both could read it.

Ekaterina said, "Oh, for the love . . ."

"Good grief, Mom. Really, why do you even waste

your time on stuff like this? You know how ridiculous this is. I'm in love with this woman and plan to marry her. I would no more do her harm than I would harm myself!"

"I know. I'm sorry. I just want you to know what I'm dealing with. Can you think of anyone who would want to stir up this kind of trouble?"

"Only Qasim," Kenny said, "and Mattie claims he's turned over a new leaf."

"It's true," Kat said, nodding. "He's been a perfect gentleman ever since I started my new role. And I don't think he's faking it. He doesn't disappear when we need help anymore. He seems to go out of his way to pitch in."

"How about the spiritual part?" Chloe said. "Does he seem any more interested in talking with kids about the Lord?"

"I can't say that he does, but then we don't get that much opportunity for that in rec. Plus now I think people sort of leave that part of it to me. Which is all right with me. It just gives me more opportunities."

"Yes," Chloe said, "but evangelism is what we're all about. It's why we're here. I want people working for us, even in your area, who care about these children's hearts and souls."

They sat in silence for a moment. Finally Kenny said, "Let's just forget this other, Mom. It's not worth the time, really."

TWENTY-FOUR

ABDULLAH HAD Yasmine's permission to show her letter to whomever he felt it necessary, but already he was repenting of promising to show it to Sarsour. It was so personal, and frankly so painful. . . .

And yet if it could somehow turn a stubborn heart toward God, he didn't have a choice.

When he and Sarsour were sitting across from one another again, the young man's countenance and demeanor had reverted to their first days together. "What is troubling you, son?"

"I don't know," Sarsour said, his mouth full of his snack and his tone evidencing that he did, in fact, know. "It's only fair to tell you that so far you have not changed my mind a whit. You are a curiosity, and I like a good story as well as the next man. But don't start thinking you are getting to me."

"Fair enough. But it is not your mind I care so much about, Sarsour. It is your heart. That is what God is after too."

"You sound like my parents."

"They know your mission, your work?"

The young man shook his head. "It would be cruel to tell them. They know I am not a believer, that I have a lot of questions and accusations against God. That hurts them enough. I don't need to nail the final lid in their coffin."

"They are not the ones who will die, son."

"Touché."

"But it is true! They entered the kingdom redeemed of the Lord, and while they will age—because they are naturals—they are promised eternity with God. They will be ushered from this kingdom to the next. How old are you, Sarsour?"

The young man shrugged.

"Come, come, everyone knows his own age."

"I am two months younger than Mudawar."

"And he is?"

"Nearly a hundred."

"Sarsour, please, we have no time to waste. You boys must come to your senses, come to the Lord. Consider all this foolishness just youthful independence and rebellion, but turn now to what you have to know is the truth."

"I know nothing of the sort!"

"Listen, let's say you're right. Let's say that despite all you TOLers dying off at the end of your hundred years you are somehow able to keep this torch burning down through the centuries as the population expands. By the last century of the Millennium, you have amassed this great army, and all right, let's say that against all odds and logic and prophecy and the very Word of God, your side prevails. Let me postulate that those of you who thought this up and schemed and strategized are still dead and still in hell and that your leader does not have the power to resurrect you. Convince me I am wrong."

"Well, Lucifer would be returned to his rightful place. He would be the king then, in charge, on the throne."

"And he would inherit the powers of God Himself?"

"Sure. Why not?"

"Because it doesn't work that way. If he was almost God, almost as good as Jesus, and had himself overesti-mated, why was he kicked out of heaven? Why didn't he stay and fight? Because he doesn't have the power, and the power will not be endowed him, regardless what happens in that final conflict. Think of the irony. Your side wins, and you all still lose."

"That doesn't make sense."

"Neither does your stubborn insistence on winning. You cannot name one prophecy of the Bible, Old Testa-ment or New, that has not been fulfilled exactly as it was foretold. Not one. And yet you have the audacity to tell me that when it comes down to the final moment in the history of natural man, a bunch of rebels from the last millennium will change everything."

Sarsour stood and moved to a window, averting his

eyes. He actually pulled back the curtains and raised the blinds.

Abdullah had to stifle a laugh. "How's the view?" he said. "From the basement." He looked past Sarsour to a wall of bricks. "Beautiful day, isn't it?"

Sarsour turned quickly. "Okay, all right, so I'm not as smart and articulate as you and I can't frame my argument the best. Mudawar can. You should be debating him."

"Oh, friend, hear me. The problem with your argument is not you! It's simply that you're wrong. When I was raging against my wife, I was as prideful as you are. I sincerely believed she was wrong and that I could somehow bring her to her senses. I was angry. I was self-righteous, even as my life was flying out of control."

Abdullah was overcome with emotion. His lips trembled and his voice grew thick. "I was almost too late in seeing it myself! Imagine if I had been killed in the chaotic aftermath of the Rapture. I'd have been lost forever. God granted me the grace to dig out my wife's letters and remind myself what she said. Sarsour, this is your chance! You won't get another. If you die at one hundred, there's no more hope for you."

Sarsour returned to his seat and seemed to study Abdullah. "Why does this trouble you so? Why don't you just leave me to my hopelessness, my wrongness, my—as you call it—foolishness. What am I to you?"

"You're my friend."

"*Ya Bek*, I am your enemy. I disagree with everything

you say. I mock your God. I accuse Him. I hold Him accountable."

"And I am instructed to love my enemy and to pray for those who spitefully use me."

Sarsour shook his head. "Talk about foolishness."

"I don't know what else to say to you, Sarsour. If you are so resolute . . ." Abdullah carefully folded Yasmine's letter and began to tuck it back into his Bible.

"Oh, let me see that," Sarsour said, reaching for it.

> Abdullah, I believe—and I am certain you agree—that God hates divorce. It was not my intention that my new faith would result in the end of our marriage. This was your choice, but I concede that staying with you and allowing you influence over our children would have also been untenable as long as you feel the way you do about me now.
>
> I know this letter will anger you, and neither is that my intention. We have talked and talked about the differences between Islam and Christianity, but please indulge me and allow me to get my thoughts down in order. Hopefully God will help me make them clear.
>
> I do not expect that you will suddenly see the truth because of my words, but I pray that God will open your heart and will one day reveal Himself to you. As I have said over and over, the difference between what you call "our religions" is that mine is not religion. I have come

to believe that religion is man's effort to please
God. I had always been bound by rules, acts of
service, good deeds. I was trying as hard as I
could to win the favor of Allah so that in the
end I would find heaven on earth.

But I could never be good enough, Abdullah,
and as wonderful as you were for many years,
you couldn't either. That became clear with your
unreasonable reaction to my coming to faith in the
one true God and Father of Jesus Christ. To you it
was anathema, despite the fact that, like me, you
had drifted even from the tenets of Islam.

I believe that to you, my converting was a
public humiliation. I regret that, but I could no
more hide my true feelings and beliefs than I
could ask you to give up flying.

Just once more, let me clarify: Christians
believe the Bible teaches that everyone is born
in sin and that the penalty for sin is death. But
Jesus paid the price by living a sinless life and
dying as a sacrifice for all who believe.
Abdullah, you must admit you have never met
a perfect person, and we each know the other
is not perfect. We are sinners in need of salvation. We can't save ourselves, can't change ourselves. I am most encouraged by your discipline
and your efforts. You are now more like the
man I married, but don't you see? You will
never be good enough to qualify for heaven,
because you would have to be entirely perfect.

Someday, when you are ready—and I hope it will not be too late—just pray and tell God that you know that you are a sinner, that you are sorry and want to repent and be forgiven. Ask Him to take over your life. The day is coming, prophesied in Scripture, when Jesus will return in the clouds and snatch away all true believers in an instant. No one will see this happen except for those to whom it happens. Those left behind will simply realize that it is all true. Christians from all over the world will disappear. I hope it does not take a tragedy like that—though it will be anything but tragic for those of us who go—to get you to swallow your pride, examine yourself, and humble yourself before God. Of course, if this does happen before you come to true faith, you will know what has occurred. And you will be without excuse. I just pray that you do not lose your life in the resulting chaos before you can become a believer, not in a religion but in a person. Jesus the Christ.

With fond memories and deep affection, praying for you,

Yasmine

Sarsour handed the document back to Abdullah. "And so you did what she said? Became a believer?"

Abdullah nodded.

"And she and your children were gone? You didn't see them until they returned from heaven? My parents had reunions like that with their friends."

"Sarsour, who could accomplish that? How could the evil one hope to prevail over a God like that?"

The young man pressed his lips together and shook his head. "I have to get back to work," he said. "We have a delegation coming from France in a few days."

"That's it then, Sarsour? The end of our discussion?"

"It hasn't been a discussion, sir. It has been a sermon. Why waste your time here with just the two of us? Why are you not out preaching to the masses? There are a lot more undecided young people out there than in here, and they have to be more open-minded than we of the Other Light. We ought to know. They are our audience, our prospects."

"*You* are my prospects," Abdullah said. "I am here in obedience to my Lord Christ, who knows best."

Ekaterina was tearful at Kenny's news that he would be gone a few days to France. "I wish I could go with you," she said.

"Me too. Pray for me while I'm gone."

"I pray for you all the time, love. Of course I will."

"I gave Ignace and Lothair some very innocuous information about COT. I merely told them where it was, how many children we hosted, how large the staff was, and that the big deal now had been the visits from biblical heroes. They were not impressed. Ignace fired back a message that said, 'Tell us something we don't know. Tell us something that not everybody in the world knows.

And tell us in person.' I think he was really surprised when I told him I would be there tomorrow. I believe they were really starting to suspect me."

"You know what I miss?" Bruce said late one night in the Negev as he and Rayford sat outside by a small fire. "Darkness."

The rest of the team slept in the massive trailer, heavy shades pulled against the daylight-like beaming of the moon.

Rayford chuckled. "You know what the Bible says about that. Men love darkness rather than light because their deeds are evil."

"Yeah, I think I was the one who taught you that, Ray. And yep, that's me. Evil."

"I know what you mean, though, Bruce. I'd love a starlit night to aid my sleep. But you've been to heaven, where there is no night, not even shadow. Were you tired of it there?"

Bruce shook his head. "Heaven is different. And I can't wait till the books are opened and all the believers go. As fascinating as this world and this kingdom are, I can't think they hold a candle to the next."

They chatted long into the night, plotting the coming weeks of their mission. Bruce told Rayford of Kenny's call. "Think of it, man. Who'd have ever thought I'd officiate your second wedding, your daughter's, and her son's?"

TWENTY-FIVE

KENNY HAD cleared several days off so he could complete his clandestine mission to Paris, but almost as soon as he got there he heard from Ekaterina, asking whether he could return and postpone his trip.

"Why? What's going on?"

"Your father has just announced our next heroic visitor. Kenny, he's your favorite."

"Not David!"

"The prince himself."

"I can't believe it! When?"

"Within the next couple of days."

"I don't plan to return until Saturday."

"I know. That's why I'm saying maybe you could—"

"But I prayed about this, sweetheart. I know this is where God wants me, and I have to think that if I make this sacrifice, He will somehow make it up to me."

"How?"

"Who knows? Maybe by giving me an audience with David as He did my grandfather. I guess someday I'll have all the time I want with all the biblical characters."

"I know you're right, Kenny. And you've taught me that God favors obedience even over sacrifice. That's just hard for me right now, because I was hoping this news would be enough to bring you back to me."

"I'll be back soon enough."

"Oh, and Kenny? This visit from David is different from all the others. We're not to tell anyone."

"You weren't even supposed to tell me?"

"Well, you're on staff. But no kids, no parents, no friends. We've all been sworn to secrecy. That priest friend of your father's supposedly told him that if even one outsider shows up, the visit is off."

"And yet we don't even know when it is."

"Not exactly, no."

"Well, I'll bet ol' Qasim makes this one for sure."

"Actually, he's off the rest of this week too."

Abdullah knocked lightly on Mudawar's door.

"Yeah!"

He pushed it open slowly. "Sorry to intrude. It's just that Sarsour mentioned perhaps a visiting delegation sometime soon and—"

"And you were wondering whether you should make yourself scarce?"

"On the contrary. I wish to offer my services to them, too. If they are friends of yours, they are friends of mine, and I am eager to meet their needs."

"They don't have needs, Abdullah. And they aren't my friends. They are my bosses. More than that, they are my mentors, the ones who got me into this. The fact is, I idolize them and want to make a good impression, and right now I can't imagine for the life of me how it's going to look if I have you ensconced in one of my offices. They're coming the day after tomorrow, and if you really want to help, I want this place sparkling by then."

"I am pleased to help."

"And then I want you out of here for a few days. No sign of you. Nothing left on your desk."

"That I will not do."

"Excuse me?"

"You heard me, Mudawar. I repeat my pledge from the first. I am here under assignment from almighty God. You may be under some illusion or delusion that you—in some moment of madness or genius—decided to allow me in. But the fact is, the Lord has ordained it."

"You don't think I can kick you out of my own suite of offices?"

"Oh, I know you can. But you also know that I would then be stationed in front of your door with my little table and my Bible and my smile, and I will be greeting your honored guests every time they enter or leave. And we both know people are somehow drawn to me."

"Yes! Out of morbid curiosity! You're a relic, Abdullah, a peculiarity."

"Whatever it takes to attract a listening ear. Once I have their attention, I merely talk about the Lord. The rest is up to Him, not this imperfect vessel."

"You are a crazy man."

"The apostle Paul would have called me a fool for Christ."

"And so, what? It's either you in here, making me look like an idiot before my mentors, or out by the front door, being the dunce yourself?"

"Either way it reflects upon you, I suppose. You have not consulted me in some time, though Sarsour has been at least cordial—"

"That's what I'm afraid of."

"—but a word to the wise: If I were you, I would represent my presence in your offices as your idea, a stroke of brilliance, going against the grain, zigging when the rest of the world is zagging. If you can't persuade your mentors there's some benefit to the cause in this, that you have somehow convinced me that my time is better spent here than trying to persuade the same target audience, then perhaps you are not qualified for the role you have been given. Give it some thought."

Kenny was in his Paris hotel room the next morning when he was informed of a message waiting for him at the desk. It read: *Meet us at the address on the reverse, 30 minutes. I & L*

The location was easy to get to by mass transit. Ignace

and Lothair nodded at him from a wrought iron table at an outdoor café as he crossed the street.

"Hey, guys," Kenny said, pretending not to notice that they didn't look happy.

"Just sit down," Ignace said. "Who do you think you're kidding anyway?"

"I don't follow."

"You don't follow. You make noises at our cousin's funeral like you might be one of us, you string us along by e-mail, we get absolute zilch from you—even though your buddy Qasim vouches for you with his life. And how hard do you think it was for us to figure out that your parents—your *parents*—started COT? And now you want us to believe you're sympathetic to the Other Light?"

Busted. What could he say? He breathed a silent prayer. "Lord, what now?"

"Take the offensive," he heard in his soul.

"Believe what you want to believe," Kenny said. "But you'd better not have wasted my time, dragging me all the way here just to tell me you don't trust me. There are plenty of people in other TOL cells who *do* trust me. And as for where I'm embedded, where do you think you'd get better information?"

The brothers looked at each other, and Ignace nodded. Lothair pulled a computer printout from inside his jacket and looked around before setting it on the table. It listed every employee of COT, their addresses, and even their salaries.

"See what we can get without you, in spite of you?"

"Fine, you've got a list you're not supposed to have, but it's not like it's highly classified. What can you do with it? You going to start assassinating these people? You know they're invulnerable, even the naturals."

Ignace leaned close, sighing and indicating that Lothair should put the printout away. The redhead stuffed it back into his pocket. "Listen, we realize that sometimes the best we can do is to be nuisances. We want access to these kids, these younger minds. So far we've been targeting older kids, but your parents and all the people at COT are brainwashing these innocents, and they'd never get a chance to hear the other side if it wasn't for us. In the meantime, we try to wreak havoc on the leadership, get their minds off their mission, give us a chance to move in, maybe provide an alternative. Now do you follow?"

"Not really, but I suppose you've thought this through."

Ignace looked over Kenny's shoulder and discreetly waved, summoning a young woman who looked strikingly like Cendrillon. "Another cousin," Ignace explained.

"Nicolette," she said as she sat, her voice husky. "A pleasure."

Kenny greeted her noncommittally.

"She's going to tell you what's going on in some of the other places."

"Mexico," she said. "Drugs, parties, alcohol. We spread the word quietly, and kids who feel oppressed by their parents or by society or by the church come in droves. We get 'em on our mailing lists and go after them with intellectual arguments."

"You can't be serious."

The three looked at Kenny with brows raised. "There a problem, Williams?" Ignace said.

"Yeah, there is. You lure them with booze and drugs and then you try to persuade them with reason? How reasonable can they be?"

"How would *you* get to them?"

"Start with the reason! Don't you respect your audience? Don't you want people with brains? At this rate, by the time we get to the last century of the Millennium, you'll have a bunch of dopers and alkies trying to compete with the army of God. Get serious."

That silenced them for a moment, but it was clear they didn't like being scolded.

"Well," Nicolette said, slowing and glancing at the brothers before proceeding, "you're not going to like how we do it in Turkey."

"Pray tell."

"Hashish."

"Brilliant. You know, this is the best news that ever hit the other side. You might as well just concede, surrender, and hand over the future to the believers. It's going to be them against a bunch of doped-up losers at the final conflict. Wow, I wonder which way that's going to go. I thought the appeal of the Other Light was that you were all scholars, intellectuals, you'd thought this through, honestly come to a variant conclusion, and you wanted to keep other young people from being lemmings that follow their parents over a cliff."

"That's pretty much it, yeah," Ignace said.

"Well, they may not fall off a cliff, but they're going to pass out."

"You got a better idea?"

"Sure! Beat the believers at their own game. Raise up impressive, bright, humble young people who are a credit to society but who disagree about the future. Wouldn't that be way more attractive to your potential recruits than thinking that this is all about getting away with illegal stuff?"

Lothair squinted at Kenny. "But how do you do that? How do you reach them? How do we make our side appealing?"

"It shouldn't be that hard. If you're right, you'll be convincing. And what you have going for you is the age of your audience. They're our ages. If they haven't become believers already, you know they're searching, wondering, thinking, wanting to use their brainpower. They're going to be vulnerable to a message that goes against all the rest of society. There's glamour in being a revolutionary. Tap into that."

The three sat as if thinking, and Ignace began to nod. "You may be on to something."

Lothair said, "You know where they're doing this, sort of . . ."

"Jordan," Nicolette said. "Those goofy-lookin' little guys in Amman."

"You're here till when, Williams, Saturday?"

Kenny nodded.

"Lothair and I were scheduled to drop in on them this week anyway. How about we all go? Maybe you can inspire 'em."

"I've never been to Jordan. Let's do it."

At the end of the day, Mudawar called Abdullah and Sarsour together. "All right," he said, "here's how it's going to work. When the top TOL guys from Europe get here, we play it like this: I found Abdullah doing his thing on the streets, and he seemed effective. I gave him a cockamamie story about daring him to work with us and see who was most persuasive, and he bought it. Now that I've got him inside our little enclave, below-ground, with precious little exposure to our audience, I've got him right where I want him.

"They're going to see it as a great idea, a model for other cells."

"I like it," Sarsour said.

"I don't," Abdullah said. "But I did urge you to think about taking credit for me, and you are certainly planning to do that. One warning, though. I am incapable of perpetuating an untruth. Anyone asks me what I'm doing here, I'll tell them the truth of how it really came about."

TWENTY-SIX

WHEN DAVID, the king of Jerusalem and Jesus' prince, strode onto COT property, Cameron buzzed Chloe and they rolled into action. Word spread quickly throughout the staff that it was time to round up all the kids and get them in place.

"Greetings, greetings," David called out. "Thanks for inviting me and for your attention. I have a most busy rest of the day at the temple, so let me get right into my story. It begins when I was the same age as many of you. It is unlikely that you can imagine what my life was like, but I had fun! Can you imagine tending sheep and fighting off wild animals? I don't know why God gave me the courage and the strength, but He did! Shepherds, you know, were the outcasts of society, and I often felt like an outcast among all my brothers—until the Lord lifted me up.

"I was the youngest of eight boys growing up outside Bethlehem, but we were of lowly estate. Indeed, being a shepherd was the lowest occupation a lad—or even a man—could have. But I loved the Lord with all my heart, and I strove to please Him. I learned to play the harp and always played my best to honor my God.

"I also learned to be strong and brave and protect the sheep from wild beasts. I longed for the day when I could serve King Saul as my three oldest brothers did and fight in his army. Once our neighboring enemies, the Philistines, gathered their armies together for battle at Sochoh, which belonged to Judah. Saul and the men of Israel, including my brothers, were encamped in the Valley of Elah and drew up in battle array against the Philistines. Now picture this: the Philistines stood on a mountain on one side, and Israel stood on a mountain on the other side, with a valley between them.

"A champion came out from the camp of the Philistines, named Goliath, from Gath, whose height was six cubits and a span. You know from hearing Noah's story how long a cubit is. Well, a span is about half a cubit, so in today's measures, we would say Goliath was about nine feet nine inches tall."

The children seemed to gasp as one.

David laughed. "Oh, believe me, *I* know how big he was, for I saw him, and I was still but a lad! He wore an immense bronze helmet and was armed with a coat of woven metal that weighed 125 pounds. I didn't weigh that myself at the time! And he wore bronze armor on his legs and carried a sword, a bronze javelin, and a spear with a head that weighed fifteen pounds. He had a shield, too, but it was so huge that he had a man walk before him who carried it.

"Goliath cried out to the armies of Israel, 'Why have you come out to line up for battle? Am I not a Philistine, and you the servants of Saul? Choose a man and let him come down to me. If he is able to kill me, then we will be your servants. But if I kill him, then you shall be our servants and serve us. I defy the armies of Israel this day; give me a man, that we may fight together.'

"Well, that was the talk of the whole of Israel, and everyone seemed to know that even Saul was dismayed and greatly afraid, for Goliath did this every morning and evening for forty days, and no one dared challenge him.

"One day my father told me to take an ephah of dried grain and ten loaves to my brothers at the camp. He also gave me ten cheeses to take to the captain of my brothers' thousand men. My father said, 'See how your brothers fare, and bring back news of them.'

"So I rose early in the morning, left the sheep with a keeper, and took the food and went as my father had commanded me. When I got there, the army was going out to the fight and shouting for the battle. I left my supplies with the supply keeper, ran to catch up with the army, and greeted my brothers.

"While I was talking with them, that champion, the Philistine of Gath named Goliath, presented himself yet again and made his challenge. And all the men of Israel fled from him and were dreadfully afraid. They said,

'The man who kills him the king will enrich with great riches, will give him his daughter, and give his father's house exemption from taxes.'

"I couldn't believe my ears. Even though I was just a child, I said, 'What shall be done for the man who kills this Philistine and takes away the reproach from Israel? Who is this Philistine that he should defy the armies of the living God?'

"My oldest brother heard this, and his anger was aroused against me. He said, 'Why did you come down here? And with whom have you left those few sheep in the wilderness? I know your pride and the insolence of your heart, for you have come down to see the battle.'

"Have you ever had your big brother or sister holler at you like that? I said, 'What have I done now?'

"I turned toward others and said that no man should dare defy the armies of the living God. Well, someone reported this to Saul, and the king sent for me and asked me to explain myself. I said, 'Let no man's heart fail because of him; I will go and fight with this Philistine.'

"The king told me, 'You are not able to go against this Philistine to fight with him; for you are a youth, and he a man of war from his youth.'

"But I said, 'I, your servant, used to keep my father's sheep, and when a lion or a bear came and took a lamb out of the flock, I went out after it and struck it, and delivered the lamb from its mouth; and when it arose against me, I caught it by its beard, and struck and killed it. I have killed both lion and bear; and this Philistine will be like one of them, seeing he has defied the armies of the living God. The Lord, who delivered me from the paw of the lion and from the paw of the bear, will deliver me from the hand of this Philistine.'

"And Saul said, 'Go, and the Lord be with you!' He tried to clothe me with his own armor, but it was much too big for me. I took it off, took my staff in my hand, chose for myself five smooth stones from the brook, and put them in my shepherd's bag with my sling. And I drew near to the Philistine."

The children were dead silent, unmoving.

"So the giant came and began drawing near to me with his shield bearer before him. Well, you can imagine what he thought when he saw me, a little red-faced boy. He said, 'Am I a dog that you come to me with sticks?' And he cursed me by his gods. He said, 'Come to me, and I will give your flesh to the birds of the air and the beasts of the field!'

"I said, 'You come to me with a sword, a spear, and a javelin. But I come to you in the name of the Lord of hosts, the God of the armies of Israel, whom you have defied! This day the Lord will deliver you into my hand, and I will strike you and take your head from you. And this day I will give the carcasses of the camp of the Philistines to the birds of the air and the wild beasts of the earth, that all the earth may know that there is a God in Israel. Then all this assembly shall know that the Lord does not save with sword and spear; for the battle is the Lord's, and He will give you into our hands.'

"When Goliath drew near, I ran to meet him. I reached into my bag and took out a stone. I slung it and struck the Philistine in the forehead so that it sank in, and he fell on his face to the earth. I had defeated him without even a sword!"

The children clapped and cheered.

"I stood over him and drew his own sword out of its sheath and killed him, then cut off his head. And when the Philistines saw that their champion was dead, they fled.

"Now the men of Israel and Judah arose and shouted and pursued the Philistines as far as the entrance of the valley and to the gates of Ekron. And the wounded of the Philistines fell along the road. Then the children of Israel returned from chasing the Philistines, and they plundered their tents.

"I took the head of the Philistine and brought it to Jerusalem and presented it to Saul."

The children cheered again, but David quieted them. "I have many stories I could tell," he said, "of how King Saul eventually turned on me and hated me and tried to kill me. Of his son Jonathan, who became my best friend. Of the time when I sinned greatly against the Lord and was abject in my sorrow and repentance until He forgave me. I was eventually crowned king of Israel, and late in my reign it came to pass that I was dwelling in my house, and the Lord had given me rest from all my enemies.

"I said to Nathan the prophet, 'See now, I dwell in a house of cedar, but the ark of God dwells inside tent curtains.'

"Later that night the Lord came to Nathan and told him to tell me not to build Him a house for Him to dwell in. He told Nathan to tell me, 'I have not dwelt in a house since the time that I brought the children of Israel up from Egypt, even to this day, but have moved about in a tent and in a tabernacle. I took you from the sheepfold, from following the sheep, to be ruler over My people, over Israel. And I have been with you wherever you have gone, and have cut off all your enemies from before you, and have made you a great name, like the name of the great men who are on the earth.

"'Moreover I will appoint a place for My people Israel, and will plant them, that they may dwell in a place of their own and move no more; nor shall the sons of wickedness oppress them anymore, as previously, since the time that I commanded judges to be over My people Israel, and have caused you to rest from all your enemies. And I will make you a house.

"'When your days are fulfilled and you rest with your fathers, I will set up your seed after you, who will come from your body, and I will establish his kingdom. He shall build a house for My name, and I will establish the throne of his kingdom forever. I will be his Father, and he shall be My son. If he commits iniquity, I will chasten him with the rod of men and with the blows of the sons of men. But My mercy shall not depart from him.'

"Then the Lord told Nathan of me, 'Your house and your kingdom shall be established forever before you. Your throne shall be established forever.'

"As you can imagine, I was overwhelmed. I went in and sat before the Lord and said, 'Who am I, O Lord God? And what is my house, that You have brought me this far?'

"Now, children, I want you to rise, and I want to teach you the proper way to worship the Lord God of Hosts, Jehovah, Messiah." David reached toward heaven and lifted his face to the sky and said, "Now what more can I say to You? For You, Lord God, know Your servant. For Your word's sake, and according to Your own heart, You have done all these great things, to make Your servant know them.

"Therefore You are great, O Lord God. For there is none like You, nor is there any God besides You. And who is like Your people, Israel, the one nation on the earth whom God went to redeem for Himself as a people? For You have made Your people Israel Your very own people forever; and You, Lord, have become their God.

"Now, O Lord God, let Your name be magnified forever. The Lord is my rock and my fortress and my deliverer; the God of my strength, in whom I will trust; my shield and the horn of my salvation, my stronghold and my refuge.

"In my distress I called upon the Lord, and cried out to my God; He heard my voice from His temple, and my cry entered His ears. He rode upon a cherub, and flew; and He was seen upon the wings of the wind. He sent from above, He took me, He drew me out of many waters. He delivered me from my strong enemy, from those who hated me; for they were too strong for me. They confronted me in the day of my calamity, but the Lord was my support.

"He also brought me out into a broad place; He delivered me because He delighted in me. The Lord rewarded me according to my righteousness; according to the cleanness of my hands He has recompensed me. For I have kept the ways of the Lord, and have not wickedly departed from my God. For all His judgments were before me; and as for His statutes, I did not depart from them.

"With the merciful You will show Yourself merciful; with a blameless man You will show Yourself blameless; with the pure You will show Yourself pure; and with the devious You will show Yourself shrewd. You will save the humble people, but Your eyes are on the haughty, that You may bring them down.

"For You are my lamp, O Lord; the Lord shall enlighten my darkness. His way is perfect; the word of the Lord is proven; He is a shield to all who trust in Him.

"For who is God, except the Lord? And who is a rock, except our God? God is my strength and power, and He makes my way perfect. He makes my feet like the feet of deer, and sets me on my high places.

"You have also given me the shield of Your salvation; Your gentleness has made me great. You enlarged my path under me, so my feet did not slip. The Lord lives! Blessed be my Rock! Let God be exalted, the Rock of my salvation! Therefore I will give thanks to You, O Lord, among the Gentiles, and sing praises to Your name.

"He is the tower of salvation to His king, and shows mercy to His anointed, to me and my descendants forevermore."

And when Cameron and the children and all the staff looked up from their prayer, David had disappeared from their midst.

TWENTY-SEVEN

ASIDE FROM having been born in the old United States of America and carted about by his globe-trotting parents during the Tribulation, Kenny Bruce Williams had spent nearly all his ninety-seven-plus years in Israel. Others he knew, especially his extended family, loved to travel. But he had never seen the appeal of being away from the very country in which the King of kings and Lord of lords physically resided and presided.

On the other hand, despite the anxiety over working undercover, Kenny had found Paris interesting. None of the historical landmarks remained, of course, but attempts had been made to reproduce some of the more familiar—like the Eiffel Tower, the Louvre, and even some of the great cathedrals.

The prospect of going to Amman intrigued Kenny, if for no other reason than that his friends Bahira and

Zaki had grown up there and had vague memories of
the culture and the food. He didn't expect to experience
much of either, but perhaps something in his travels
would somehow find its way into his work with the kids
at COT.

On the plane with Ignace, Lothair, and Nicolette,
Kenny for the first time became aware of the stares and
glares of people—mostly naturals, some glorifieds—who
must have recognized the alternative clothing of the
TOLers for what it was.

Kenny had known so little negativity in his life—of
course, he barely remembered much of the Tribulation,
as it ended with the Glorious Appearing when he was
still about four months shy of his fifth birthday—that it
had been his practice to catch people's eyes, even strangers', and smile. That would not do now. His pretend
compatriots were rebels, misfits, outcasts. They kept to
themselves, looking serious, or if they did meet someone's gaze, they proffered a hateful scowl. Kenny found
that nearly impossible, so he just kept his eyes focused
on the floor most of the time.

Ignace, who sat next to Kenny, spent most of the
2,100-mile flight scribbling on papers he had apparently
received from the leaders of various TOL cells around
the world. But every time Kenny glanced toward them,
Ignace covered them and shot him a look.

Finally, with about twenty minutes to go until touch-
down, Ignace packed up his stuff and leaned over. "Here's
the deal with Amman: We're fairly new there, so even
though we've got two of our brightest recruits in that

office, not much is happening. They use the name Theological Training Institute as their front, but free speech is virtually unheard of in Jordan, so these guys lie low and do most of their work over the Internet. They're building a database of people who are at least intrigued, so we want to find out how that's going. Truthfully, we had been steering them toward hosting secret parties where kids who are fed up or questioning the status quo can come and feel like they're really rebelling. We told Mudawar—he was a recruit from my own international blog and is our top guy there, really gifted—to offer them contraband stuff.

"But the more Lothair and I think about your idea, about taking the high road, the more sense it makes. I mean, I didn't sign up Mudawar, and he didn't sign up his assistant, based on dope or booze or women or anything like that. Like you said, we appealed to their minds. And that *is* the kind of recruit we want. So once we're through with all the formalities and we get their progress report, you give 'em your pep talk, okay?"

Kenny nodded. This couldn't be worse. All he had intended with his little speech two days before was to allay their suspicions. He had done it so well he had inspired them to a better approach for recruiting. He sure didn't want to be responsible for their amassing a higher class of dissidents.

———

Cameron and Chloe sat in the office, poring over employment records. "Strange," Cameron said. "You realize that this Qasim Marid has been gone all three times we had the Bible heroes here."

Chloe leaned to look at the records. "That's some coincidence, Cam."

"It's got to be more than that. What are the odds? It's almost like he doesn't want to be here when they are. But who wouldn't want to hear those guys?"

"Hey," she said, "what did you do with the master list?"

"Which?"

"The printout with all the staff names and addresses."

"You know I don't go into the files, Chlo'. You've got it backed up on disk, right?"

"Of course, but no one else is supposed to have access to the hard copy. Oh, Cam, we're not going to have start putting locks on the doors, are we? Not after almost a hundred years with no mischief."

———

Abdullah was amused by Mudawar and Sarsour. For the first time since he had met them, they looked clean and tidy. Oh, Mudawar was still oily; it was as if he couldn't help that. But his hair was combed, and his fatigues, like Sarsour's, were clean and crisp. They had spent the entire previous afternoon cleaning up the offices, and now they scoured the suite, making sure they hadn't missed a thing. Every sheet of paper tacked to the wall hung square. Every stack of books or papers was neat and straight.

Abdullah knew he had endeared himself even more to them by helping with the cleanup. "A suggestion?" he said.

"Sure, what?" Mudawar said.

"You don't want it to look artificial. I mean, you want your mentors to believe you actually work here, right?"

"Yeah, so? We're not going to slop it up just so it looks lived in."

"No, I'm just saying that when they arrive, you shouldn't be standing around like you're posing for school pictures. You should be on your way to or from some important project."

"Good idea. Look alive when they get here, Sarsour. Don't act like you've got nothing else to do."

"But I don't. What's more important than entertaining them?"

"Just look busy! And you, old man—I haven't decided exactly what to say about you yet, so blend into the woodwork unless spoken to. Understood?"

Another young man and young woman—whom Ignace identified as TOL operatives from Az Zarqa, northeast of Amman—picked up the Jospin brothers, Nicolette, and Kenny at the airport in a plain white van. Kenny was struck by how the colleagues greeted each other. He detected no warmth or enthusiasm. It was all business.

"By the way," Kenny said, "I might as well head straight back to Israel from here. I'm not much more than forty miles away. What would be the best way to get there?"

The driver said, "I can run you there. We have business in Beersheba anyway."

"Really?" Kenny said. "Another cell?"

"The only one in Israel. They're pretty squirrelly about it, as you can imagine. Right there in enemy territory."

"Well, you can drop me close to my home, but needless to say, I can't draw any attention to myself."

"That goes double for us," the driver said. "We'll just drop you where you tell us."

When Abdullah heard the loud knock, he and Mudawar and Sarsour immediately rushed to the TV monitor to get a look at the visitors. "There are the brothers," Mudawar said, "and that must be the girl they've told me about. I don't recognize the others."

"Should I open it?" Sarsour said.

"Take a breath, man," Mudawar said. "Don't look too anxious."

Abdullah froze. What could he do? Where could he hide? Unless his eyes were deceiving him, that was Cameron and Chloe's son, Kenny! What could this mean? He rushed back to his desk, swept his Bible and papers and other personal effects into his bag, and moved quickly to the front door. When Sarsour opened it, Abdullah stepped behind it, and as the others were going through the introduction formalities, he slipped out.

He bounded up the stairs to the street and headed back to his apartment, fearful beyond all reason.

Minutes later he was pacing in the small place with Yasmine pleading with him to sit down.

"I can't," he said. "I cannot. I have known that precious boy since he was born! What am I supposed to do with this information? Ask his parents? Or would I be telling them?"

"You had better be certain first, Abdullah. You have no doubt?"

"It was him all right. I caught a live glimpse of him too and heard his voice. There is no question."

"Strange."

"It's worse than strange, Yasmine. It's catastrophic and has dire implications."

"Ask Bahira and Zaki. They're his friends."

Abdullah reached the message systems of both kids' phones, informing him they would return his call at the end of their workdays. "Yasmine, what was the name of that infiltrator? He will know. Perhaps Kenny is in league with him."

"Yes, that has to be it!" Yasmine dug around until she found the contact information for Qasim Marid.

Abdullah phoned. "I have a very delicate question for you, Master Marid. Is there another infiltrator from Millennium Force?"

Qasim sounded wary. "An infiltrator where?"

"You tell me. Within TOL, of course."

"Why do you ask? Of whom are you speaking?"

"Sir, please! If you know, just tell me."

"Well, first I must swear you to secrecy."

"From whom?"

"From everyone! Your friends, even your children. May I count on you for that?"

"If it will ensure the safety of the person in question, certainly."

"I have your word you will speak of this to no one until further notice?"

"Yes, yes, of course!"

"We, shall I say, *had* another infiltrator, yes."

"What a relief! Was it—?"

"Please, do not mention names other than in person. The bad news is that this infiltrator, I have just learned, has turned."

"Turned?"

"He is full-fledged TOL now. He has entirely bought into their philosophies."

"Oh no!"

"It is sad but true, sir. I am in the midst of damage control now. All I can do is all I can do, and I must tell you, that you are aware of this is a great complicator. Please reassure me that you will not share this information with a soul until you hear back from me."

Abdullah could barely speak. "You have my word," he managed.

The Amman office of the Other Light looked efficient enough, Kenny decided, even if the occupants seemed quirky. For as bright as Ignace had made them out to be, they seemed obsequious. The top guy, the pudgy Mudawar, acted the sycophant around Ignace, having to stop and catch his breath, he spoke so quickly.

Ignace had paused during the tour and stared at a clean desk in the back of the third room. "Someone work here?" he said.

"Oh, uh . . . yeah . . . I mean, no. No one. Well, sometimes if we have special projects, you know. I've been known to work here if I need room to spread out. And you have too, haven't you, Sarsour?"

"What?"

"Worked here, right here where this extra space is. We like to keep it free for . . . you know. You have, right? Worked here?"

"Not in a long time. Not since—"

"Well, I settled in there recently for one of my all-night newsletter-writing stints. And I know Sarsour has worked there too . . . at least he used to, before. Recently."

Finally Ignace's entire entourage crowded into Mudawar's office, some in chairs, some sitting on the desk, others leaning against the wall. Ignace asked Mudawar to give them an update on their recruit list and strategy, then reminded him that "Kenny here is one of our only two operatives embedded near Jerusalem. We've got real potential for a cell in Beersheba, but that's going to take time.

"Kenny has interesting recruitment ideas I wanted him to outline for you, not because you need it, necessarily, and certainly not because you've been doing it wrong. If anything, you've been going about this better than we have, and we didn't even know it until Kenny pointed it out."

Mudawar was beaming. "Really?"

"Yes. Kenny?"

"Well, I was just mentioning to Ignace and the others that it seems to me the best strategy for recruiting the young disaffected of our world is not through this bait-and-switch technique of luring them to parties and illicit activities and substances. We want them for their minds, and so that is where we ought to be aiming. . . ."

Within minutes everyone was furiously taking notes, and Kenny was having a major crisis of conscience. He knew he had to keep this up to avoid giving himself away, but he would never forgive himself if his counsel had the effect TOL so desired—building a better, smarter network of brighter adherents.

TWENTY-EIGHT

KENNY COULD not have been happier to be getting home a day earlier than he expected, and he knew Ekaterina would be pleased too. His hope was to surprise her and be waiting at her home when she returned from work.

Imagine his surprise when her parents greeted him with less than enthusiasm. They appeared grim, preoccupied. Kenny remained upbeat, exulting over the change in his schedule that allowed this. "Is something wrong?"

"Well, we don't know," Mrs. Risto said. "Ekaterina sounded rather upset, said Mr. Steele had called an emergency meeting of some little group of yours and asked her to be there."

Kenny almost blurted the name of the Millennium Force, but he was surprised enough that Raymie would have invited Ekaterina. What in the world was up, and why hadn't he heard directly from Raymie? Raymie knew that Kat knew about the Force, because Kenny had told him himself.

"Do you know where they're meeting?" Kenny said.

The Ristos shook their heads. "We don't appreciate this, you know," Ekaterina's father said. "This whole period is supposed to be a time of peace and tranquility. I don't know what this little group is all about, but it can't be positive if it has to have emergency meetings that its members—specifically you—know nothing about, and that an outsider—specifically Kat—is asked to attend, and which upset her so. She's enough on edge because you were gone. Now what is all this?"

"I don't know, sir, but I'll find out. Kat's peace of mind is my top priority too, so I'll get to the bottom of this as fast as I can."

On his way home, Kenny tried calling everyone, starting with Ekaterina. Her phone immediately went to her message system, as did Raymie's and Bahira's and Zaki's. Finally, as he was entering his own house, Kenny reached his mother.

"Oh, Kenny! Where are you?"

He told her. "What's going on, Mom?"

"I wish I knew. It's like our office has been vandalized."

"What do you mean?"

"Well, those silly things like the phony personnel report on Kat and the ridiculous note about you could have come from anywhere within the interoffice mail system. But someone walked off with our employee list, and now we've gotten another crazy report."

So the list Kenny had seen in Paris had not been the

result of a computer hacking; someone had provided the actual printout. He didn't even want his mother to know that yet. "What crazy report?"

"Oh, it's so upsetting, I'm not even going to try to tell you about it except in person. Can Dad and I come see you tonight?"

"Well, sure, but right now I'm looking for Kat. She's supposed to be meeting with the Millennium Force, but I don't know where."

"*You* don't know where? Just call Raymie and—"

"'C'mon, Mom, you don't think I've thought of that? Now what's this report?"

"Like I told you, it's not something I want to talk about over the phone."

"Just tell me what it's about."

She hesitated. "Well, it's about you. But that's all I'm going to say for now."

Kenny dropped his stuff in his room and noticed something strange. The chair before his computer was out, away from the desk. He tended to be fastidious about stuff like that. He always pushed the chair back in and left the mouse in the same position. It looked skewed too.

Great; now I'm imagining things.

He tried calling everybody again. What were the odds they had all turned their phones off without it being on purpose? They didn't want to hear from him! Why? They couldn't have known he was going to be home earlier, or he would have been invited to the meeting. Wouldn't he?

Frustrated at being so helpless, he struck out for the

Valley Bistro. The Force didn't always have its meetings there, but it was worth a shot. At least it was a place Kat would know how to get to, and maybe they made it easy for her.

Kenny arrived to find them in the back room with, of all people, Qasim Marid. In an instant, Kenny knew something was terribly wrong. Raymie was pale and appeared grim. Zaki looked shell-shocked, as did Bahira. Qasim appeared stunned to see Kenny, but of course Kenny was most curious about Ekaterina. Her face was red, her eyes puffy. As soon as she saw him, she gathered up a sheaf of papers that appeared to be the same as everyone else's and bolted from the restaurant.

Kenny followed, but she was sprinting. "Kat!" he hollered. "Wait just a minute!"

She stopped and whirled, pointing at him. "I don't want to talk to you, Kenneth Williams. I don't ever want to see you again."

He stepped closer. "Kat, wait. I deserve to know—"

"Don't you dare!" she said. And she turned and kept going.

Kenny staggered back into the bistro and into the back room. "I want to know what's going on," he said. "And I want to know now."

Bahira was the only person who would look at him. And she looked like death. "You've been found out is all," she said.

"Found out?"

Raymie looked up. "We know where your true loyalties lie," he said. "You can end the charade."

Kenny plopped into the seat Kat had vacated. "I'm listening," he said. "What are the charges?"

Raymie said sadly, "You can have my copy. I don't need to see any more." He slid it across to Kenny and stood. The others rose also. "Why don't you look this over, and if there's anything more to be said, well, you know where to find us."

"Well, but, what—?"

"We're leaving, Kenny. The ball is in your court."

"Can't we talk about this, whatever it is?"

Raymie shook his head as the others left. "Not right now. We're not in the mood."

Kenny fingered the pages and looked at the first page as a waitress came and asked if he wanted anything. All he could do was shake his head as he read a memo dated three days prior:

To: Ignace Jospin, Executive Director
The Other Light International
Paris, France

From: Operative 88288, Kenneth Bruce Williams
Israel

Re: Progress

First, Ignace, it was great to reunite with you and your brother despite the sad occasion of your cousin's death. It had been too long, and communicating like this is never as good as in person, especially when we share such a bond.

I very much look forward to seeing you and
Lothair in Paris and thank you in advance for
making available to me the lovely Nicolette
again. The nights can otherwise be lonely in a
strange city, even one as beautiful as your capital.

You'll be pleased to know that my parents
remain wholly in the dark. It's nice that they
are so naïve. I don't doubt their sincerity, but
the blind devotion believing parents have in
their offspring makes duping them so easy. My
dull-witted mother remains convinced that I
share her beliefs and points to the night she
claims to have "led" me to Jesus. Well, Mom,
you have to mean it if you pray that prayer.

I trust you got the personnel printout. My
mother is making noises about putting locks on
the doors; my access to her office won't cross
her mind this Millennium.

My uncle Raymie suspects nothing. I'm sure
he was brought in on the Risto personnel matter, plus the later defaming note about yours
truly. Imagine if they even dreamed I planted
both those myself.

Rest assured your fears over the new girlfriend are unfounded. She's no Nicolette, but
she's cute enough and more naïve than my
mother. Her parents are homely, swarthy little
people who worship the ground I walk on. Her
father was apparently a spectacularly unre-
markable tradesman, and her mother is basi-

cally a nondescript homebody. They will not be
an issue. I may even go through with marrying
this girl, which will only make my work for
you at COT that much easier. She is in another
department, which merely broadens my reach.

I'll provide a virtual core dump of other vital
information when I arrive. Keep Nicolette
warm until I get there. I'll see you soon.
Loyal to the Other Light forever,

KBW

Kenny was nauseated. Where did one begin to try to
defend himself against such a detailed, devastating document? He scooped up the pages and stood, woozy and
feeling utterly alone. His parents would visit that evening.
That loomed as an oasis. Surely they wouldn't believe a
word of this.

But who wrote this, and where did they get their information? The nuances, the detail, made it so much worse.
And yet it was so dead-on that Kenny was surprised
someone didn't see through it. What were the odds that
almost every line would incriminate him?

Naturally Kenny had never faced a crisis like this, but
in the past when he had what now appeared minor, petty
issues, he'd turned first to his mother, then maybe to
Raymie or his dad. Who could he turn to now? For all
they knew, he was what the document purported: a turn-
coat. Hardly anyone had been spared.

"Lord, You're all I have left," Kenny prayed as he
headed toward home. "Please tell me You're still here."

He nearly wept with relief when he felt the peace only Jesus could give, but still Kenny had no idea how to dig himself out of this.

And what was that vehicle that had crossed at the corner ahead of him? It looked like the van that had delivered him back to Israel. When it stopped, turned around, and came toward him, he stopped and stared. The window was lowered and Nicolette leaned out.

Kenny wanted to run, to warn her to stay away from him, but he couldn't jeopardize his cover with TOL, regardless of whether they were behind trying to ruin him.

She jumped out and approached. "We missed our turn," she said. "Ignace wants to fly out of Tel Aviv."

"Back the way you came," Kenny said, still reeling and desperate to cover. "That'll take you to the main route toward Tel Aviv and the airport."

"You're a peach," Nicolette said, leaning close to kiss him on the cheek.

"Yeah, yeah, see ya," Kenny said, only realizing as she pulled away from him that Lothair had been hanging out the window and had shot a picture of the kiss.

TWENTY-NINE

CAMERON WILLIAMS sat steely eyed and somber in Kenny's living room as Chloe wept. He didn't know what to think. His son was denying everything, which he would do whether innocent or guilty. Admittedly, the document that Qasim Marid claimed he had retrieved off Ignace Jospin's desk in Paris had so many glaring incriminations in it that it could easily have been a setup. But who would do such a thing, and who would know enough details to pull it off?

"There's not a doubt in my mind that Qasim is behind this for all kinds of reasons," Kenny said. "But how would I ever prove that?"

"Call me a typical mother," Chloe said, looking pleadingly at Cameron, "but I believe him."

"Of course you do, and I want to, too."

"You *want* to, Dad? My word is not good enough for you? You always taught me to live in such a way that if someone brought a charge against me, no one would believe it. What have I done, how have I lived, that makes no one but my mother believe me?"

"Yes, Cam," Chloe said. "That's a good question."

Cameron sighed. "Maybe I know something you don't, Chloe."

"Oh, great!" Kenny said. "There's more?"

"I got an anguished call from Abdullah this afternoon. He saw you at TOL headquarters in Amman today, Kenny."

"What? What was he doing there?"

"So you *were* there?" Chloe said.

"Of course I was! Didn't everyone know where I was and what I was doing? I was undercover, infiltrating."

"And—" Cameron said.

"Oh no, Dad. What now?"

"Qasim delivered our copy of the memo to COT. Raymie and I had it evaluated by a computer techie. It was sent from your computer, Kenny."

Kenny just sat shaking his head.

"There has to be an explanation," Chloe said. "Kenny, I need to hear it."

"What can I say, Mom? It wasn't me. You know we've never locked our doors around here. Anybody could have done it."

Cameron was as conflicted as he'd been since the Glorious Appearing. How he wanted to believe Kenny! But the evidence against him just kept mounting.

"What recourse do I have, Dad? Is this a case I can take before the judges?"

"Only if someone charges you with a crime. Has anyone done that?"

"I wish Qasim would. He's the one who seems to gain the most from this."

"What is he gaining?"

"He makes me look bad. He costs me Kat."

"Where is Ekaterina, by the way?" Chloe said.

"Where do you think? Anywhere but here. She won't answer her phone, won't see me. I guess I can't blame her, but I thought we knew each other better than this."

"Well," Chloe said, "those things you said about her parents . . ."

"*I* didn't say them! I love her parents. Listen, something else is going to surface, and I need your help." Kenny told them about Nicolette and the picture. "I just know they'll deliver it to Kat. Since I can't get anywhere near her, could you warn her?"

"I don't know," Cameron said.

"Of course I will," Chloe said. "And she's going to want to know what to do about work. I'll assure her that she can come and not worry about running into you."

"And why is that? You're finding me guilty too? firing me?"

"Call it a suspension," Cameron said. "Just till we can figure this out."

"What can I do, Dad, take a lie detector test? You know what this means if it's true? I'm an infidel, an unbeliever. That means I die at one hundred and go to hell. Do you really believe that about me?"

"No," Cameron said. "I don't. But I don't know what to do about your reputation now or countering all this evidence."

They sat in silence a long time. Finally Kenny spoke. "It seems that with all the people you know, all the people you've worked with, we have access to spiritual power few others have. If everybody who's worked with you and believed in you and supported you in the past would cooperate in prayer, I don't believe Jesus would let this injustice stand. Do you?"

Cameron and Chloe looked at each other. Then Cameron addressed his son. "They would all have to know everything, Kenny. They would have to see all the evidence."

"Dad, I've got nothing to hide. What have I got to lose? I believe Jesus is here and on His throne and that lies will be exposed. I'm open to anything."

But that night Kenny couldn't sleep. He sat at his computer and composed a message to the Millennium Force and copied it to Ekaterina.

> Dear friends, you can't know what I'm going through, but perhaps you can imagine. Think how it would be if you were in my place and wholly innocent. I am, you know. Let me get that on the record from the start. I confess I'm hurt, deeply wounded, that you assume me guilty. I suppose all I can do now is to endure a little more than two more years until I turn one

hundred. And when I am still here the next day, you'll know that I am a believer, that I belong to Christ, and that while I am not perfect—as I am a natural—I could not be guilty of this.

Kenny didn't feel much better even after transmitting his defense, so he wrote separately to Ekaterina:

My dearest love, I can only imagine how phony and hollow that sounds coming from me now. You are convinced I am guilty, and I don't know how to prove otherwise. Perhaps there is some deep pocket of love for me in your heart that misses what we had together and longs to believe all things, as the Bible says.

Kat, I fell in love with you almost from the beginning. I can't even remember, nor do I wish to, life before you. I thanked God for you every day and looked forward to that great day when we would marry and be able to spend the rest of our lives together.

Do me a favor tonight, will you, and read the love chapter, 1 Corinthians 13. And while you are raw and aching, I know this may sound empty to you too, but I want you to know that one day in the future, when the truth comes out, I will not hold it against you that you didn't trust me. I'd like to think that I would not have believed such charges about you, no matter how convincing, but I don't

know. Regardless, I will forgive you, so don't
let anything keep you from coming back to me.
Whatever happens, you will always be my life-
time love, and there will never be another.

With my soul,

Kenny

Kenny lay wide-eyed on his back, staring at the ceiling.
He didn't know why he was so desperate to sleep with
no obligations in the morning. Finally he rose and
grabbed his Bible, taking it back to bed and reading
what he had recommended to Ekaterina:

> Though I speak with the tongues of men and of
> angels, but have not love, I have become sounding
> brass or a clanging cymbal.
>
> And though I have the gift of prophecy, and
> understand all mysteries and all knowledge, and
> though I have all faith, so that I could remove
> mountains, but have not love, I am nothing.
>
> And though I bestow all my goods to feed the
> poor, and though I give my body to be burned, but
> have not love, it profits me nothing.
>
> Love suffers long and is kind; love does not envy;
> love does not parade itself, is not puffed up; does
> not behave rudely, does not seek its own, is not pro-
> voked, thinks no evil; does not rejoice in iniquity,
> but rejoices in the truth; bears all things, believes all
> things, hopes all things, endures all things.
>
> Love never fails. But whether there are prophe-

cies, they will fail; whether there are tongues, they will cease; whether there is knowledge, it will vanish away.

For we know in part and we prophesy in part. But when that which is perfect has come, then that which is in part will be done away.

When I was a child, I spoke as a child, I understood as a child, I thought as a child; but when I became a man, I put away childish things.

For now we see in a mirror, dimly, but then face to face. Now I know in part, but then I shall know just as I also am known.

And now abide faith, hope, love, these three; but the greatest of these is love.

Kenny found himself weeping and longing for heaven, where Jesus had promised to wipe away all tears from his eyes. "Lord, I need You," he said. "I need Your help."

"Lo, I am with you always, even to the end of the age."

And, finally, Kenny was able to doze.

———

Abdullah called the Other Light headquarters in Amman before heading out the next morning.

Sarsour answered, "TTI."

"TTI indeed," Abdullah said. "Are your guests gone? Is the coast clear for me to return?"

"Oh, Mr. Ababneh! Yes! And you have no idea how

much Mudawar wishes to see you. He is so appreciative
of your acceding to his request yesterday and keeping
him from an embarrassing situation. Of all the kind
things you have done since you have been here, that
was the kindest. Anyway, yes, please come in."

Kenny arose not refreshed but with an interesting new
outlook. It was as if the Lord had spoken to his heart
even as he slept. It was the strangest feeling—something
that those like him were unlikely to grasp without an
ordeal such as the one he was enduring. He was getting a
taste—albeit a very small and entirely less violent one—
of what it must have been like for Jesus to be betrayed
and abandoned by His friends. Of course, Jesus was
mocked and spit upon and struck, had a crown of thorns
thrust into His scalp, had His side riven by a sword, and
was eventually put to death.

And He was more than innocent. He was perfect,
sinless. It went without saying that Kenny could not say
the same about himself, but he knew he could face the
day. His soul was pierced by the loss of the love of his
life, and all he could do was pray that truth and time
would walk hand in hand and that eventually Ekaterina
would return to him.

Meanwhile, the Lord seemed to be impressing upon
Kenny to redeem the time. Nothing would be served by
defending himself and moping about in misery—Jesus
certainly never did either of those. Though he was not

hungry, Kenny forced himself to pick fresh fruits and vegetables and to eat them with bread and wine. Normally he would have enjoyed this bounty from the Lord, and while he was grateful for it, he was eating only out of a sense of duty. He needed fuel to function correctly, and he wanted to fill his hours—until his vindication, however long that would take—with some sort of work for the kingdom.

This day that would mean planning and writing and preparing curriculum that would make him a better Bible teacher, a better leader for the young charges at COT that he prayed would once again someday be entrusted to him. Only the Lord would be able to keep his mind on the task and off Ekaterina and his troubles.

For the first time since he had begun his unusual assignment in Amman, Abdullah was greeted warmly not only by Sarsour but also by Mudawar. The latter actually emerged from his office with a smile and a two-handed shake for Abdullah.

"Come into my office a moment, sir," Mudawar said. "Sit down. I must tell you, I don't understand you. I disagree with you. You should be my enemy, and in many ways you are. But you honored me by your absence yesterday. I have to say I would not likely have afforded you the same courtesy. And I didn't expect it from you. Indeed, you had warned me that you would do nothing of the kind. In fact, when finally, at the end of the day, I walked my guests out to their car, I expected you to be sitting in front of our door, prepared to shame me.

"Now, you must tell me. Why did you not, and where in the world were you?"

THIRTY

THE UNIQUE ministry the Lord had assigned Rayford
Steele and his team in Osaze had gone more swimmingly
than any project Rayford could recall, but that very fact
niggled at him every spare moment. Had he erred in
believing that this period, this millennial kingdom with
Jesus on the throne of the world, would be a time of
unmitigated peace?

Clearly things were different than they had ever been.
But while it seemed that in every city and town and
outpost, citizens were eager to hear from the Lord, willing to work with those He had sent, and desperate to be
sure their young people made decisions for Christ, that
angelic visit from Anis had both inspired and rattled
Rayford.

For if the Lord Himself was in charge, why did

Rayford and his little band need a rear guard? From whom were they being protected?

Everyone had been affected by the drought and famine that had resulted from Egypt's disobedience. And so everywhere Rayford and the others traveled, things seemed to turn around immediately. The preachers preached, the builders built, the consultants consulted, and everyone on the team got the chance to lead someone to salvation virtually every day.

It soon became apparent to Rayford, however, that those with natural bodies—himself, Chaim, and Mac—had way less stamina than the glorifieds. Without consulting anyone else, Rayford began planning a long break after what he expected to be a huge meeting in Siwa the next evening. The naturals needed it, and perhaps some respite from the work would calm his troubled mind.

Successful as it was, the work was not easy, partly because Rayford and the others remained committed to living in the motor home. They could afford to stay elsewhere, but crowded as it was, it seemed the most prudent use of their resources.

As they sat debriefing after a particularly stressful but also successful day of ministry, Chaim reported that the welcoming committee in Siwa expected one of the biggest crowds of their entire effort. "Apparently there will be protestors, too," he said. "But we've never worried about opposition before."

In the middle of their confab, the awful news about Kenny arrived by fax from Israel. Rayford distributed the document to the others, then phoned Chloe for further details. He told her of the planned break and promised to be back as soon as possible.

When the others had read the document and Rayford had told them what Chloe had said, he added, "There is no question Irene and my daughter and I are biased, so I would ask that we simply accede to my grandson's request that we covenant together in prayer and seek the Lord over this."

And so it was that Rayford and Irene and Chaim and Tsion and Mac and the Barneses knelt and prayed. Tsion began, and then Chaim, and soon all were praying at the same time. Several minutes later they prayed in succession again, but Rayford noticed a change. Whereas they had begun haltingly, seeking God's wisdom, asking Him to shed light on the truth, now they seemed to be praying for Kenny, for strength, for endurance. One by one, those with glorified minds and bodies—those who had been in heaven—expressed in their prayers that the charges against Kenny did not resonate with them.

Finally Mrs. Barnes closed the prayer meeting. "Lord," she said, "I barely know this boy, but I know You and You know him, and You've made it clear to my spirit that he belongs to You. I pray swift justice for him and for those who seek to destroy him. In the name of Jesus . . ."

And they all chorused their amens.

For some reason, despite how long Rayford had lived in this new world, it still surprised him to emerge from the heavily curtained mobile hotel to a moon brighter than the sun had once been. But with a wide-brimmed hat and dark wraparound sunglasses, he could pretend. And an hour's amble at midnight often cleared his head.

This night, however, after whispering his intentions to Irene, Rayford found the night wasn't much cooler than the day had been. He rolled up his sleeves as he moseyed along, trying to pray, trying to imagine the future, and, yes—despite the interest and challenge and novelty of the Millennium, longing for heaven. Such complications as the clearly bogus charges against Kenny would not invade such a paradise.

Rayford had learned much about the Lord and about the future, yet still he did not understand God. Why was it that some days He seemed closer than even His throne in Israel, answering Rayford before his prayers were voiced, and other days—like now—He seemed distant and silent? Perhaps heaven would provide those answers.

The occasional car and light truck passed Rayford in the wee hours, one driver stopping to see if he needed a ride. While on his way back to the camper, Rayford was startled to not see it in the distance where he thought he'd left it. Shrugging and assuming he had merely misjudged the distance and that it would appear on the horizon around the next bend, he lowered his head and continued trudging.

Rayford looked up quickly at a sound and saw a plain black sedan racing toward him. It skidded into the dust on the other side of the road as the window rolled down and an Egyptian with a leathery, lined face leaned out and hollered in a raspy, ancient voice, "Are you Rayford Steele, the man of God?"

Rayford considered joking that he was at least half right, but the man seemed so urgent that he simply said, "I am."

The man emerged quickly and crossed the road, leaving the door open. "I am Ishmael," he said, embracing Rayford tightly and then shaking his hand in a firm grip. "I have need of you."

"But how did you find me and—?"

"I asked around and stopped by your motor home. I was told I'd likely find you on the road. You must come with me. Believers are being persecuted and the undecided harassed."

"Where? And what can I do?"

"Come! Come!" Ishmael said, pulling Rayford across the road to the other side of the car and opening the door.

Rayford noticed dark green blankets covering lumpy mounds in the backseat. "Where are we going?"

"Not far, but we must hurry. And thank you in the name of the Lord. Sit in the front; I have foodstuffs filling the back."

Rayford settled in and was buckling his seat belt as Ishmael rushed to slide behind the wheel. Before the driver had even shut his door, Rayford felt the cold steel of a weapon pressed against his neck. He turned far enough to see a young man and woman who had emerged from under the blankets. "What is this?"

"Just cooperate and you will not be hurt," Ishmael said, his voice suddenly sounding younger as well. The man covered his own face with his hand and pulled away what appeared to be a buildup of rubber cement and hair. His face was youthful and smooth.

As the car spun in the dust and then lurched onto the road, the man behind Rayford said, "Put your hands behind your neck and interlace your fingers."

Rayford hesitated.

"Do it now," the young woman said, producing handcuffs.

Still Rayford waited. "You could shoot me through the brain or I could leap from this car and still God would spare me," he said. "Surely you know that."

"Risk it then," Ishmael said.

Rayford considered it. What a message that would send! He could envision himself tumbling and rolling in the dirt, then jogging unharmed back to the others. But the Lord suddenly spoke quietly to his heart. "Comply. I am in this."

How could it be? God was in this?

Rayford locked his fingers behind his head, and the young woman cuffed him. He knocked off his own hat returning his manacled wrists to his lap and used his elbows to balance as the car careened through the countryside, dust billowing behind them.

"So you fooled my compatriots like you fooled me," Rayford said. "They believe I'm assisting you in some spiritual emergency?"

"Hardly," the young woman spat.

Ishmael shushed her with a raised hand. "Do not speak to the hostage," he said.

"I'm a hostage now? And who do you think will pay a ransom for me?"

"We have no need of ransom," Ishmael said. "We require only you."

Rayford became aware of the tightness of the cuff on his left hand and tried to maneuver his wrist to relieve the pressure. Immediately the young woman leaned over the seat and checked it herself, unlocking and loosening it before securing it again.

"Rehema!" Ishmael shouted at the black-haired girl. "What are you doing?"

"It does not need to be so tight," she said, a whine in her voice.

"He is not here to be coddled!"

"What am I here for?" Rayford said.

Ishmael kept his eyes on the road, now moving at more than a hundred miles an hour. "You are here so you will not be there."

There? "And where is that?"

"Siwa."

"You intend to hold me the entire weekend?"

"Perhaps longer."

"And may I ask for what purpose?"

"To prove our god is greater than yours."

Rayford couldn't stifle a laugh. "Good luck."

"So far, it's working."

"How will keeping me from Siwa accomplish anything?"

"You made the mistake of advertising."

"All of our visits are advertised. We want the people

to know we're coming so they can prepare their hearts and minds, not to mention mustering teams of volunteers to help us improve their cities."

"You have done nothing more than frighten the people into believing God will strike them dead if they don't comply with His wishes."

Rayford shook his head. "It seems God Himself may have persuaded them of that. So you are with the Other Light."

"We don't call ourselves that."

"You don't? You're not TOL? I was unaware there were other rebel factions."

"Oh, we are TOL, but our O does not stand for *other*. It stands for *only*. Consider us the enforcers, the hard-liners. We aver that we are not fighting your God. We treat Him as if He doesn't exist."

"So you're pretty much idiots."

Rayford saw Rehema cover her mouth.

"You're not in a position to insult us, Mr. Steele."

"Come now. You were born in this Millennium, but surely you know the history, have seen the power of God, know Jesus is on the throne."

"So the rulers would have us believe."

"But you don't."

"We don't, and we will prove it, as we also are advertising. We have publicized that our god will keep you from appearing in Siwa, proving once and for all that you claim to represent a God who is capricious, unjust, and nonexistent."

"He does not exist and yet He is capricious and

unjust? Detaining me will prove nothing. God will do what He chooses."

"But the hearts of the people will no longer be swayed. Or if they are swayed, they will be swayed our way."

"Toward Lucifer."

"Yes, toward our god, who shall overcome."

"Overcome what or whom? A God you say does not even exist?"

"He will lead us to overcome all who oppose him. Even now, centuries before he is released, massive preparations are under way."

"Released by whom?"

"We believe he will release himself."

"From confinement by whom?"

"He incarcerated himself to prove a point."

Rayford laughed aloud. "If he did that, he's proved *my* point!"

"Your point?"

"That you're idiots. *Now* who's capricious? You really believe your all-powerful leader locked himself away for a thousand years and will eventually emerge to prove he's in charge?"

Ishmael shook his head. "When you see what is happening in his name, you will not be so cavalier."

Ishmael finally slowed about a half mile from a lonely intersection, then turned right onto a road lined on either side by black-uniformed, armed soldiers. They stood at attention and saluted as the sedan passed. Ishmael waved and waved. The route led to an underground entrance wide enough for the car, and Rayford was intrigued by

the quick plunge into utter darkness and a coolness he
had not experienced for years.

The decline must have continued more than three
hundred yards, but Rayford soon quit trying to calculate
how far below the surface they must be. They rolled to
a stop before a small structure that reminded him of a
modular home, and Ishmael signaled for several personnel to take Rayford from the car.

"When did you last eat?" Ishmael said.

"About six hours ago."

"Good. Let him wait another eighteen for just enough
food to keep him functioning. And take his shirt, shoes,
and socks. Chilly, Mr. Steele?"

"Of course."

"Your slacks and undershirt should be enough. A little
chill will keep you alert."

Rayford was led to a cavernous opening that proved
incongruous, as it sported walls bearing huge flat-screen
TV monitors and high-tech desks and workstations but
was ringed by dirt-floored cells enclosed by prison bars.
Each cell bore a prisoner—a man, a woman, or a young
person, all sitting on steel mesh beds. Each wore an
expression of fear and resignation. And each had one
armed guard posted outside his or her cell.

Rayford found himself grateful beyond measure that his
guard was Rehema. "You know what your name means,
do you not?" he said as she gently guided him inside,
removed his handcuffs, and pulled the cell door shut.

"Do tell," she whispered, her face a mask of boredom
but her eyes dancing.

"'Compassionate.' And you have already proven to be that."

She shrugged and sat with her back to the bars, her weapon tucked between her knees. Rayford sat on his metal frame, already beginning to shiver, and talked loudly enough so only she could hear. He asked her to tell him about herself, but she demurred.

"Come now," he said. "I can tell you're smarter than this. More curious than this. It's written all over you that you know better."

"My back is to you," Rehema said, turning her head to make herself heard. "How can you tell what's written all over me?"

"What did you mean when you said 'hardly' when I asked if Ishmael had also fooled my team?"

"So much for how much you know," she said. "We never even found your team."

"Then how—?"

"We've been following you. Not a week passes that you don't venture out in the night. We merely waited for you. We sent one team to neutralize your people, and we picked you up."

"My people have also been seized?"

"No, I told you; we couldn't find them."

"You saw me leave the motor home and then lost track of it? It's a big, slow, ponderous thing—"

"Believe me, I know. Ishmael is irritated to the point of exasperation. You must not tell him I said anything."

"Yeah, I'm going to tell on you, get you into trouble."

She giggled.

"What happens in here, Rehema?"

"Monitoring, tracking." She pointed to the screens, where Rayford could make out huge manufacturing operations in progress. "Munitions plants all over the world. In virtually every country."

"All planning for the big war at the end of the Millennium?"

She nodded. "It will make the so-called Armageddon look like child's play."

"Jesus Himself took care of that."

"So you would have us believe."

"And this buildup of armaments is for what?"

"For Lucifer, who will lead the charge."

"Against the nonexistent God?"

Rehema hunched her shoulders as she seemed to throttle a laugh again. "I know how it sounds," she said. "But the battle is against the believers in the God who is not there."

"But we believe so deeply that we have obeyed His edict against weapons of war. You and yours would attack an unarmed people?"

"Better safe than . . . you know."

"And you will not even be there. How old are you?"

"Ninety."

"A mere child. Does it mean nothing to you that all your older compatriots are dead? Does that not tell you anything?"

She fell silent.

"It does tell you something, doesn't it? How do your fearless leaders explain that one? The God you claim does not exist—and yet whom you oppose—somehow curses those who reject Him for a hundred years, and no one gets the picture?"

She shook her head slowly. "No wonder you call us idiots."

"Don't be an idiot, Rehema. Think."

Again she was quiet for several minutes. Rayford knew he shouldn't be hungry until morning, but just knowing he would not be given any food until dinnertime the next night gave him pangs. And he was shuddering. He rubbed his arms and brought his knees up to his chest, wrapping them in his forearms.

"We're not all atheists, you know," Rehema said.

"Of course I know. How could you be?"

"I couldn't. You're right. I've seen friends and relatives die, right on schedule. Only a fool denies that."

"So you believe in God."

"I believe He exists. I just don't like Him much."

"Let's talk about it."

"I'd better not."

"Then I'll talk and you listen."

"Is it going to bother you when I eat? They deliver my meal to me right in front of you. It's part of the deal."

"Of course it'll bother me, but I'll survive."

But Rayford had underestimated the power of her simple sandwich. He smelled it as if it lay under his nose, and he imagined every bite. He looked away, tried to think of something else, and concentrated on his recitation of history—especially his own. He talked of his life, his family, the Rapture, being left behind. And while

Rehema appeared interested and even at times enthralled, she furtively passed the last few bites of her sandwich through the bars to him.

Rayford eagerly wolfed it down, worrying aloud about the cameras that might reveal her deed and get her into trouble.

"What's the worst they can do to me?" she said. "They need me. We're still in the minority, and history proves I'll be around only ten more years anyway."

Rayford smiled. "Whose side are you on? You're proving my points."

When Rayford began telling her of his own salvation and all his experiences during the Tribulation, Rehema finally turned to face him. He surprised himself by how much Scripture he had committed to memory over the years, and as he held forth, he quoted passage after passage of prophecy that had come true just as the foretellers had predicted.

Finally Rehema said, "How could anyone doubt God after all that?"

"They couldn't," Rayford said. "To oppose Him they had to acknowledge that He existed but that they simply wanted to go their own way. Like you."

With that Rehema stood and turned her back, pacing before his cell.

THIRTY-ONE

I<small>RENE WAS</small> awakened just before dawn by a gentle rap on her door.

"Forgive me," Chaim said. "I was looking for Rayford."

Irene sat up and pulled back the blind, making her cover her eyes. "He went out for a walk around midnight," she said. "I don't recall his returning."

"I'm sure he's about," the old man said, smiling. "It's not as if we moved."

———

Rayford would not have been surprised to find it was noon, as long as he had been talking, as uncomfortable as he felt, and as tired as the young Rehema looked. She was fairer-complexioned than most in the compound, despite her dark brown eyes and hair so black it could have been dyed but clearly wasn't.

Rayford's watch, however, read 0700 hours. By now his people would miss him, wonder about him, worry about him, pray for him. Where had they gone that he had been unable to see the vehicle and that Ishmael's troops had also missed them? It wasn't like them to venture out after settling in for the night.

Rehema appeared weary. Rayford was too, of course, but worry and earnestness fueled him. "When does your shift end?" he said.

"Oh," she said, "we're twenty-four hours on, twenty-fours hours off, and I only just began before we apprehended you."

"You're not serious. You're stuck with me until midnight?"

She nodded.

"Poor girl. You're going to know more about me than I know about myself, because I plan to talk until I cannot go on."

She chuckled. "That will keep me awake. Keep me out of trouble. But I am supposed to be talking to you, propagandizing you, selling you on the inevitability of our cause and the certainty of our victory in the end as evidenced by all the work you see being accomplished on the screens. This will continue for centuries until we are invincible."

"Oh, dear one," Rayford said, "you have already lost. Victory is ours. You have so little time, really. Follow your heart and mind, change your course, join the forces of the one true and living God before it is too late."

Rehema turned and faced Rayford. "You are a nice

and well-intentioned man. But it is you who are out of
time." She looked at her watch. "In fewer than seventeen
hours, your God will have been shown incapable of
delivering you from our hands in time for your meeting.
Then we will know whose god is worthy."

"I already know, and so do you. And now I will tell
you about my daughter and my son."

"Oh! I'd love to hear about your children! I have
a son too."

"Surely not. You're much too young. I would not have
guessed you were even married."

"I did not say I was."

"How old is he?"

"Four."

"And you wish him to live to be only one hundred?"

Rehema set her jaw and looked away. "Tell me of your
children," she said.

———————

Abdullah sat across from Mudawar in his office, leaning
toward him earnestly. "So you feel, as you have expressed
it, that you 'owe me one.'"

"Yes. You earned it. You deserve it. One for your side.
What will it be?"

"I have no idea what you have in mind. You know my
heart's desire: that you and Sarsour come to faith."

"Come now, Abdullah. That would not be a favor;
that would be surrender, defeat. And we both know it's
not going to happen. Now take advantage of my

largesse. I was thinking more in terms of your borrowing our list of recruits. Big sale, today only, limited time only, while they last! You get one shot at communicating with the very people you're so worried about. That's fair, isn't it? I don't fear that, and—like I say—you've earned it. Of course, I would have to see what you're saying to them before I allow it to go out."

"I would be a fool to pass up that opportunity, so I accept and thank you. But there is one more thing."

"Try me."

"I confess I did not absent myself yesterday for your benefit."

"Really? Well, it worked to my benefit nonetheless, so our deal is still valid."

"The truth is I thought I recognized someone in the entourage and didn't want him to see me."

Mudawar sat back and seemed to study Abdullah. "The one from Israel?"

"That's the one."

Mudawar nodded. "You know him?"

"I believe I do."

"From?"

"We go way back. I am a friend of his family."

"And you're telling me they are unaware that he works for us."

Abdullah could not speak, could not move. *It's true then.*

"Well," Mudawar said. "This *is* a complicator. If you know him, you know where he works, and it should be no stretch for you to understand now that he is a mole, a double agent if we were using spy vernacular. He has his people believing he's infiltrating us, while in reality it is the other way around."

"You know I will have to expose him," Abdullah said. "I cannot allow such damage to the kingdom and to the people I love."

"Oh, Master Ababneh, are you really so naïve? Do you believe that after all the time you have spent in our offices, coming and going and doing us favors, that you retain an ounce of credibility among your own? Do you not suspect that with our closed-circuit cameras and our hidden still cameras that we can build an airtight case for you yourself having flipped?"

"Don't be ridiculous! I am well past one hundred years old. A natural my age has a built-in pedigree with the Lord. The fact that I remain alive testifies that I am His and He is mine."

"And thus you are incapable of sin? Oh, it will surprise believers, horrify them even. But how will you explain it? You don't wear the robe of the righteous. You don't speak Hebrew, at least not when you are with us. These cameras have sound, you know."

"But everything I have said in here would implicate you, not me."

"Everything? You don't think we could find something, anything, in all the time you've been here that might portray you as our friend rather than our enemy? Anyway, you can tell the world that we let you set up shop here, knowing full well who you were and what you were about. Who in his right mind would believe it? You hardly believed it yourself!"

Silently Abdullah was praying desperately. Had this idea been his own and not the Lord's? Had his foolishness damaged the work of the kingdom?

"Now, why don't you work on the message you'd like to send to our list, and I'll take a look at it when you're finished."

Abdullah stood quickly, afraid that if he said anything more he would multiply the damage. When he opened the door, Sarsour—who had plainly been standing close enough to hear—quickly moved away. Abdullah walked to his desk, his knees weak, sat, and buried his head in his hands. He couldn't believe this was happening and that he had helped perpetuate it.

Would the Lord want him to actually take Mudawar up on his offer? The idea of communicating to the very audience TOL targeted was too good to pass up, but would Mudawar find a way to use it against him? Of course he would.

Abdullah's mind was too jumbled to even think about crafting a message. Soon it would be time to make his daily run for Mudawar's coffee and Sarsour's snack. Should he continue to do that, to serve his enemies out of love while they stabbed him in the back?

———————

Chloe was miserable, trying to function while her mind was entirely on Kenny. She knew Cameron believed him deep down too, but Cam's detached manner frustrated her. She would not be happy until Kenny was vindicated.

During the morning break, Ekaterina dropped in. As soon as the women saw each other, they both dissolved into tears.

"Pardon my saying so, Mrs. Williams," Ekaterina said, "but you look as bad as I feel."

"This is like a death in the family," Chloe said. "And we'd better have no more of those."

"I'm sure glad you told me about that picture before it showed up in my e-mail last night."

"Who sent it?"

"Who knows? Anyway, I came by to tell you that I've asked Mattie for the afternoon off. I can't work, can't concentrate. I'm doing more harm than good here."

"You'll be even more miserable at home, Kat. What will you do?"

"If I tell you, will you promise not to tell anyone else?" Chloe nodded.

"Anyone?"

"Whatever you say, Kat."

"I have to see Kenny."

"Well, good. I think that's good. Does that mean that you've decided—?"

"It doesn't mean anything. I still don't know what to think, but I owe him a face-to-face."

As Abdullah slowly made his way toward the street coffee vendor, nothing was making sense to him. He had somehow painted himself into this corner, and the Lord seemed silent. Did that mean He was disappointed in Abdullah? He hadn't felt that way for years.

He jumped when Sarsour touched his shoulder and whispered, "Can we talk, around the corner?"

"Certainly, son. What is it?"

They found a small table under a shade tree. Sarsour looked deeply troubled, his face clouded over. He kept peeking around, as if to be sure no one was watching. "Mudawar told me to follow you, keep an eye on you. I suppose he was afraid you were leaving to inform on us and that you would be gone for good."

"It may come to that, Sarsour. I suppose you heard our conversation."

The young man looked down and nodded. "I knew you were coming back. You didn't take your Bible. Plus you have never let anything get in the way of your being kind to us, not even this. Returning with Mudawar's coffee will be like heaping coals of fire on his head, will it not?"

Abdullah couldn't hide his surprise. "You're quoting Scripture to me now?"

"I told you how I was raised. Until I left home my parents took me to worship all the time."

"You hated it."

"Most of it. But that doesn't mean I didn't learn a few things."

It was clear to Abdullah that Sarsour had something on his mind. He kept furtively glancing about, taking a breath as if to speak, then seemingly thinking better of it. "What is it, son? You can talk to me."

Sarsour suddenly sat forward and rested his elbows on the table, burying his face in his hands. "I visited my parents last night."

"Yes?"

He nodded miserably. "Just as I was about to knock, I noticed through the curtain that they were praying."

"Really?"

"They knelt beside each other at the couch. I can't tell you the effect it had on me. It wasn't as if I hadn't seen this frequently all my life. They both love the Scriptures, and I often saw them reading. But standing there at the front door and seeing them like that, I was overcome with the knowledge that they were praying for me."

"How did you know?"

"I don't know. I just did. I felt low. Ashamed. Mr. Ababneh, I felt worthless and guilty."

"About what?"

Sarsour lowered his hands and snorted. "You know my profession and you ask that?"

Abdullah put a hand on Sarsour's shoulder and smiled. "Well, we both know that *I* know you're worthless and guilty. I'm just wondering what brought this truth to you."

The young man took a deep breath and let it out. "It had been a long time since I felt God had spoken to me."

"And now you did? What was He saying, Sarsour?"

"Nothing specific. I just felt His presence."

"Of course you did. Your parents must have been praising Him. You know what the Bible says about that; He inhabits the praise of His people. He was there."

Sarsour nodded. "I know. That just made me feel worse, so I turned to go. One of my parents either saw me or heard me, because suddenly the door opened, and my mother called out to me. She said, 'Sarsour, have you ever felt like an answer to prayer?' Well, I sure hadn't, and I didn't then, but of course I went inside. What else could I do? Even my father wept when he saw me. I asked them what was going on.

"My mother said they had both been troubled in their spirits about me all day. I laughed and said that was nothing new, but she said no, it was something deeper and more specific, as if I was going through some new crisis. How could they have known?"

"What was your crisis, Sarsour?"

"Just everything that happened yesterday—the visit, your disappearing, our pretending not to know that the man from Israel was an infiltrator."

"What?"

"Oh, surely *you* know, Mr. Ababneh. You are friend of the family. We do have a plant at that Children of the Tribulation ministry in Israel, but it's certainly not Kenny Williams."

"Who is it?"

"Qasim Marid."

Abdullah fought to keep his composure. He wanted to leap and shout, and he couldn't wait to clear Kenny's name. "You know I cannot sit on this information, Sarsour. This will cost you your job. Why are you telling me this?"

"Because I have had enough, and God is speaking to me. You know, for a long time I really thought the Other

Light was a valid alternative. At first they seemed like honest, honorable people. But to mislead you as Mudawar has, and to tell you outright lies as he did this morning, well—that combined with what happened to me last night. This is not working for me."

"What happened to you last night?"

"Just seeing my parents praying, knowing they were praying for me and then having them confirm that . . . I didn't say much to them, but I couldn't wait to get back to my place and see if God was still trying to talk to me."

"And?"

"He was. Of course. He always has. I had just shut Him out for so long."

"What was He telling you?"

"You know, sir. He wants me. And when I overheard your conversation with Mudawar this morning, it was the last straw. I couldn't believe it when he told me to follow you this morning. I was going to anyway, but that would have tipped him off that something was up."

"We'd better get back before he comes looking for you," Abdullah said.

"I don't care if he does. I'm not setting foot in that place again without being a believer. I was hoping you'd pray with me."

———

Kenny had sketched out some handicraft projects for the kids that would help drive home the current lessons from

the life of David. It hadn't been easy to concentrate.
There had been times when he slid off his chair to the
floor, moaning in frustration and crying out to God for
relief. A knock at the door made him wipe his face and
straighten up.

He peeked out to see Ekaterina. *Thank You, Lord.*

Mudawar was amused to see Abdullah and Sarsour
return together, delivering his coffee. "So much for you
being assigned to surveillance again," he said. "How
long did it take him to spot you?"

"Not long after I tapped him on the shoulder."

"What're you saying?"

"I want to help him with his missive to the TOL
membership."

"You? What would you say?"

Sarsour glanced at Abdullah, who was packing up his
stuff. "I'd say that if the number two man in our cell
headquarters can get his mind changed about Jesus,
anybody can."

"You're not serious."

"Dead serious."

"I *knew* this would happen!" Mudawar pointed at
Abdullah. "This is all your fault! Like an idiot, I let you
in here, and now this. Well, I suppose you know you're
fired, Sarsour."

"I had an inkling I might not still qualify for a job
I wouldn't want."

"What will you do? You can't do anything else."

"Maybe I'll get a job at COT. I'm guessing they're going to need to replace Qasim."

———————

Kenny had not felt awkward in front of Ekaterina since the day they had met. Until now. They sat across from each other.

"It's only been half a day and I miss you," she said.

"I know. Me too."

"I'm so sorry, Kenny. If you'll have me back, I'm here."

"You believe me?"

"Of course. I can't believe I ever doubted you. Nothing in your life or character jibes with that e-mail. If I'm wrong and you wrote that, well, then I'm a fool. I love you."

She rose and approached him, but before he could stand, she sat on his lap and buried her head in his chest. "I just want the truth to come out so everyone will know. You know the others are suffering too."

"The others?"

"Raymie, Bahira, Zaki."

"Not Qasim?"

"Don't talk to me about Qasim."

"Why?"

"Because if you're innocent, he's guilty."

"I'm glad someone else recognizes the obvious." Kenny's implanted phone chirped. "Let me answer this, hon," he said, shifting.

She stood.

"Well, yes, hello, Mr. Ababneh. Good to hear you too. . . ."

THIRTY-TWO

"REHEMA, I need you to call my wife and assure her and the others that I am well. And, of course, I need to know the same is true of them."

"And why would you think I would do that for you?"

"Because I would do the same for you. You are a mother. You have family. You may see yourself as an operative of the rebellion, but I know better. I can see in your eyes that you know the truth. I have told you everything I know about God and Christ and faith and prophecy, about the world as it once was and now is, and about my family. You know God is real, and you know He will somehow get me out of here in time to get back to my people and my assignment."

Rehema pressed her lips together. "That would persuade me."

331

"Would it?"

"Of course."

"But you're not otherwise convinced?"

No answer.

But she asked for his wife's number and turned away to call.

Irene Steele was, of course, puzzled by and suspicious of the call from the young woman who identified herself as Rayford's guard.

"He's wondering where we're hiding?" Irene said slowly, carefully considering whether she should reveal anything. She decided she could do Rayford no harm. "Tell him that he will find us where he left us. We will wait in plain sight."

"You are crafty people, Mrs. Steele," Rehema said.

"If you wish to think so. But it strikes me that God has blinded your compatriots, as we have not moved since my husband left us. And would you remind him that we must be on the road to Siwa by no later than one in the morning if we wish to fulfill our obligations there?"

"I'll tell him, ma'am," Rehema said, "but if he is with you, I likely will be too."

"Is that so?"

"Oh yes. My career, my future, my very life depends on keeping him from that appointment. So if he makes it, it will be either with my help or with me under his protection against my former superiors."

Irene chuckled. "He has convinced you of the error of your ways, has he?"

"Very nearly."

"We will welcome you warmly into the family of God, dear."

"What?"

Irene could tell Rehema was overcome. "Did you not hear me?"

"I heard you, Mrs. Steele. It's . . . it's . . . it's just that no one has ever said that to me before."

———————

"What is it?" Rayford said, noting that Rehema was fighting tears.

The young woman merely shook her head and held up a hand as if she needed a moment before she could speak. Finally she said, "If I get you out of here, can we stop for my son?"

"First things first," Rayford said. "Do you understand what you are saying?"

"Of course. I have more reason to believe in your God than you ever did. There is more evidence, more proof, more of everything than you ever had. I know who I am and what I am."

"And what is that?"

"A sinner in need of God."

"Then you also know what you need to do. Do you understand the consequences?"

Rehema nodded solemnly. "TOL does not lightly hold their own."

"And you also realize that I could not allow you to release me and go to find your son while other believers remain here."

"What are you saying?" Rehema said.

"What kind of a zealot would I be to escape and leave others to whatever fate awaits? If we do this, we take everyone."

"That would require an act of God. There are more than thirty others, each with his or her own personal guard."

Rayford smiled. "You have heard every story I can remember. Where would you think such a miracle might rank on my list of supernatural events?"

Rehema looked about. "I feel as if every eye is on me, every camera, every hidden microphone."

"I hope they are. I hope Ishmael and whomever else he wishes to enlist as a henchman has heard every word. The Scripture is clear that 'You shall know the truth, and the truth shall make you free.'"

As if on cue, the bureaucrats and other guards looked up as a cadre of armed guards rushed from every direction, joining in the middle of the compound and then heading, led by Ishmael, toward Rayford's cell, weapons at the ready.

"Surrender your rifle and sidearm, Rehema," Ishmael said.

As Rehema allowed them to be unstrapped and taken, she glanced in panic at Rayford.

"You have one chance and one chance only to renounce all you have heard and said here," Ishmael told her. "Proclaim your loyalty to TOL and be reassigned, or join the prisoners to whom you seem so sympathetic."

"You're asking me to choose sides?"

"Precisely."

"I choose the true and living God and His Son, Jesus."

Stripped of her weapons and ammunition belt as well as her boots, Rehema was shoved into Rayford's cell and shackled both to him and to a steel ring embedded in the wall. She was shuddering, but he drew her close and whispered, "The better for us to be able to pray."

And with the withdrawal of TOL troops, they did pray, and Rehema became a child of God.

"My son is in a TOL day care center six miles from here," she said.

"God knows," Rayford said.

———

Tsion Ben-Judah made the decision to keep the news of Rayford's incarceration from the brothers and sisters in Israel. "They have enough to occupy themselves for now," he said. "And besides, we know this is only a temporary setback. Have you looked out the window?"

The others crowded around as Tsion raised the blinds. Marching resolutely down the road was a robust figure.

Bruce Barnes whispered, "I don't believe it."

"Of course you do," Tsion said. "And you should not even be surprised."

"Anis?" Chaim said.

"My man," Tsion said.

"He's more than a man," Bruce said. "And you, above all, know it."

Rehema knelt awkwardly with Rayford, their cuffs not only tethering them together but also pinning them to the wall, as he led her in prayer again. When they finished he asked her what time it was.

Through tears she reported, "It's 2200 hours."

"Two hours before midnight. We must soon be on our way. Does your son usually spend the night at day care?"

She shook her head. "I pick him up on the way home."

"How many will your car hold?"

"Four."

"We'll need more vehicles and drivers."

"Assuming we can get the keys. How is this supposed to happen, sir?"

"I have quit asking or even wondering. The Lord works—"

"In mysterious ways. Don't look so surprised. Even unbelievers have heard all the clichés."

The old man and the young girl turned carefully and sat next to each other, backs against the wall, manacled arms raised. "This is the best part of being on the right side," Rayford said. "Waiting and watching to see what God will do when there seems no possible solution."

Rehema sighed. "And you never wonder, never worry."

"Not anymore. Don't wonder; don't worry. Just wait and watch. And obey."

"Obey whom?"

"Whomever He sends. Whatever He does. Just be prepared to act in faith."

Rayford found his head bobbing as he fought drowsiness when midnight approached. He was aware that Rehema remained tense and alert. That was understandable. All of this had to be foreign to her.

"I'm scared," she said. "Mostly for my son. What will become of him?"

"Jesus is a lover of children," Rayford said. "Trust Him. Obey Him. May I teach you a song?"

"Are you serious?"

Rayford began humming, then singing "Trust and Obey."

> "When we walk with the Lord in the light
>   of His word,
> What a glory He sheds on our way.
> While we do His good will, He abides with us still,
> And with all who will trust and obey. . . ."

Rehema looked at him with what appeared amazement, but she listened until he trailed off and finally dozed.

At the stroke of midnight, Rayford was awakened when Rehema struggled to her feet, yanking painfully on his arm.

"Who's that?" Rehema said, pointing with her free hand. "And how did he get in here?"

There stood Anis in the midst of the chaotic compound, calm, serene, confident, authoritative. He raised both arms, as if directing a church choir, and Rayford noticed that all the prisoners seemed to know it was their cue to stand. Ishmael approached, brandishing his weapon and calling for aides to apprehend the intruder. But as others joined him, forming a half circle around Anis and demanding that he identify himself and surrender, the man of God did not even acknowledge their presence.

Suddenly the screens on the walls and the computer monitors flickered and went dark, and a low rumbling began. It soon grew into a shaking and rattling, and the armed guards grabbed frantically for anything to stay upright. As the lights went out and emergency lamps came on, the foundations of the place rumbled and rattled, and as one the cell doors broke from their latches and swung open, chains and handcuffs falling from all the prisoners.

Ishmael screeched that guards would shoot to kill any who even dreamed of leaving their cells, but Rayford noticed that all eyes were on the stoic Anis, who began directing the prisoners out one by one.

"Shoot! Shoot!" Ishmael raged. "Fire!" But no one responded, and not even the man himself seemed able to raise his weapon.

Soon the prisoners were following Anis past guards who appeared paralyzed with fear. They moved into the parking area where the rolling stock stood, and Anis divided the freed men and women and young people into threes and fours, handing them keys and pointing them to various cars. Some guards tossed away their weapons and tore off their hats and shirts, joining the throng leaving the complex.

Anis directed Rehema to her own car and assigned an older woman to join them, telling Rehema where to drop her.

The caravan of cars slowly fell into line and snaked its way to the surface, where armed guards calmly opened the gates and allowed them out. They sped off in all directions, Rehema quickly reaching top speed and asking Rayford to sing his song once again.

And as he sang, "Trust and obey, for there's no other way to be happy in Jesus, but to trust and obey . . . ," Rehema delivered the woman to her joyous, weeping family, then headed directly to the care center, where her son stood in the doorway, backpack full, eyes heavy-lidded. He politely met Rayford, climbed into his car seat, and fell asleep.

Rehema drove directly to the camper, where Rayford introduced her and quickly recited the story. As the others welcomed her to the fold, it was decided she would accompany them to Siwa. Within another hour, they were on their way.

The following evening, she became one of many formerly imprisoned believers who testified of the miraculous midnight prison break. Siwa enjoyed a revival unmatched by any other city in Ozase.

Rayford and his team mobilized the local teams and finally set out for Israel and their long-awaited break.

———

Qasim Marid was, of course, fired from the Children of the Tribulation ministry, and he died at one hundred.

He was replaced by Abdullah Ababneh's friend Sarsour, who endeared himself to the staff and Cameron Williams's extended family over the next nine centuries.

Ignace and Lothair also died at one hundred—as did Mudawar—and became the Other Light martyrs, still revered by billions of adherents more than nine hundred years later.

Kenny and Ekaterina Williams's wedding was performed by Bruce Barnes, and the couple produced eight sons, six daughters, and more than eighty grandchildren over the next two hundred years. The couple expanded the work of COT to Greece, as had been Ekaterina's dream, until they grew too feeble to carry on.

By the end, the ministry was maintained by the glorifieds, as the naturals finally saw the ravages of time catch up with their bodies. When the naturals reached ages higher than about seven hundred, they began to slow and notice the diminution of their senses, particularly hearing and sight.

On his eight hundredth birthday, Mac McCullum was honored when it seemed that all his former friends and loved ones and associates were invited to celebrate with him at COT in Israel—and most showed up. He asked for the microphone and announced "what I believe is a brilliant idea. It probably came from the Lord, but until we know for sure, I'll take credit for it. Let's make a pact, all of us, that we find a way to move right back here to witness the end of the Millennium. If everybody can work that out over the next two hundred years, at my thousandth we'll have us a mighty reunion, and all you glorifieds can help feed us naturals. How 'bout that?"

The idea was met with laughter and high spirits and then forgotten for several years until Rayford raised it with Chloe and Cameron. "You've expanded," he said. "And the earth's population has exploded as we all knew it would. Let's free up a building here where you young ones can keep an eye on us oldsters and keep us from having to be warehoused somewhere else. Kenny and Kat can't walk without canes anymore. Mac and Chaim are in wheelchairs and I soon will be. Abdullah's the only one who still has a little spring in his step, but we know that won't last. What do you say?"

Cameron apparently liked the idea, for when virtually the same crowd returned for Mac's millennial bash, The "six oldsters," as they had come to be known, were lined up in their wheelchairs, facing the horizon.

"This here's like a funeral where the dead guy won't go," Mac said, as dear ones from the past began a long procession past Rayford, Kenny, Ekaterina, Chaim, Mac, and Abdullah.

Rayford had to have the visitors remind him of their names and their connection. His heart was full as he was greeted by Loretta, Bruce Barnes's secretary; Floyd

Charles; David Hassid; T Delanty; Mr. and Mrs. Miklos
from Greece; Ken Ritz; Hattie Durham; Annie Christo-
pher; Steve Plank; his own parents—looking centuries
younger than he; Amanda and her first husband; Albie;
Hannah Palemoon; Zeke senior and junior; the Sebastian
family—George, Priscilla, and Beth Ann; Razor; Enoch
Dumas; Leah Rose; Eleazar Tiberias; his daughter,
Naomi; Chang Wong; Otto Weser; Lionel Whalum;
Ming Toy and Ree Woo; and so many others.

"You know what I want?" Rayford said.

"Tell me, Dad," Chloe said.

"I want a picture of the original Tribulation Force."

Chloe rounded up Bruce and Cameron, and the three
glorifieds posed behind Rayford's chair.

The instantly produced photograph stunned even
Rayford. It depicted three robust young people frozen
in the prime of their lives and a long, bony man with
drooping jowls, liquid eyes, and no hair, weighing barely
over a hundred pounds, veins prominent on the backs of
his hands, bundled in a sweater despite the desert heat.

THE LAST DAY OF THE MILLENNIUM

THIRTY-THREE

THE EARTH teemed with billions of people, and the end of
the Millennium was vastly different from the beginning.
That was no surprise to Rayford, who kept up with the
news, often sitting before the television with Chaim
Rosenzweig. "We don't have one trained soldier," he
said. "And we don't need one. Not a hair on the head of
a believer will be harmed by the biggest fighting force the
world has ever seen."

Daily for the past three years, the news had abounded
with stories of millions of adherents to the Other Light,
growing bolder by the minute. Their printing presses and
electronically transmitted messages blanketed the globe,
recruiting new members, amassing a weapons stockpile
and training a fighting force a thousand times bigger
than had been aggregated for the Battle of Armageddon
a millennium before.

Rayford was amazed that God allowed such a brazen, wanton act of defiance on the parts of so many as they symbolically thumbed their noses at Jesus and the earthly rulers He had chosen from the ages. Even in Israel, tanks rumbled through the streets, uniformed soldiers marched, and missiles and rockets were paraded before the faithful.

Television broadcasts from around the world showed the same and worse—what seemed like entire people groups dressed in the all-black uniform of the fighting forces of the Other Light. Of course they were all younger than one hundred and thus relegated to the status of children—rebellious, articulate, passionate, defiant, furious children. But they were also brilliant and had written songs and poems and speeches anticipating the day their leader, the Other Light personified, would be—in their words—"foolishly released" by his captor.

"The so-called God Almighty will rue the day He returns to us our leader, for it will mean the greatest comeback, the most decisive defeat, the most gargantuan victory of any foe over another in the history of mankind."

Warships, tanks, personnel carriers, bombs, rockets, launchers, and all manner of battle paraphernalia from tents to food and medical supplies had been arriving at Holy Land ports daily for months, vast encampments growing around the entire expanded city of Jerusalem.

Rayford was stunned that even many of the faithful were outraged and terrified by this. Oh, it was awful, terrible and disconcerting to see the plains filled with warriors and their tools of war. But the only reason the government allowed it was because they knew—as did Rayford and his friends—the schemes of the marauding invaders were futile.

"All this time, Rayford," Chaim said, his voice weak. "All this waiting. And the prophecies are clear that this will be entirely anticlimactic. Think of the irony of that."

Rayford remembered when the airwaves had been full of praises to the Lord Christ, who ruled the earth from His throne. Now it was as if people on both sides of the conflict had forgotten that He was still there, still sovereign, still destined to triumph. Debates, speeches, charges and countercharges filled the airwaves now.

And the enemy continued to arrive. Every nation on earth sent fighting forces. And while many believers fled the Holy Land, others vowed to fight the Other Light to the death.

The only question on the final day was the timing of God's release of His archenemy of the ages.

That became obvious soon enough when the countless followers of the Other Light announced that their centuries-long project to manufacture weaponry unlike anything that had ever been seen on earth had resulted in all that could be seen, blotting out much of the landscape of Israel and surrounding the City of David.

For a thousand years there had been no wars or rumors of wars, no nation rising against nation; now TOL had emerged with a highly organized, trained, precision-tuned army of hundreds of millions. It finally became obvious that God had released Satan, according to the Scriptures, when the warriors from all over the world, "whose number is as the sand of the sea," were finally in place, gathered for battle.

For months they had been arriving, first in small groups and finally in great battalions, carefully following orders and surrounding "the camp of the saints and the beloved city."

As the entire world looked on—many by television, many from what they hoped were safe distances—the colossal fighting force suddenly came alive with a buzz of anticipation. Clearly Satan had been released and was in their midst, preparing to show himself and lead them. The cosmic battle of the ages between the forces of good and evil, light and darkness, life and death, was about to commence.

Rayford and his friends gathered on the veranda of Cameron's estate, where they were allowed to see this all unfold. And Rayford knew it was only by the supernatural grace of God that his thousand-plus-year-old eyes were able to see every detail. It was as if God Himself was revealing everything to the theater of Rayford's mind.

The millions-strong enemy created a cacophony of rumbling and jangling, sending dust billowing as far as the eye could see. And suddenly rising from within those masses and marching to the fore came Satan himself, as a shining light, a gleaming sword raised high.

"And now," he shouted, somehow able to be heard for miles, "I come to claim what has been rightfully mine since the dawn of time: the very throne of God!"

As Satan advanced toward the temple, the noise of his endless troops drowning out the sounds of nature, God Himself seemed to allow Rayford to stand taller than he had in centuries. It was as if he were a young man again, and he longed to join his Savior on the front lines. He was aware that his friends also stood tall beside him, eager, anticipating, knowing the side of the righteous would prevail.

Despite all the attacks of the evil one throughout the aeons of time, his efforts were doomed to an ill end. And as Rayford Steele and his compatriots looked on—all of them sinners redeemed by the blood of the Lamb who sat on the throne—Jesus rose to face His challenger for one last time.

The Alpha and Omega, the King of kings, the Lord of lords, the Lion of Judah, the Mighty God, the Everlasting Father, the Prince of Peace, the Rock, the Savior, the Christ stood in the courtyard of His temple.

Satan, silenced for a thousand years, shrieked, "Charge!"

Jesus responded quietly, *"I AM WHO I AM."*

And with that, the clouds rolled back and the heavens opened, and orange and yellow and red mountains of white-hot, roiling flames burst forth. Satan's entire throng—men, women, weapons, everything—was vaporized in an instant, leaving around the holy mountain a ring of ash that soon wafted away in the breeze.

Satan looked about him and slowly lowered his sword. He appeared to have something to say and even drew breath to say it, but he fell silent.

And Jesus spoke. "You, O evil one, were once full of wisdom and perfect in beauty. You were in Eden, the garden of God. Every precious stone was your covering: the sardius, topaz, and diamond, beryl, onyx, and jasper, sapphire, turquoise, and emerald with gold. The workmanship of your timbrels and pipes was prepared for you on the day you were created.

"You were my anointed cherub. I established you; you were on the holy mountain of God. You were perfect in your ways from the day you were created, till iniquity was found in you.

"You became filled with violence, and you sinned. Worse, you led countless others to unbelief. Therefore I cast you as a profane thing out of the mountain of God. Your heart was lifted up because of your beauty; you corrupted your wisdom for the sake of your splendor; and now I cast you to the ground, I lay you before kings, that they might gaze at you.

"You defiled your sanctuaries by the multitude of your iniquities. All who knew you among the peoples are astonished at you; you have become a horror, and shall be no more forever."

Satan dropped his sword and fell shuddering to his knees.

From within the temple, King David emerged and said with a loud voice, "This is Christ Jesus, who, being in the form of God, did not consider it robbery to be equal with God, but made Himself of no reputation, taking the form of a bondservant, and coming in the likeness of men. And being found in appearance as a man, He humbled Himself and became obedient to the point of death, even the death of the cross.

"Therefore God also has highly exalted Him and given Him the name which is above every name, that at the name of Jesus every knee should bow, of those in heaven, and of those on earth, and of those under the earth, and that every tongue should confess that Jesus Christ is Lord, to the glory of God the Father."

David retreated, and Jesus merely lifted a hand and opened His palm. A seam in the cosmos opened before Satan. Flames and black smoke poured from where the Beast and the False Prophet writhed on their knees screaming, "Jesus is Lord!"

Satan cried out, "Jesus is Lord! Jesus is Lord!"

Jesus closed His fingers and Satan was thrown into the abyss, the seam sealing to muffle the screams of the three who would be tormented day and night forever and ever in the lake of fire and brimstone.

Suddenly Rayford got an idea of what it had been like for Irene and Raymie to be raptured. He found himself lifted from the veranda, muscle and flesh and hair restored to the way he had looked and felt at about age thirty. His clothes had been exchanged for a gleaming white robe, and as he and all his friends and loved ones ascended through the ceiling and the roof and flew toward the holy mountain, Rayford knew from his depths that his mind, too, had finally been glorified.

The only thing that mattered now was to praise and glorify Jesus, the lover and Savior of his soul. As he and the billions who had lived through the Millennium ascended, he saw descending the most beautiful and massive foursquare city of transparent gold, so stunning that Rayford knew his finite mind would never have been able to take it in.

As the elect and redeemed of the ages happily gathered in the new Jerusalem, they watched in awe as the final resurrection occurred below them. From every nook and cranny on the earth and from the seas and below the earth came the bodies of all the men and women in history who had died outside of Christ.

And descending from the heavens came Jesus, sitting on a great white throne. With the saints above Him and the resurrected dead amassed in the heavens around Him, the very earth and sky flew from Him. Fire from the heavens and from within the earth ignited the globe, and in a flash it was incinerated and blown into tiny flaming particles that hurtled through space.

Rayford now understood the Scriptures that foretold of this great judgment, as below him he saw the dead, small and great, standing before Jesus. These were those whom, according to Revelation 20:5, "did not live again until the thousand years were finished." As the Bible had foretold, the sea had given up the dead who were in it, and "Death and Hades delivered up the dead who were in them." All these billions of the sinful dead now resurrected stood in shame before Jesus. Rayford worshiped with all who had escaped this fateful hour.

Arrayed before Jesus were three great books: the Book of Life, containing the name of every person who had

ever lived; the Book of Works, containing every righteous or evil deed they ever committed; and the Lamb's
Book of Life, containing only those who had trusted in
Christ for their salvation. Rayford's glorified mind
allowed him to understand that he was, of course, listed
in the Book of Life, but he had been forgiven for any
misdeed associated with his name in the Book of Works.
And that he and everyone with him in the beautiful city
of God were listed in the Lamb's Book of Life, while all
the desolate souls hovering about the throne were not.

What a contrast! Everyone with Rayford had longed
to see Jesus and lived for the day they would be with
Him in paradise. Those waiting for judgment looked as
if they dreaded even looking at Him, as if they would
have given anything to be anywhere else in the
universe.

In his new state, Rayford also instinctively understood God's economy of time. Dealing fairly with that
massive throng for even just a few minutes each would
take—in the earthly measure of time—millions of years.
But to God, a thousand years is as a day and a day as
a thousand years. The Lord somehow dealt with each
person individually, calling out his or her sins and
transgressions and assigning punishment—all would
suffer in the lake of fire, but some worse than others,
such as those scoffers who had led others astray, especially children. Yet in what seemed a matter of
moments, it was over. The unbelieving dead had been
judged according to their works, by the things which
were written in the books. Then Jesus cast Death and

Hades into the lake of fire, and all not found written in the Lamb's Book of Life were cast into the lake of fire.

Rayford had the feeling that the many verdicts he had just heard would have horrified him in the old days. And yet now, hearing the offenses of those who had rejected and rejected and rejected the One who was "not willing that any should perish" and seeing Jesus' own tears as He pronounced the sentences, Rayford understood as never before that Jesus sent no one to hell. They chose their own paths.

Now, with the earth and its atmosphere obliterated by fire and the wicked dead banished to the lake of fire for all eternity, all that remained was the new Jerusalem and Jesus on His throne. And in an instant Jesus created an entirely new earth, onto which the Holy City descended.

Suddenly Rayford saw what John the revelator had seen more than three millennia before: a new heaven and a new earth, for the first heaven and the first earth had passed away. There was no more sea. A loud voice from heaven said, "Behold, the tabernacle of God is with men, and He will dwell with them, and they shall be His people. God Himself will be with them and be their God. And God will wipe away every tear from their eyes; there shall be no more death, nor sorrow, nor crying. There shall be no more pain, for the former things have passed away."

Then Jesus said from the throne, "Behold, I make all things new. It is done! I am the Alpha and the Omega, the Beginning and the End. I give of the fountain of the water of life freely to him who thirsts. But the cowardly, unbelieving, abominable, murderers, sexually immoral, sorcerers, idolaters, and all liars have their part in the lake which burns with fire and brimstone."

Jesus stood and faced the billions of believers, stretched wide His arms, and announced, "You chose to believe in Me and accept My death on the cross for your sins. My resurrection from the dead proved this sacrifice was acceptable to My Father. Therefore, on the basis of your faith, I invite you into the eternal city the Father and I have been preparing for you."

Rayford hardly knew where to look. Below him was the new earth, majestic, endless, beautiful, as the original Garden of Eden must have looked. And all around him the great city bore the very glory of God. Her light was like a most precious jasper stone, clear as crystal. She had a great and high wall with twelve gates, and twelve angels at the gates, and names written on them, the names of the twelve tribes of the children of Israel: three gates on the east, three gates on the north, three gates on the south, and three gates on the west.

The wall of the city had twelve foundations, and on them were the names of the twelve apostles of the Lamb. The city was laid out as a square, its length as great as its breadth. The wall was of jasper, and the city was pure gold, like clear glass. The foundations of the wall were adorned with all kinds of precious stones. The twelve gates were twelve pearls: each individual gate was of one pearl. And the street was also pure gold, like transparent glass.

There was no temple in it, and Rayford knew why. The Lord God Almighty and the Lamb were its temple. The city had no need of the sun or of the moon, for there would be no more night, no need for a lamp nor light of the sun, for the Lord God, the Lamb, would be the light.

The only residents of the new heaven and new earth were those written in the Lamb's Book of Life. And they would reign forever and ever.

NOTE FROM
DR. TIM LAHAYE

JERRY AND I felt uniquely led of God to take on this challenging task of presenting what we believe is the truth of end times prophecy in fiction form. Our prayer was that it would take admittedly complex and often confusing elements of Scripture and help them come to life in your eyes.

As you can imagine, this has been the most daunting and yet enjoyable and rewarding experience of our lives. We've attempted to follow the Scriptures carefully in a time-honored pattern of taking the Bible literally wherever possible. When it was obvious that the Scripture was symbolic, we carefully considered context and compared it to similar passages to try to determine what was truly intended by the original writers. We never tried to alter Scripture but sincerely attempted to use fiction to cast light on prophetic truth.

By now there should be no question, but for the record let me say that yes, we believe what we have portrayed here will happen someday. Our deepest prayer is that this sixteen-book story has drawn you closer to God and caused you to either receive Him as your Savior or more deeply commit yourself to Him if you were already a believer. Thousands of readers have told us they became believers through reading these books, which makes everything else associated with them—media coverage, controversy, best-seller lists—pale in comparison. There's nothing any novelist enjoys more than to hear that his work has changed a reader's life. Well, when readers tell us that, they mean it literally.

If you have a similar story of these books' impact on your life, we would love to hear from you. Just write us in care of the publisher.

One of the closing verses of the Bible says, "Let him who thirsts come. Whoever desires, let him take the water of life freely." This makes it clear that salvation is a matter of the will—whoever wishes may come. If there is any question in your mind as to whether you have received the living Christ, I urge you on the basis of His challenge to change your will and receive Him as your Savior today.

ABOUT THE AUTHORS

Jerry B. Jenkins (www.jerryjenkins.com) is the writer of the Left Behind series. He owns the Jerry B. Jenkins Christian Writers Guild (www.ChristianWritersGuild.com), an organization dedicated to mentoring aspiring authors, as well as Jenkins Entertainment, a filmmaking company (www.Jenkins-Entertainment.com). Former vice president of publishing for the Moody Bible Institute of Chicago, he also served many years as editor of *Moody* magazine and is now Moody's writer-at-large.

His writing has appeared in publications as varied as *Time* magazine, *Reader's Digest, Parade, Guideposts,* in-flight magazines, and dozens of other periodicals. Jenkins's biographies include books with Billy Graham, Hank Aaron, Bill Gaither, Luis Palau, Walter Payton, Orel Hershiser, and Nolan Ryan, among many others. His books appear regularly on the *New York Times, USA Today, Wall Street Journal,* and *Publishers Weekly* best-seller lists.

He holds two honorary doctorates, one from Bethel College (Indiana) and one from Trinity International University. Jerry and his wife, Dianna, live in Colorado and have three grown sons and three grandchildren.

Dr. Tim LaHaye (www.timlahaye.com), who conceived the idea of fictionalizing an account of the Rapture and the Tribulation, is a noted author, minister, and nationally recognized speaker on Bible prophecy. He is the founder of both Tim LaHaye Ministries and the Pre-Trib Research Center.

He also recently cofounded the Tim LaHaye School of Prophecy at Liberty University. Dr. LaHaye speaks at many of the major Bible prophecy conferences in the U.S. and Canada, where his prophecy books are very popular.

Dr. LaHaye earned a doctor of ministry degree from Western Theological Seminary and an honorary doctor of literature degree from Liberty University. For twenty-five years he pastored one of the nation's outstanding churches in San Diego, which grew to three locations. During that time he founded two accredited Christian high schools, a Christian school system of ten schools, and Christian Heritage College.

There are almost 13 million copies of Dr. LaHaye's fifty nonfiction books that have been published in over thirty-seven foreign languages. He has written books on a wide variety of subjects, such as family life, temperaments, and Bible prophecy. His current fiction works, the Left Behind series, written with Jerry B. Jenkins, continue to appear on the best-seller lists of the Christian Booksellers Association, *Publishers Weekly, Wall Street Journal, USA Today,* and the *New York Times.* LaHaye's second fiction series of prophetic novels consists of *Babylon Rising* and *The Secret on Ararat,* both of which hit the *New York Times* best-seller list and will soon be followed by *Europa Challenge.* This series of four action thrillers, unlike *Left Behind,* does not start with the Rapture but could take place today and goes up to the Rapture.

He is the father of four grown children and grandfather of nine. Snow skiing, waterskiing, motorcycling, golfing, vacationing with family, and jogging are among his leisure activities.

CROSSINGS®
THE BOOK CLUB FOR TODAY'S CHRISTIAN FAMILY

A Letter to Our Readers

Dear Reader:

In order that we might better contribute to your reading enjoyment, we would appreciate your taking a few minutes to respond to the following questions. When completed, please return to the following:

Andrea Doering, Editor-in-Chief
Crossings Book Club
401 Franklin Avenue, Garden City, NY 11530

You can post your review online! Go to www.crossings.com and rate this book.

Title _____ Author _____

1 Did you enjoy reading this book?

❑ Very much. I would like to see more books by this author!

❑ I really liked_____

❑ Moderately. I would have enjoyed it more if_____

2 What influenced your decision to purchase this book? Check all that apply.

  ❑ Cover
  ❑ Title
  ❑ Publicity
  ❑ Catalog description
  ❑ Friends
  ❑ Enjoyed other books by this author
  ❑ Other _____

3 Please check your age range:

  ❑ Under 18   ❑ 18-24
  ❑ 25-34   ❑ 35-45
  ❑ 46-55   ❑ Over 55

4 How many hours per week do you read? _____

5 How would you rate this book, on a scale from 1 (poor) to 5 (superior)?
_____

Name_____

Occupation_____

Address_____

City_____ State_____ Zip_____